The Slow Mirror
and Other Stories

To Sheldon,
I thought you might
enjoy this.
ZBR

The Slow Mirror and Other Stories

New Fiction by Jewish Writers

*(ed) by Sonja Lyndon
and Sylvia Paskin*

Five Leaves Publications
*in association with the European
Jewish Publications Society*

The Slow Mirror and Other Stories

*Published in 1996 by Five Leaves Publications
PO Box 81, Nottingham NG5 4ER, in association with
the European Jewish Publications Society*

*Designed and set by 4 Sheets Design & Print
Printed in Great Britain by Antony Rowe*

ISBN 0 907123 81 3

*Five Leaves Publications
acknowledge financial assistance
from East Midlands Arts*

*The European Jewish Publications Society is a registered charity which makes
grants to assist in the publication and distribution of books relevant to Jewish literature, history, religion, philosophy, politics and culture. EJPS c/o The Joseph
Levy Charitable Foundation, 37–43 Sackville Street, London W1X 2DL.*

Cover painting:
The Artist's Brother Harry Holding an Apple
by Mark Gertler (1913), courtesy of Edgar Astaire

Contents

Foreword

The Slow Mirror was selected as our title for a number of reasons, some of which we have held over for the Afterword, to give our readers the chance to discover for themselves the significance of Richard Zimler's image. We were inspired by the richness of associations conjured up by the word mirror: the notion of the mirror as a symbol of consciousness and an instrument of contemplation seemed very apt for our purposes and led to the creation of a framework for our introductory remarks.

Mirror, mirror...

In the story of Snow White, the Queen consults the mirror about her beauty and is horrified to be told that she has been ousted from her position as the fairest in the land by her step-daughter. Echoes of the Narcissus story are clearly in evidence, and the wicked step-mother's fate, like that of Narcissus, is to finally become swallowed up by her own self-love. However, as Bruno Bettelheim points out in *The Uses of Enchantment,* the young Snow White is also the victim of narcissism, for twice she is ensnared by the disguised Queen through her own vanity, once with the gift of suffocating lace stays, and once with the gift of a poisoned comb. Bettelheim makes a distinction, however between the narcissism of the adult Queen and that of the child, Snow-White. For the child, narcissism is a natural stage of its development, he maintains, before adding the warning note that: "The child must gradually learn to transcend this dangerous form of self-involvement."

The last statement struck an interesting chord with us in connection with the work contained in this anthology. It seemed to us that the notion of *self-involvement* was highly applicable to a genre of Jewish writing that has exploded on the American literary scene in the second half of the twentieth century. This genre has displayed all the narcissism of infancy in its attention-seeking, scatalogical brashness, beneath which can be sensed the child's plea for inclusion and recognition. Much of this writing has stemmed from the largely male pens of Jewish writers of a particular generation; many of whom, according to one of our contributors, the American writer Nessa Rapoport, still "had the immigrant experience to draw on and quarrel with... the music of Yiddish in their ears... a tangible neighbourhood anti-semitism to sharpen their mordant wit. Their novels taught a generation of Jews to understand itself — torn between the

1

world of European parents and the wild, seductive promise of America, with its non-Jewish women and its non-neurotic men."

Provocative and fresh as this genre of Jewish narcissism has been, its attenuation would be tantamount to arrested development. There comes a point when a "Jugendstil" is no longer appropriate, particularly for a new generation of writers who may be at more than one remove from the Jewish world that nurtured Philip Roth and Woody Allen. Thus the American-born Richard Zimler, the author of the title story in this collection, writes about "the trade off between comfort and curiosity", stating that whereas, as a reader, "it's probably easier for me to feel comfortable inside a work of fiction featuring Jewish characters... I am no longer interested in what I call the humorous-macho school of Jewish American fiction, this genre of humour and the psychology of the narrators involved. It all seems tired and clichéd."

The majority of contributors to this anthology, by virtue of either belonging to a different, younger generation or of having been nurtured in environments outside the United States, bear the hallmark of a far less self-conscious school of Jewish writers. The Jewishness of their writing is often a subtle phenomenon, so much so that we foreswore the label *New Jewish Fiction* and have chosen instead the less problematic and more appropriate subtitle *New Fiction by Jewish Writers*. This subtitle is not without its own difficulty, however, for although the twenty-six writers in this volume are very happy to find themselves alongside each other, the majority of them do not see themselves primarily as Jewish writers. Tony Dinner is one of the exceptions: "I think of myself as a Jewish writer. Of course I have a great love of, and have absorbed many influences from, writers who are not Jewish; but my primary orientation is towards Jewish tradition and literature, especially Biblical. The secular writers who mean most to me are those whom I would describe as being *inside out,* like Spinoza, Heine, Freud, Singer, Rubenstein."

Nessa Rapoport is similarly unequivocal about her identity as a Jewish writer: "As a Jewish writer, I am not of the minimalist school of fiction. I am most interested in the possibility of a literature whose spine and sinews would be not simply Jewish experience, but Jewish materials and Jewish dreams..."

This is in stark contrast to a writer like Robert Lasson who defines himself primarily as "a gastrointestinal Jew, with an abiding love of the Yiddish language" or Jack Gratus who writes that that things ethnic set his teeth on edge and who has never really thought of himself as a Jewish writer because: "to my mind, a Jewish writer is one who consciously writes for a Jewish readership. Not that there is anything wrong in that. In all literature the writer has been able to make certain assumptions

2

based on a common culture. Today, however, such a community of like-minded Jews does not exist in the diaspora — if it ever did."

Whether or not they are conscious of their Jewishness during the act of writing clearly differs from writer to writer and from one piece of work to another. Nevertheless, however unconscious the writer may be, and however seemingly divorced the writer's subject matter might be from anything overtly Jewish, the end-product may be suffused with what has been called by some a *sensibility* and by others, such as Cynthia Ozick, a *substratum,* that is recognisably Jewish. Thus Dan Jacobson comments that although his story *The Circuit* is devoid of any human characters, it is in his opinion, the most Jewish story he has ever written. And Gabriel Josipovici detects a Jewish sensibility in writers such as Proust and Muriel Spark "who are half Jews, and never thought of themselves as Jews" as well as "in the work of Kafka as much as of Malamud, of Perec as much as of Agnon...Aharon Appelfeld is for me a Jewish writer whereas Amos Oz is an Israeli writer."

For a number of the writers in this anthology, then, their Jewishness is barely reflected in their work, some indeed prefer their mirrors to be covered.

The covered mirror.

The Jewish tradition of covering the mirrors in a household of mourning has a number of interpretations. One of the more obvious ones is the requirement on the mourner to transcend all forms of vanity, to cease from dwelling on the self, to dwell instead on a higher, more spiritual plane. The mirror is regarded as the means of achieving social acceptance, a convention that is to be disregarded at a time of mourning, during which a sense of withdrawal and a period of loneliness are natural and unavoidable concomitants.

The latter interpretation sits well with the act of writing, which of necessity involves social withdrawal and more often than not a degree of self-imposed loneliness. The prohibition on self-contemplation is a more problematic analogy; the writer needs both to know and not know the source of his or her imaginative outpourings. Achieving the right balance of consciousness and unconsciouness is one of the mysteries of any act of creation.

For many writers in this anthology the Jewish content of their work is very much a product of their unconscious. Carol Bergman states: "I know that I am haunted. I am not aware of the resonances as I am writing. Ghosts travelled with my parents across the Ocean. Their shadows stay;

3

they're glued to me." As a New Yorker she has the additional problem of not being easily able to sift out the Jewish from the native American strands of her work: "There is so much cultural cross-fertilisation in New York that although the voice in my stories is distinctly contemporary, distinctly American and very Jewish-New York, Afro-Americans speak like this too, as do the Latinos, and I speak like them. We trade/share vocabulary, idiom, rage."

For Tamar Yellin, writing from rural Britain, the Jewishness of her stories emerges not so much in her themes, as in a sense of dislocation that she identifies in her work which, she states: "is by no means a negative thing: indeed I feel it's essential to creativity."

Jack Gratus writes: "At the point when writers sit down and work, compelled by our personal angel or demon, we bring with us our baggage and a large part of that consists of the traditions of the group to which we belong, whether we choose to draw on these traditions or not. Our stories will be 'Jewish' only in the sense that some Jewish readers may respond to them in a way that perhaps non-Jewish readers may not. Anything more self-conscious is likely to be kitsch."

Part of this baggage is the culture and literary tradition in which writers have been reared, which for most of the writers in this anthology is both Western and Christian. Frederic Raphael writes: "I was born in the United States, came to England when I was seven, was educated in the Classics and have lived in western Europe nearly all of my life..... The experience of British and American literature is my crucial experience as a writer. Malraux said that one became an artist by looking at art, not by looking at life. It is, as they say, *un peu vrai*."

Through the looking glass

> *Let's pretend there's a way of getting through*
> *it, somehow...Let's pretend the glass has*
> *got all soft gauze, so that we can get through.*

Taking our cue from Alice let us enter the other world of *The Slow Mirror* and its myriad images. What does the mirror hold? The wide spectrum of themes and preoccupations in this anthology cannot fail to reflect the diversity of what it is to be Jewish at the most latter end of the 20th century, in the middle of which is planted the poisoned tree of the Holocaust whose roots still remain to be eradicated. These roots may be detected in an awareness of racism that permeates Shelley Weiner's *The*

4

Vote where mutual need and dependency between a madam and her maid is resolved with a certain equivalence when they journey together to a foreign land. Elaine Feinstein's spartan journey back in *Christmas in Berlin* also provides us with a chilling reminder of how the past and present inter-relate. The uncertain immigrant Angelina from Haiti in Carole Malkin's *The Silence of Dishes* is a sharp reminder of what it is to be on the outside and in exile. Not that exile always needs to be dramatic; Tamar Yellin's protagonist and alter ego, Mr. Kafka, are lost and suffused by the white highlands whilst "down in the valley, in the poor town, live the Asians, Pakistanis, Muslims from Karachi and Lahore". Nor is all exile negative — Rozanne Rabinowitz's *Maza Zoftig* is a compassionate and sensuous story of the delight of connection through tongues both in flesh and language. Deena Linett's *Seder* hosts unsual guests who are also exiles — Hymie Rodriguez from Cuba and Estrillita Chu from the Philippines. The meal they share with Molly Greenblatt, Professor of Philosophy enriches her understanding of what it means to be Jewish. Robert Lasson's *Tale of A Shamos* is a challenging account of how one man uses the past to his advantage — he subverts it, betrays it and still suceeds...

As one would imagine food plays a central role in at least one of the stories — Onkel Mendl and Tantie Rosa's holy strudel in Zvi Jagendorf's *Strudelbakers 1951* becomes 'a perfect child' for this ill-matched couple who seek to surmount their refugee status in post-war Britain by achieving material success. A strudel has another role to play in Frederick Raphael's poignant revelation of an an odd quasi-familial arrangement in *Going Back*.

Families, who needs them? Certainly not the betrayed daughter in Rachel Castell Farhi's excoriating view of family life in *Life with Letter 'F' Missing* — a mother struggling to survive in an alien culture and a mixed marriage, pays a high price for remaining intact. The self-deprecating 'hero' of Jonathan Wilson's *Dead Ringer* attempts through a veil of testicular ache to acknowledge the brief life and long death of a baby brother.

The Slow Mirror yields images of love in all its guises: love between the generations in Stephen Walker's warm and witty *Mr. Silberman Meets The Pope*, the search for love in Michelene Wandor's Gothic feminist fable *The Devil in the Cupboard,* the fatal attraction of obsessive love in *A Suburban Tragedy* by Jack Gratus, love between men in Shaun Levin's charged, erotic story of transvestism, desire and shoes — love between two women in *Maza Zoftig*. The engendering of sexual desire is explored in Moris Farhi's bucolic *Lentils in Paradise,* which reminds us that France is not the only country where they order things differently.

Other stories fall into more ambiguous areas — *The Hand of God* by Gabriel Josipovici and *The Sphinx, The Dream And The Death of T* both provide points of entry into the fragile momentous terrain of artistic creativity; *Great Men* by Nessa Rapoport explores the impossibility of living two lives at the same time. Marci López-Levy provides a cool, wry visit to contemporary urban hedonism.

Carol Bergman's *Grateful* depicts a shadowed and tenuous relationship across two generations against the vibrant background of New York. In stark contrast is Dan Jacobson's intensely powerful Orwellian parable, Ellen Galford's science-fiction voyage to Jews in Space is both a playful and thoughtful take on Jewish self-obsession, and the magic realism of Richard Zimler's title story is a mysterious, many-layered meditation on memory and loss.

We invite you now to pass through our glass slowly, to take in all that it holds.

Grateful

Carol Bergman

Francie is talking and I am trying to get out of my sweaty clothes, pull out my basket, organize the shampoo and towels. It's hard to concentrate when she's here and inevitably things get left on the bench or on the floor, lockers don't get locked, locks got misplaced. This is a high class gym so how come the place is always a mess? I say this to Francie. How come this place is such a mess? So, what else is new, she asks. I don't know if this is the answer to my question or something else. Usually, she only hears what is in her own mind. First swim, then bridge, then eat, she says. Usually at Muriel's Cafe with the other "girls." Curry noodle salad, her favorite. I know her whole routine. She takes up all the space on the bench, pulling up her hose, nattering to the obese woman in colour coordinated workout clothes about the upcoming presidential elections.

The pool's wonderful, Francie says, we should be grateful for what we have and, by the way, do you swim, have you ever lifeguarded, have you ever nearly drowned? Then comes the story about how she nearly lost it out in Far Rockaway when she was a kid. She was only three when she followed her older brother into the surf. He was supposed to be looking after her, but he forgot. Fortunately, a lifeguard saw what was going on and went after her. "That's when I decided to become a lifeguard," Francie says.

"When was that?"

"When do you think? I was born in 1912," she says. "My father went off to fight somewhere in Germany, the front they called it, those fucking Nazis, and never returned." Jeesus can Francie swear.

Then she continues, moves on. Get dressed or undressed, about to leave or just arrived, one story segues into another. It doesn't matter where you come in, you can always find your way, like a soap on TV. You get to know the characters, that's the amazing thing. You get hooked. Francie, her parents, her sister, her brothers, her grand nieces and nephews, her friends. She's got no kids of her own, never been married even, I learned that in a day or two. Time for a new *shtick*, Francie, I told her once, when I was in a bad mood. Hard day at the office, no men in my life, the usual New York story. Fortunately, she's hard of hearing and didn't catch what I said.

"What was that you said, dear?" She was rouging her cheeks at the time and didn't pay attention to my answer. Anyway, I changed it and said

7

something about the weather.

Two weeks in, I remember now, I went into the membership office and asked if I could move my basket to get away from her. We'll see what we can do, they said. Then nothing happened. Call me at work, call me anytime, I said. I come here to relax and there's this woman driving me nuts. She does pedicures on the bench and sits there with her politically correct vagina hanging out. Her breasts are down to the floor. Jeesus, do I come here for this?

Next time in the locker room, the day after I went into the membership office, Francie shook my hand. I'd betrayed her and we both knew it.

"Shalom," she said. "That's, how are ya doing in Hebrew." I don't know how she assumed I would know what she meant, but she did. Then she asked my name. "What do you call yourself?" she asked. "I say this because when I was young they called me Frances, but now I'm just Francie."

"Phoebe," I said. "Pheeb, for short."

"You see. You see," she said. "They did it to you, too."

"Did what?"

"Shortened your name. Made it sound sweet. Made it sound like you're a *goy*. I was important when I was Frances. Now look."

"You're not important?"

"Not in that way," she said. "You know what I mean. This basket yours?"

"Yup," I said.

"Isn't it always the way," Francie said. "Only two people here and we've got our baskets one on top of the other. Well, I'll be out of your way in a minute, dear. What did you say your name was?"

"Phoebe, Pheeb for short."

"Going for a swim? Hope you're going for a swim, Phoebe dear."

"Not today. Stairmaster. Bike. I need to work up a sweat," I said.

"Well, see you in the pool. Ta-ra-da." And she was off.

Not long after our first introductions, I went into the pool and saw her there in the slow lane. I was wearing my goggles so she didn't recognize me. I just slid in and started to do my laps. I knew it was her because she wasn't wearing goggles. Also the rouge on her cheeks, semi-permanent like a tattoo, was visible from a length away. I looked up occasionally or stopped to blow the fogging out of my lenses and watched her swim. She moved gracefully, her thin long arms were like a dancer's arms and came out in a soft arc over the water. No splashes or crashes like some folks. And she kicked with her heels just under the surface, not too high, not too low. Perfect, I'd have to say, if you care about these things, which I do.

Once in a while, Francie got out of the water and wandered over to the

8

whirlpool. She'd disappear for a while and then come back and swim some more. What I enjoyed about watching her was the transformation. In the pool, her age was meaningless, the water held her as it held me and her arthritic limbs moved easily. Out of the pool, she was old again, bent, her toes curled under and around the ball of her foot like the bound feet of Chinese women not so long ago. It was the pointed shoes she'd worn when she was young, she explained, when I asked her about it.

And this is what began to get to me, this is what surprised me. I was interested in her body, though I couldn't bare to look at it. She never covered it up, just sat there, as I've already said, with all to see. So this is old. When she's there, I can hardly think about anything else. I've never had a grandmother, up the chimney in the crematoria before I came along, and my own mother is a button-up for sure, so I look in wonder. The nooks, crannies and wrinkles shadow me. The way her pubic hair is thin and so much visible under it like a translucent scrim.

Keep swimming and you'll be all right, Francie always says. Then she goes to dry her hair and I can hear her saying the same thing to the women there. Her voice is deep, a mezzo voice, and hasn't thinned with age like all the rest of her.

So, today, I'm thinking again I don't want to see her anymore, I want to have my basket moved. I hear her voice close up to my ear. "Been swimming, Phoebe dear?"

"Not today, Francie," I say. I sip on my V-8 can and bend down to unlace my shoes.

"It's really a shame you not swimming, Phoebe dear. They've done studies but I suppose you know. What happens to us when we get old. Best thing is not to be alone. Not to ever be alone."

And then I do something I never thought I would. I ask Francie where she lives, what her arrangements are, whether she has anyone in her life. Once I speak these words, I can't stop the answer, it's there in front of me, palpable as flesh and bone.

"My sister calls me every morning to say hello," she says. "Just picks up the phone and says Good morning, Francie, how are you today? No matter how I feel, I tell her I'm just fine. I don't want her coming in from Jersey to keep me company. She's got a husband, grandkids. I come here, play bridge, swim, get home late as I can before I have to go to bed. Be grateful for what you have Phoebe, dear."

But she doesn't ask me what that is, what it is I have exactly. A job, friends, lovers. Maybe this is all the sum of it and what petrifies me when I meet Francie on the bench and see my own sad future there. It is only the years that stand between us, between me and loneliness, between me and laps of solitude in the pool.

9

"How about you come out to dinner with me one day, Phoebe dear," she says. "I'll tell the girls I have a date, give them something to talk about."

Because of the state of my inward reverie, I hear myself mouth yes.

She takes out a pad of paper from her bag and insists I write down my particulars — name, phone numbers at work and home. I contemplate changing the digits but end up writing them straight. "Do you mind if I call you at work?" she asks. "I always enjoyed people calling me at work. We made plans that way, you see. Oh we had lots of plans. Skating, movies. Did I tell you I was a secretary? And oh they loved me there. Frances will do it Frances will do it, they said. I was a problem solver, you see. That's why they kept me there so long. They let me work til I was seventy. Did I tell you that? Gave me a party and sent me on a cruise. Can you imagine? On a cruise."

After we are dressed, our baskets tucked away, Francie says to wait a minute, she has to put her lipstick on. Then she takes me by the arm. By the arm. Jeesus, I never imagined Francie touching me. But it feels OK, really, it feels OK. And that's the way we walk right out the door, one arm looped into another arm, past the women folding towels, mostly from the Caribbean with one or two stories of their own, past the security guards downstairs and out into the burning concrete street.

"Let's go to dinner now," she says. "There's Muriel's, right there, let's go."

So here we are at Muriel's. I begin my stories, she intertwines with hers. She wants to know what I have to say, what I am doing with my life. She looks into my eyes, sucks on her curry noodles, looks into my eyes again. "Why aren't you married, Phoebe dear" she asks. "I don't want you ending up like me."

Then and there I decide to move aside, to get the check and rush away, make excuses if she decides to call to make more plans. "I want to pay," she says. I say "no, I cannot let you pay."

"Look, Phoebe dear," she says, "you don't know this but I have money stashed away. $75,000 just last year went to this and that and that. Charities, my accountant says. Why not spend a bit on this here meal and see a face light up?"

After dinner in front of the TV, I get undressed for bed. Before putting my nightshirt on, I stand in front of the mirror and contemplate my skin, my fat, my hairy parts. I admire my muscles, strike a body builder's pose. I imagine Francie tucked in bed and compose a eulogy for her funeral, a peculiar little quirk of mine. I imagine people dead. I imagine people gone. Francie was a doodlebug, I say. And it goes on like that, the words unformed but filling up my heart. Then, at the gravesite, I rehearse a three-act scenario. I throw in cards, a pair of goggles, Francie's stretched out bathing suit, a plastic container of left over curry noodles from our one night on the town.

10

The Dream The Sphinx And The Death of T.

Tony Dinner

1.

It was after his second visit to the brothel that he had the dream.

2.

T. sat in the shade of the linden tree. It was already hot. The sun was prowling like an animal. T. was transfixed as though seeing for the last time the street, the people passing by on the pavement, those sitting alone or together at the cafe, and the waiters gliding like seals in an out of his sight. The waiters knew him well. He had been coming here for years. They called him simply "The Painter". He gradually became aware of the intensity of his vision, of his seeing. It had a great deal to do with inwardness, with the enigma of being.

3.

Physical beauty had never been enough for him. It needed to be transfigured, animated by an ardent spirit. What moved him, though, was the silence, the mystery that lay just out of reach. But in his painting the sheer bodily joy of applying paint, of being there, at the centre of the struggle, of the drama that he was trying to resolve in the immense space around him, around us all, excited him immeasurably. A young couple, sitting nearby, had their tongues in each other's mouths. When they drew apart, they laughed in delight, absorbed in contemplation of themselves. T. smiled. It had been many years.

4.

The dream contained odd, disjunctive elements which he was trying to divine. There was a wild-game park, acacia trees with hovering vultures with a boy asleep in the shade of one of these, and the endless, dry savannah. There were giraffe, zebra, and the elephant moving like a mighty, slow-pumping river. There was also the dream within the dream. All he could remember was that he was at a brothel. He was vaguely aware of a swarm in a variety of couplings, treblings, quadruplings. At the back, in the centre, a man stood naked, his legs strong and firmly planted, with his huge phallus erect. He

11

was masturbating himself with his right hand. A neophyte, clad in black stockings, suspenders and high-heeled shoes, the iconic madonna of sex, knelt beneath him, her mouth agape, ready to receive the sacred semen, and fertilise the world. This was his image of God. Suddenly he noticed a tall, elegant woman across the vestibule. She wore a full-length evening dress of the darkest blue, with long, blue gloves. She had short-cropped hair and large, dark eyes. She half-smiled at him, like a sphinx, and seemed to beckon him to follow her. She turned and walked slowly up the wide stairway. He saw that her back was bare, her white flesh shimmering like a moon on water. He felt impelled to follow her. In the boudoir she undressed herself and then undressed him. He was conscious of how sleek and firm her body was, and how old, creased and infirm was his own. He thought at that moment, he remembered, of his mother's body, her long legs, her narrow breasts, and the bones of her shoulders. Her body haunted him all his life even now as an old man. He recalled her eyes, her vivid, moist gaze that penetrated to his soul and which he carried around with him always as the paradigm of the look of love. He experienced again that exquisite pleasure that he had when he first beheld his mother naked, that he knew was reserved only for those who were truly blessed. The woman looked deep into his eyes, clasped him round and drew him down into her darkness.

5.

T. sipped his bitter, muddy coffee. He relished the taste of its ferment, its passion. Lunch had come and gone and the afternoon was drifting by in a haze. Why could he not tear himself away? His painting was awaiting him. It was a large canvas, which he had named "The Silence", and he had been working on it for over a year now. He was moving more surely into its depths and coming, he felt, near to its close. He must be careful not to rush it. Even at this late stage, especially at this late stage, it could be spoiled irreparably. Perhaps that was why he did not hurry back to it. Restraint, discipline, he must hold on to these. Each time he began a painting, he approached the vast, white, empty space with awe. The first mark that began the journey, and the last that signified the journey's end always made him tremble with trepidation.

"More coffee, *signor*?" the young waiter, whose name was Jorge, asked. T. nodded. "Yes. Yes, more. Please."

6.

T. liked this cafe. He liked sitting outside on the pavement in the heat, beneath the shade of a tree, at the small, round tables. He liked sitting

alone in a crowd. He often came here to puzzle things out. He liked the
sound of chatter and laughter, sifting through his reverie. He heard the
hum of a violin. Was it Brahms? Some gypsy music? It was pleasant, whatever it was. He rubbed his hands together. They were permanently
stained with paint. They were sore again today. He found it difficult to
make a fist with his right hand. Arthritis. He did not know how much
longer he could continue. He knew he might soon have to call it a day.
Suddenly, at his side, was a man in a shabby coat, with sparse, ruffled
hair, holding a violin and a hat for coins. Their eyes caught each other in
that ferocious gaze that entrapped you in another's life. The man
half-smiled. He, too, had those deep, sorrowful, dark eyes that betokened
persecution, loss, lamentation, sweetness. T. involuntarily looked away,
embarrassed. He knew who the man was, as the man knew him. They
recognised each other in an instant—brothers in the city of lost dreams.
The man's sadness was simply unbearable to him. Another alien in this
city of aliens—another forlorn being, at the turn of the century, as the
clock was about to strike the year 2000. To meet him like this, this
refugee, this refuge, from the tormented past! Why had the man come to
this city? Whichever city he was in, T. knew that sooner or later they
would be bound to meet each other.

"Play for me," T. asked the man, putting a note into his hat. "Play an
old tune for me."

"For us both," the man responded softly. "Perhaps for all of us."

7.

Memories he had suppressed for a long time surfaced from his childhood.
He was in the wild, with the burning African earth at his feet, and the
light and sound transcendent, sharp, sensuous, mythic, unforgettable.
But he had been drawn to the city; the city was where he had come to live.
It was his arena, and his paintings were about its calumnies, its despairs,
its terrors, its labyrinthine ecstasies. The city was his place of contest, for
better or worse.

8.

T. sat on until he noticed it was already evening. The neon signs and the
street lights vibrated in the gloom. He wanted to get up but he was too
lethargic. His legs felt heavy as though rooted to the earth. The pain in

13

his hands was now also in his arms and was so acute it was consuming him. He called for a double cognac. Jorge had gone and another waiter whom he did not know brought his order.

"It will warm you, *signor*," the waiter said. "It will put fire back into your blood."

Would he return to the brothel that night for the third and last time? Or would he go home and complete his painting? He did not yet know. He continued to sit.

Lentils in Paradise

Moris Farhi

Paradise was Sophie's gift to Selim and me. She took us there frequently. I was about seven; Selim a year or so older. Paradise was the Women's *Hamam* — Turkish Baths — of Ankara.

Sophie cherished us as if we were her own; and we loved her just as much. In fact, I can now admit, we loved her more than we loved our mothers. We reasoned that since she was under no obligation to hold us dear, the fact that she did, meant we were worthy of affection. Consequently, we never believed the loose talk from parents and neighbours that, given the law of nature whereby every woman is ruled by the maternal instinct, Sophie, destined to remain unmarried and childless, needed, perforce, to treasure every child that came her way, even curs like Selim and me.

Sophie was one of those young women from the Anatolian backwoods who, having ended up with no relatives and no home, found salvation in domestic service in the sizeable metropolises, Istanbul, Izmir, Adana, and the new capital, Ankara. Often payment for such work amounted to no more than the person's keep and a bed in a corner of a hallway; wages, if they existed, seldom exceeded a miserable *lira* or two a month. But, in the early 1940s, when Turkey's policy of neutrality in the Second World War, had brought on severe economic problems, even this sort of employment was hard to find.

My parents, I am glad to say, paid a decent wage despite the constant struggle to make ends meet. For Sophie was an Armenian, a member of a race that, like the Jews, had seen more than its share of troubles. Sophie herself, as her premature white hair and the scar that ran diagonally across her mouth testified, was a survivor of the passion suffered by the Armenians at the hands of the Turks and the Kurds during the First World War.

Selim and I never accepted the distinction that Sophie was a servant. With the wisdom of young minds we dismissed the term as derogatory. We called her *"abla"*, "elder sister". At first — since Selim was not my brother, but my friend who lived·next door — I insisted that she should be known as *my "abla"*, but Sophie, who introduced us to everything that is noble in humanity, took this opportunity to teach us about true justice. Stroking our foreheads gently, she impressed upon us that since Selim and I had been inseparable since our toddling days, we should have

15

acquired the wisdom to expel from our souls such petty impulses as greed and possessiveness. She belonged to both of us, what was more natural than that?

*

The event that led us to Paradise occurred the moment Sophie set foot in our house.

She had arrived from the Eastern Anatolian province of Erzurum. The journey, mostly on villagers' carts, occasionally, using up her few *kursh*, on dilapidated trucks, had taken her about a week. And for another week, until she had heard on the grapevine that she might try knocking on my mother's door, she had slept in cold cellars procured for her, often without the owners' knowledge, by sympathetic countrywomen. She had washed in the drinking fountains of the open-air market where she had gone daily in search of scraps; but, lacking any spare vestments, she had not changed her sweat-encrusted clothes. Thus, when she had arrived at our flat, she had come enveloped in the pungent smell of apprehension and destitution.

My mother, seasoned in matters of disinfestation — she had attended to my father whenever he had come on leave from the Army — immediately gathered, from her own wardrobe, a change of clothes and guided Sophie to the shower, our only fixture for washing. We had hardly settled in the sitting room — I remember we had visitors at the time — Selim's parents, some neighbours and, of course, Selim — when we heard Sophie laughing. My mother, who had taken to Sophie instantly, looked well satisfied, no doubt interpreting the laughter as a happy omen.

Moments later, the laughter turned into high-pitched giggles. Giggles became shrieks; and shrieks escalated into screams.

As we all ran to the hallway fearing that Sophie had scalded herself, the toilet door flew open and Sophie burst out, wet and naked and hysterical.

It was Selim's father who managed to contain her. Whilst my mother asked repeatedly what had happened, he threw a raincoat over Sophie and held her in a wrestler's grip until her screams decelerated into tearful, hiccupy giggles. Eventually, after sinking onto the floor and curling up, she managed to register my mother's question. As if relating an encounter with a *djinn*, she answered, in a hoarse whisper: "It tickles! That water tickles!"

The ensuing laughter, manifesting as much relief as mirth, should have offended her; it didn't. Sophie, as we soon learned, believed that laughter had healing qualities and revered anybody who had the gift of humour. But it had never occurred to her that she herself could be comical. The

16

revelation thrilled her. And, as she later admitted to me, her ability to make us laugh had been the factor that had convinced her to adopt us as her kin.

The afternoon ended well. When Sophie, hesitantly, asked whether she could finish washing by the kitchen tap, my mother promptly took her, together with the women visitors, to the *Hamam*.

Thereafter, Sophie became a devotee of the Baths. And she used any excuse, including the grime Selim and I regularly gathered in the streets, to take us there. My mother never objected to this indulgence: entry to the *Hamam* was cheap — children went free — and Sophie, Selim and I, sparkling after so much soap and water, always appeared to confirm the adage: "only the clean are embraced by God".

In those days, Turkish Baths had to struggle hard to maintain their Ottoman splendour. The travail was particularly evident in Ankara. This once humble townlet which, with the exception of an ancient castle on a hillock, had barely been touched by history, was rising fast as the symbol of the new, modern Turkey. As a result some "progressive" elements saw the Baths as totems of oriental recidivism and sought to reduce their popularity by promoting Western-style amenities.

Yet, here and there, the mystique prevailed. After all, how could the collective memory forget that, for centuries, Istanbul's spectacular *Hamams* had entranced and overawed flocks of discerning Europeans.

And so the tradition survived; discreetly, in some places; openly in others. And when new Baths were built — as was the case with most of the establishments in Ankara — every attempt was made to adhere to the highest provision.

Two cardinal standards are worth mentioning.

The first predicates that the primary material for the inner sanctum, the washing enclave itself, must be marble, the stone which, according to legend, shelters the friendly breezes and which, for that very reason, is chosen by kings for their palaces and by gods for their temples.

The second standard stipulates the following architectural features: a dome, a number of sturdy columns and a belt of high windows, a combination certain to suffuse the inner sanctum with a glow suggestive of the mystic aura of a mosque. Moreover, the high windows, whilst distilling apollonian light, would also deter peeping-toms.

Our Women's *Hamam*, having adhered to these standards, was the epitome of luxury.

Let me take you in, step by step.

The entrance, its most discreet feature, is a small, wrought-iron door located at the centre of a high wall like those that circumvent girls' colleges.

The foyer is lush. Its dark purple drapes immediately promise exquisite sensual treats.

To the right of the foyer there is a low platform with a kiosk. Here sits the manageress, *"Teyze Hanim"*, "Lady Aunt", whose girth may well have coined the Turkish idiom, "built like a government". She collects the entrance fees and hires out such items as soap, towels, bowls and the traditional Turkish clogs, *nalins*.

At the bottom of the foyer, a door leads into the spacious communal dressing room. As if to prolong your anticipation, this is simply trimmed: whitewashed walls, wooden benches and large wicker-baskets for stacking clothes.

Another door opens into a passageway which has boards on its floor. Here, as you walk, the clogs beat an exciting rhythm. Ahead is the arch which leads into the baths' marbled haven.

The next moment you feel as if you are witnessing a transfiguration. The mixture of heat and steam have created a diaphanous air; the constant sound of running water is felicitous; and the white nebulous shapes that seemingly float in space profile kaleidoscopic fantasies in your mind. This might be a prospect from the beginning of days — or from the last. In any case, if you adore women and crave to entwine with every one of them, it's a vision that will remain indelible for the rest of your life.

Thereafter, slowly, your eyes begin to register details.

You note that the sanctuary is round — actually, oval. You are glad. Because had it been rectangular, as some are, it would have emanated a masculine air.

You note the large marble slab that serves as a centrepiece. This is the "belly stone". Its size determines the reputation of the particular establishment; a large one, as that in the Women's *Hamam*, where people can sit and talk — even picnic — guarantee great popularity.

You note the washing areas around the "belly stone". Each is delineated by a marble tub — called *kurna* — wherein hot and cold water, served from two separate taps, is mixed. You note that the space around each *kurna* accommodates several people, invariably members of a family or a group of neighbours. These people sit on stocky seats, also of marble, which look like pieces of modern sculpture, and wash themselves by filling their bowls from the *kurna* and splashing the water onto their bodies. Sometimes, those who wish to have a good scrub, avail themselves, for a good baksheesh, of one of a number of attendants present.

You note that, beyond the inner sanctum, there are a number of chambers which, being closer to the furnace, are warmer. These are known as *"halvet"*, a word which implies "solitude", and are reserved for those who wish to bathe alone or to have a massage. For the elite customer, the latter is performed by Lady Aunt.

But, of course, above all, you note the bathing women. Wearing only bracelets and earrings, they look as if they have been sprinkled with gold. Tall or short, young or old, they are invariably Rubenesque. Even the thin ones appear voluptuous. Covered with heavy perfumes and henna, they carry themselves boldly, at ease with their firm-soft bodies. They are, you realize, proud of their femininity — I am speaking in hindsight — even though — or perhaps because — they live in a society where the male rules unequivocally. But if they see or think someone is looking at them, they are overcome with shyness and cover their pudenda with their bowls. You note little girls, too, but, if you're a little boy like me, you're not interested in them. You have already seen their budding treasures in such outworn games as "mothers and fathers", "doctors and patients".

*

I feel I have related our entry to Paradise as if it were a commonplace occurrence, as if, in the Turkey of the 40s, little boys were exempt from all gender considerations. Well, that's only partly true. Certainly, over the years, I came across many men of my generation who, as boys, had been taken to the women's baths either by their maids or nannies or grannies or other elderly female relatives — though never by their mothers; that taboo appears to have remained inviolate.

In effect, there were no concrete rules on boys' admission into Women's *Hamams*. The decision rested on a number of considerations: the reputation of the establishment, the status of its clientèle, the regularity of a person's — or group's — patronage, the size of the baksheeshs to the personnel and, not least, the discretion of Lady Aunt.

In our case it was the last consideration that tipped the scales in our favour. We were allowed in because the Lady Aunt who ran the establishment had been well-versed in matters of puberty. She had ascertained that our testicles hadn't yet dropped and would convey this view to her patrons when necessary. The latter, always tittering cruelly, accepted her word. Mercifully, dear Sophie, incensed by this artless tresspass on our intimate parts, would lay her hands over our ears and hustle us away.

Selim and I, needless to say, were greatly relieved that our testicles were intact. But the prospect that they would drop off at some future date also plunged us into great anxiety. Thus, for a while, we would inspect each other's groins every day and reassure ourselves that our manhoods were not only still in place, but also felt as good as when we had last played with them that morning, on waking up. We would also scour the streets, even in the company of our parents, in the hope of finding the odd fallen testicle. If we could collect a number of spare testicles, we had reasoned, we might just be able to replace our own when calamity struck. The fact that, in the past, we had never seen any testicles lying around did not deter us; we simply assumed that other boys, grappling with the same predicament, had gathered them up. Eventually, our failure to find even a single testicle bred the conviction that these organs were securely attached to the body and would never fall off; and we decided that this macabre "lie" had been disseminated by women who had taken exception to our precociousness in order to frighten us.

*

And precocious we were. We had had good teachers.

Selim and I lived at the very edges of Ankara, in a new district of concrete apartment blocks designated to stand as the precursor of future prosperity. Beyond, stretched the southern plains, dotted here and there with Gypsy encampments.

Gypsies, needless to say, have an unenviable life wherever they are. Historic prejudices disbar them from most employment. The same condition prevailed in Ankara. Jobs, in so far as the men were concerned, were limited to seasonal fruit picking, the husbandry of horses, road digging and the portering of huge loads. Gypsy women fared better; they were often in demand as fortune tellers, herbalists and faith healers; and they always took their daughters along in order to teach them, at an early age, the intricacies of divination. The occasional satiety the Gypsies enjoyed, was provided by the boys who begged at such busy centres as the market, the bus and railway stations, the stadium and the brothels.

The last was the best pitch of them all. Situated in the old town, at the base of the castle, the brothels consisted of some sixty ramshackle dwellings piled on each other in a maze of narrow streets. Each house had a small window on its door so that customers could look in and appraise the ladies on offer. Here, on the well-worn pavements, the beggars set up shop. They knew that, after being with a prostitute, a man, particularly if he were married, would feel sinful; and so they offered him instant redemption by urging him to drop a few *kursh* into their palms to show Allah that, as the faith expected of him, he was a generous alms-giver.

Some of these wise Gypsy boys became our friends; and they taught us a great deal.

Above all, relating all the causerie they had overheard from punters and prostitutes, they taught us about the strange mechanics of sex: the peculiar, not to say, funny, positions; the vagaries of the principal organs and

20

the countless quirks which either made little sense to anyone or remained a mystery for many years.

And this priceless knowledge served as the foundation for further research in the *Hamam*.

*

Breasts, buttocks and vaginal hair — or, as was often the case with the last, the lack of it — became the first subjects for study.

Our Gypsy friends had instructed us that breasts determined the sexuality of a woman. The aureole was the indicator for passion. Those women with large aureoles were insatiable; those with what looked like tiny birthmarks were best left alone as they would be frigid. (What, I wonder today, did frigidity mean to us in those days?) For the record, the woman with the largest aureole we ever saw was, without doubt, the prototype of lethargy; nicknamed "the milkman's horse" by Lady Aunt, she always appeared to be nodding off to sleep, even when walking. By contrast, the liveliest woman we ever observed — a widow who not only allowed us generous views of her vagina, but also appeared to enjoy her exhibitionism — had practically no aureoles at all, just stubby, pointed nipples like the stalks of button mushrooms.

And buttocks, we had learned, were reflectors of character. They were expressive, like faces. Stern buttocks could be recognized immediately: lean cheeks with a dividing line that was barely limned, they looked like people who had forsaken pleasure. Happy buttocks always smiled; or, as if convulsed by hysterical laughter, wobbled. Sad buttocks, even if they were shaped like heavenly orbs, looked abandoned, lonely, despairing. And there were buttocks which so loved life that they swayed like tamarind jelly and made one's mouth water.

Regarding vaginal hair, there was, as I mentioned, little of it on view. In Turkey, as in most Muslim countries, the ancient Bedouin tradition whereby women, upon their marriage, shave their pubic hair, has almost acquired the dimensions of a hygienic commandment.

Our research into vaginal hair, in addition to its inherent joys, proved to be a lesson in sociology. A shaven pudenda not only declared the marital status of the particular woman, but also indicated her position in society. To wit, women who were clean-shaven all the time were women wealthy enough to have leisure — and the handmaids to assist them — therefore, were either old aristocracy or *nouveau riche*. Women who carried some stubble, thus betraying the fact that children or household chores or careers curtailed their time for depilation, were of more modest backgrounds.

21

To our amazament, as if the chore proved less of an inconvenience if performed in company, there was a great deal of shaving going on in the baths. No doubt the fact that, for a small baksheesh, a woman could get an attendant to do a much better job, thus liberating her to gossip freely with friends or relatives, contributed to the preference.

*

Our main study — eventually, our *raison d'être* for going to the Baths — centred on the labia and the clitorises. Both these wonders, too, possessed mythologies. Our Gypsy friends apprised us.

The myths on the labia centered on their prominence and pensility. The broad ones, reputedly resembling the lips of African peoples were certain to be, like all black races, uninhibited and passionate. (What did those adjectives mean to us? And what did we know of black races?) Lean labia, because they would have to be prized open, indicated thin hearts. Pendulous ones represented motherhood; Gypsy midwives, we were assured, could tell the number of children a woman had had simply by noting the labia's suspension. Those women who were childless but did possess hanging labia were to be pitied: for they found men, in general, so irresistably attractive that they could never restrict their affections to one individual; consequently, to help them remain chaste, Allah had endowed them with labia that could be sewn together.

The perfect labia were those that not only rippled down langourously, but also tapered to a point at the centre, thus looking very much like buckles. These labia had magical powers: he who could wrap his tongue with them, would receive the same reward as one who walked under the rainbow: he would witness the Godhead.

*

As for clitorises, it is common knowledge that, like penises, they vary in size. The Turks, so rooted in the land, had classified them into three distinct categories, naming each one after a popular food.

Small clitorises were called *"susam"*, "sesame"; *"mercimek"*, "lentils" distinguished the medium sized ones — which, being in the majority, were also considered to be "normal"; and *"nohut"*, "chick-peas", identified those of large calibre.

Women in possession of "sesames" were invariably sullen; the smallness of their clitorises, though it seldom prevented them from enjoying sex to the full, inflicted upon them a ruthless sense of inferiority; as a result, they abhorred children, particularly those who were admitted to the Baths. Women blessed with "lentils" bore the characteristics of their namesake, a staple food in Turkey. Hence, the "lentilled" women's perfect roundness were not only aesthetically pleasing, but also extremely nourishing; in effect, they offered everything a man sought from a wife: love, passion, obedience and the gift for cooking. Those endowed with "chick-peas" were destined to ration their amorous activities since the abnormal size of their clitorises induced such intense pleasure that regular sex invariably damaged their hearts; restricted to conjoining only for purposes of conception, these women were to find solace in a spiritual life. And they would attain such heights of piety that, during labour, they would gently notch, with their "chick-peas", a prayer-dent on their babies' foreheads thus marking them for important religious duties.

*

I can hear some of you shouting, "Pig — clitorises have hoods. Even if you find a clitoris the size of an Easter egg, you'll have a tough time seeing it! You've got to, one: be lucky enough to have your face across your lover; two: know how to peek past the hood; three: have the *sang-froid* to keep your eyes open; and four: seduce it into believing that, for you, she is the only reality in life and everything else is an illusion."

So, let me confess, before you take me for a liar, that, in all likelihood, neither Selim nor I ever saw a single clitoris. We just believed we did. Not only the odd one, but, by that unique luck that favours curs, hundreds of them. And the more we believed, the more we contorted ourselves into weird positions, peeked and squinted from crazy angles, moved hither and thither to fetch this and that for one matron or another. We behaved, in effect, like bear cubs around a honey pot.

Of course, I admit, in hindsight, that what we kept seeing must have been beauty spots or freckles or moles or birthmarks and, no doubt, on occasions, the odd pimple or wart or razor nicks.

Naturally, when we described to our friends all that we had feasted with our eyes, they believed us. And so we felt important. And when we went to sleep counting not sheep but clitorises — we felt sublime. And when we woke up and felt our genitals humming as happily as the night before — we basked in ultimate bliss.

*

An aside here, if I may. We never investigated Sophie's features. She was, after all, family, therefore, immaculate, therefore, non-sexual. Now, looking back on old pictures, I note that she was rather attractive. She

23

had that silky olive-coloured skin that makes Armenians such a handsome race. Moreover, she had not had children, hence, had not enjoyed, in *Hamam* parlance, "usage". Consequently, though in her mid-thirties, she was still a woman in her prime. (Sophie never married. When my family moved from Ankara, soon after my *bar-mitzvah*, she went to work as a cook in a small taverna. We kept in touch. Then, in 1976, she suddenly left her job and disappeared. Her boss, who had been very attached to her, disclosed that she had been seriously ill and presumed that she had gone home to die in the company of ancestral ghosts. Since neither one of us knew the exact place of her birth, our efforts to trace her soon floundered.)

*

Alas, our time in Paradise did not fill a year.

Expulsion, when it came, was as sudden and as unexpected as in Eden. And just as brutal.

It happened on July 5th. The date is engraved in my mind because it happens to be my birthday. In fact, the visit to the Baths on that occasion was meant to be Sophie's present to me.

As it happened, on that particular day, the Women's *Hamam* was exceptionally full. Selim and I were having an awfully hard time trying to look in many directions all at once. Such was our excitement that we never blinked once. It was, in effect, the most bounteous time we had ever had. (Given the fact that it was also our last time there, I might be exaggerating. Nostalgia does that.)

We must have been there for some time when, lo and behold, we saw one of the women grab hold of an attendant and command her, whilst pointing at us, to fetch the Lady Aunt. It took us an eternity to realize that this nymph of strident *fortissimo* was the very goddess whom Selim and I adored and worshipped, whose body we had judged to be perfect and divine — we never used one adjective where two could be accommodated — and whom, as a result, we had named "Nilufer" after the water-lily, which, in those days, we believed to be the most beautiful flower in the world.

Before we could summon the wits to direct our gaze elsewhere — or even to lower our eyes — Nilufer and the Lady Aunt were upon us, both screaming at lovely Sophie, who had been dozing by the *kurna*.

Now, I should point out that, Selim and I, having riveted our eyes on Nilufer for months on end, knew very well that she was of a turbulent nature. We had seen her provoke innumerable quarrels, not only with Lady Aunt and the attendants, but also with many of the patrons. The old

24

women, comparing her to a Barbary thoroughbred — and, given the ease with which she moved her fleshy but athletic limbs, a particularly lusty one at that — had attributed her volatility to her recent marriage and summed up her caprices as the dying embers of a female surrendering her existence to her husband, as females should; one day, a week hence or months later, when she would feel that sudden jolt which annunciates conception, she would become as docile as the next woman.

And so on that 5th July, Selim and I had been expecting an outburst from Nilufer — though not against us. She had seemed troubled from the moment she had arrived. And she had kept complaining of a terrible migraine. (The migraine, Sophie wisely enlightened us later, shed light on the real reasons for Nilufer's temper: for some women severe headaches heralded the commencement of their flow; what may have made matters worse for Nilufer — remember she was not long married — might have been the disappointment of the passage of yet another month without conception.)

It took us a while to register Nilufer's accusations. She was reproving us for playing with our genitals, touching them the way men do. (I am sure we did, but I am equally sure we did it surreptitiously. Had she been watching us the way we had been watching the women, seemingly through closed eyes?)

Sophie, bless her dear heart, defended us like a lioness. "My boys," she said, "know how to read and write. They don't have to play with themselves."

This nonsequitor enraged Nilufer all the more. Stooping upon us, she took hold of our penises, one in each hand, and showed them to Lady Aunt. "Look," she yelled, "they're almost hard. You can see they're almost hard!"

(Were they? I don't know. But, as Selim agreed with me later, the feeling of being tightly held by her hand was sensational.)

Lady Aunt glanced at the exhibits dubiously. "Can't be. Their testicles haven't dropped yet..."

"Yes. Thanks for reminding me," yelled Sophie. "Their testicles haven't dropped yet!"

"They haven't!" Selim interjected bravely. "We'd know, wouldn't we?"

Nilufer, waving our penises, shrilled another decibel at Lady Aunt. "See for yourself! Touch them! Touch them!"

Shrugging like a long-suffering servant, Lady Aunt knelt by our side. Nilufer handed over our penises like batons. Lady Aunt must have had greater expertise in inspecting the male member; for as her fingers enveloped us softly and warmly and oh, so amiably, we did get hard — or felt as if we did.

25

We expected Lady Aunt to scream the place down. Instead, she rose from her haunches with a smile and turned to Sophie. "They are hard. See for yourself."

Sophie shook her head in disbelief.

Nilufer celebrated her triumph by striding up and down the Baths, shouting: "They're not boys! They're men!"

Sophie continued to shake her head in disbelief.

Lady Aunt patted her on the shoulder, then shuffled away. "Take them home. They shouldn't be here."

Sophie, suddenly at a loss, stared at the bathers. She noted that some of them were already covering themselves.

Still confused, she turned round to us; then, impulsively, she held our penises. As if that had been the cue, our members shrank instantly and disappeared within their folds.

Sophie, feeling vindicated, shouted at the patrons. "They're not hard! They're not!"

Her voice echoed from the marble walls. No one paid her any attention.

She remained defiant even as Lady Aunt saw us off the premises. "I'll be bringing them along — next time! We'll be back!"

Lady Aunt roared with laughter. "Sure! Bring their fathers, too, why don't you?"

And the doors clanged shut behind us.

And though Sophie, determinedly took us back several times, we were never again granted admission.

Life With The Letter 'F' Missing

Rachel Castell Farhi

ONE

My mother had an old typewriter with the letter 'f' missing. This grand machine, a 1940's Imperial built from cast iron with ivory keys like a piano's, would move with us from place to place, poky bedsit to dingy flat until it came to rest on the kitchen table of a Notting Hill boarding house. Wherever it went and however much older and more responsible I became, Mother wouldn't let me touch it.

"That's my machine," she would say possessively, "It was a gift from Mr Levenstein's office." Of course, it wasn't and even as a very young child, I could sense there was something shady around the subject of the typewriter and how it came to be with us. My father wouldn't go near it, preferring to sulk behind the *Daily Mail* when he came home from work rather than hear my mother boast of its acquisition to me for the umpteenth time. Ever since I can remember, she bored me with these tales of her working life in the Jerusalem of the British Mandate, of how the past was a better country than the one she lived in now, of the fun she'd had despite the war and, of course, the men she'd flirted with like a dark-eyed Levantine butterfly until one had caught her in his English net. The butterfly catcher was my father, a gentle, honest man who behaved decently in all things but, like the majority of his gentile peers, he had inherited a mild anti-Semitism that could not reconcile itself with having a Jewish wife. In my father's case, his prejudice presented itself as a quiet embarrassment at all things Jewish, including my mother.

It wasn't difficult to be embarrassed by my mother. I used to think that her loud voice with its vulgar Israeli pronunciation of English was as natural to her as the frightening blackness of her hair. But looking back, years after her death, I now believe it was a show, a put-on to flaunt her disdain for the exile she found herself in. The English, my mother said, hadn't wanted foreign brides coming here after the war, and she hadn't wanted the English. Like marriage to my father, it was a mutually undesired circumstance which persisted because there was no other way to have it.

The typewriter was a symptom of all that was wrong between my parents. There were two versions as to how it had come into our possession, both told by my mother at different times and the script of which varied according to how recalcitrant she was feeling. Whatever the telling, I would be held hostage to her pantomime, her loud voice and semaphoric gesticulations. I sat caught between the kitchen table where the machine was, eating my bread and butter, and the window onto the street-market below, overlooking middle class hippies dropped out amongst those of us too poor to leave for somewhere better.

Jimmy Young was on the radio, his voice bright with a breakfast box cheeriness that told Britain's housewives that today would be a better day than yesterday had been. My mother hummed along to the silly jingles as she bashed in the shell of a boiled egg for me and then went back to plucking her eyebrows. For someone who claimed not to have adapted to twenty years of living among the British, she had managed to pick up a good few of their habits, including boiled eggs for breakfast and the vanity of her beehived neighbours.

The typewriter looked mutely at me as I sucked on my egg. "Mum," I ventured cautiously, "Will you teach me how to type?" I waited for the explosion. My mother's reactions to otherwise normal questions could never be predicted but usually involved her losing her precarious temper. She stopped plucking, her stubby chipped-red nails holding the tweezer with a single curly hair in its grip, and looked at me as if I had threatened her.

"So, you want to be a typist like Mummy was," she said as if my request had flattered her. Jimmy Young had obviously done his stuff and I was in for a good day with her. "Alright, I'll teach you. I'm a very good teacher. I would have gone to study for a teaching certificate at the Sorbonne in Paris if bloody Hitler hadn't invaded France." She scowled her regret at this lost opportunity which could have changed her life entirely. "But first, let me tell you how I got the typewriter..."

Mr. Levenstein was a lawyer who had survived the concentration camps and had come to Jerusalem to set up a small practice after the war. This part remained the same in each telling of the story.

"I was only twenty," she would say, "But Mr. Levenstein would only pay the higher wage to an older girl so my father forged my birth certificate." She would chuckle at this point, proud of her father's cunning which had earned her an extra pound a week, then she would cast a disdainful look at my father shaving in the mirror over the kitchen sink, as though he were incapable of an equal guile to benefit me. "Anyway," she continued, leaning across the crumbs conspiratorially, "This was when the British were in Palestine, before I met your father. Mr. Levenstein was a gentleman, a *yecke*, a bit of a fuddy-duddy but he was alright really, even if he did wear a three-piece suit in blazing June. The camps had made him permanently cold, he said, that's why. Poor man. The Nazis cut off his fingers. *Zhuum!* Just like that." And she would make a sudden gesture of a knife coming down with her hand, like a karate chop, to slice the

28

invisible. "Boom! No more fingers." The breadcrumbs scattered across the red formica as her hand came down and I jumped with fear. She flashed a smile at me, the whiteness of her perfect teeth breaking out of red lipstick and for a brief moment I saw how beautiful she must have been when my father first saw her in a dusty Jerusalem street as she passed the military checkpoint. She was past her best now, of course, fat, past her prime through those failed pregnancies and the illegal abortion she'd procured before Richard was born. But the very thought that my mother was less than the paragon she made herself out to be was a betrayal and I would not have let myself think it then.

Dad slipped quietly out to catch the bus to work as she thumped into her storytelling reverie without noticing him leave. He caught me a glance from the kitchen door, his thinning hair Brylcreemed back over his forehead, a cigarette in the hand that held his briefcase. "Bye, kitten," he said jovially and I knew he meant me but my mother waved him off absently as though the greeting belonged to her. Daddy and I had an understanding, a quiet recognition of one another as two of a kind, and this feeling of mutual respect and sensitivity for what the other was thinking had grown out of baby love into undemonstrated affection.

From the window I watched Dad skip down the steps of the house and walk through the market traders setting up their stalls, his bony blue-veined fingers pulling his cigarette to his mouth with the urgency of breathing through an oxygen mask. My mother said he lived on his nerves but I didn't know what that meant. Still, if Dad did it it must be okay. Anything my father did was white, anything my mother, black with an occasional concession of grey.

"...Mr. Levenstein," I drifted back into listening to my mother after my father disappeared from sight. "He learned to write all over again, holding the pen between his stumps, *kacha*." She imitated using her tweezers. "And his writing was horrible, only I could read it. So of course he trusted me completely." I found this part hard to believe but as usual said nothing. "Anyway, he wasn't a well man and one day he told me he was giving up the practice to go and live with his sister on a kibbutz in the Negev. The Red Cross found his sister living like a prostitute in Paris... still, that's another story..." My relief at not having to hear about this fallen woman was immense. "So, he give me a week's notice and said I could help myself to whatever I liked from the office as a leaving gift. Well, I thought, what's he going to do on a kibbutz? Can't pick dates with no fingers? Can't type with no fingers, either. Who needs a typewriter in Beersheva? So, on the night the office closed down, I hung about outside with Shalom, that bum of a brother of mine, went back in and made him take the typewriter for me. We had a taxi waiting. Oy, it was so heavy, I kept

29

telling Shalom, 'don't drop it down the stairs, it's worth money' but he knew that anyway, the little crook." She sat back triumphantly and her bosom heaved a breath.

"Mr. Levenstein's leaving present!" she said looking at the typewriter. "When your father brought me to England, I brought it with me. That's my lifeline, that typewriter is. My independence. 'Always have a trade, even if you're a girl,' my father said. If you can type, you'll never be out of a job. It's true, they always want shorthand-typists here. So I'll teach you how to be one, Sarah. And one day, if you get fed up with your man, you can give him a good kick up his back-arse and tell him to fuck off I can manage quite nicely by myself. You don't need a man, Sarah. They only want to get into your pants anyway and then it's goodbye. Filthy creatures."

The good mood was gone, replaced by some whirlwind of cruel memory which I knew nothing about but which was strong enough to invade any moment when I thought my mother and I might be happy. Her face turned thunderous with anger and I noticed her hands quiver. The familiar nausea of fear which always seemed to happen at mealtimes to put me off my food, crept up my gullet and into my mouth, filling me up. I wanted to escape, to be down there with the market people whose noise and shouts I could hear like a faraway echo of all that was commonplace, all that was normal, all that was to be despised as being part of the *goyim*, so it was wrong to desire it. Instead, I was trapped behind the kitchen table with that black monster machine blocking my exit and my mother, manic, in front of me.

"Filthy bastards," she kept saying to me. "You don't need them, Sarah. You'll never need them as long as you've got me. I'll keep the wolves away from my pretty girl. My little one." And she advanced towards me, her hands outstretched. I waited for the blow, the one that was meant for whoever but not for me but this time it didn't come. Regaining control, stopping herself, my mother's hands turned to a caress, stroking my cheek softly.

"I think I'd better take one of my pills," she said quietly, "and then we can go out."

I knew better than to remind her about the typing lesson, even though I really wanted to have a go. I wished I was back at school where the bullying from the girls on the estate seemed better than this because at least I knew when it would happen, at breaktime. But the summer holidays had only just begun and August stretched before me like one long lunchtime. It would be hours before Daddy came home and Rich, from college. We were alone, cat and mouse, and the smug typewriter. It was 1969 and I was ten years old.

30

TWO

She used to go through our pockets when she thought we weren't aware of it. I was never quite sure what she was looking for and I don't think she was either, until the day came when she would find it. It was Rich who got into trouble first. She'd found the stub of a cinema ticket for a midweek matinee performance of *Midnight Cowboy* and had gone berserk. Rich was supposed to be at college on Wednesdays. Why were you at the cinema? Who went with you? Who put you up to this? Was it that Tony Smith? It was, wasn't it? I'll get on the phone to his mother, I will. I'll break you two up, see if I don't.

My brother sat on the sofa, silently taking in the accusations without bothering to defend himself. He was seventeen and had just started his first job as a clerical assistant with the local council. Wednesdays were his day-release to college to take an extra O Level and I knew he hated going. Richard detested academic stuff and couldn't wait to leave school and go to work. My parents had both tried pushing him further, Dad even had some idea about university but Rich wasn't having it. His resistance took the form of illness and he conveniently developed asthma shortly before joining the Sixth Form, so the pressure was released and he went to work instead.

That afternoon, Rich sat dejectedly waiting for a hiatus in our mother's tirade, his slim fingers, younger versions of my father's, fiddling anxiously with a lock of his hair. The TV was on in the background, its sound deliberately turned up to fool the neighbours against the shouting.

"Give me that phone," she yelled, "I'm going to speak to Tony's mum. Does she know what her little boy gets up to instead of going to school? It's a disgrace. If we were living in Israel now, you'd be in the army, boy. They'd make a man of you, instead of......instead of a poof!"

"I'm not a poof," Rich said determinedly. "And Tony's not a little boy. He's seventeen, same as me. And college isn't school, you ignorant cow!"

She whacked him one across the face. Her nails drew blood. "How dare you! How dare you call me names!" she kept saying, truly surprised that Rich had done so. I was surprised too, shocked that he had answered back to a parent because I was still in awe of them but I felt quietly proud as well. The violence disturbed me, though.

I wanted to cry.

After she had hit him, Rich got up and went to wash his face. "Do it properly," mum ordered, "And roll up a piece of cotton wool to stick to the wound, like you'd cut yourself shaving. Dad doesn't need to know about any of this, not if you promise me not to hang around with that lousy Tony Smith and bunk off college."

She rose to her feet and went over to Richard, her manner completely changed. It was as if she had been satiated by the act of aggression, that seeing the blood drawn of another had somehow cooled her own. "How about some eggs and bakes for tea?" she said kindly, putting her arm around Rich's waist as if he were not her son. "You know," she continued. "You should take me to the cinema instead. I look young enough for people to think I'm your girlfriend, not your mother."

We heard keys in the front door jangle. Dad was home.

"Why's the telly on so loud?" he asked. "Mrs. Galliano's just given me an earful about it on the way up. We don't want to antagonise the neighbours now, do we?"

THREE

On the day my mother hadn't intended to snoop through my father's pockets, she came across the thing she'd been waiting for. It was *Pesach* at the same time as Easter and as Catholic Mrs. Galliano downstairs was making a big thing of her festival, my mother, not to be outdone, decided to celebrate Passover. I didn't understand Passover, for as so many things in Judaism that she failed to forget completely, she didn't seem to remember enough to pass it on.

"We buy *matzohs*," she said and I remembered those tasteless crackers that seemed to surface annually which I would spread thick with Anchor butter. Every year it was the same. Mother would buy this box of *matzoth* and make me eat one slice of it a day for seven days. Only after I'd eaten the *matzo* did she let me have some bread.

There was another strange ritual which I assumed was religious in its basis. My mother hated housework and she never cleaned the house, except where it showed. Turning out cupboards and dusting corners were left to me but she never forced me to do it, either, waiting instead for a childish impulse to 'keep house' to emerge. But just before the purple *matzo* box featuring a timeless Mr. Rakusen would appear instead of a *seder* plate to mark the start of the festival, she would suddenly be overtaken by a frenzy of cleaning out the oddest places. Blankets would be inspected for fluffballs, brushes groomed and coat pockets shaken out to dislodge crumbs and old sweets. Dad used to suck toffees between smoking cigarettes and his coat pocket was always a lucky dip for a candy, smelling as it did of coconut and tobacco.

I'd asked for a sweet one day and she'd gone to fish one out of his coat when the card dropped out.

It was an ordinary business card with a name, address and profession listed on it in black type. At first, she just looked at it, eyes narrowed in thought as if trying to remember whose it was. She clearly didn't want me in the room but it was too late for me to slip out before she noticed me and I stood in the doorway, holding tightly onto the doorknob.

"Do you know anyone called Gloria Taylor?" she asked me.

"No." It was true, I didn't. She put the card back in my father's coat pocket, throwing me a sweet as she drew her hand out. She went very quiet, unnaturally quiet all afternoon, then suddenly she offered to give me the typing lesson I'd so long been waiting for.

"Fetch some paper, Sarah, and we'll make a start." I wasn't really in the mood that day but it seemed a rare opportunity. Besides, my mother's calm disturbed me and instinct told me she ought to be distracted by being occupied. Dutifully, I fetched the paper and we made up a little office space on the kitchen table where the lunch things had been. I sat very upright in my chair, the chair that faced the typewriter. I'd never sat in it before.

She showed me how to insert the paper and I heard the satisfying clicking rumble of the carriage as it wound the sheet around itself. The typewriter was noisy, as sonorous as a musical instrument and I liked the way every impression I made on the keys told the world how busy I was. Mum told me to type my name a few times, to get used to the feel of it.

Saarah Joseph ine airley
Sarah J osephine airley
Sarah Josephine airley

"There's no 'f' " I complained but mother didn't think that was important.

"It broke off during one of our moves," she explained. "Still, the typewriter's cost us nothing. What more do you want? Just fill in the 'f's by hand afterwards."

Without really knowing what to do, my mother tried drilling me into learning the keyboard by touching certain keys without looking at them and typing nonsense words. It was devastatingly boring and I longed to type something of my own and get to know the keyboard that way.

"DFD. DDD. DRF. FRD," she kept saying, beating out time with a fork on the table as though taking me through musical scales. "Faster. Faster." she kept saying, "Don't look at your hands!" The keys were heavy to depress and my fingers small. Soon my hands ached with being stretched but still mother wouldn't let up on me.

"DFD. DRD.DFD.DFF."

"Please, mum, my hands are hurting. Can I stop now ?" She didn't seem to hear me and just kept on repeating the words. Gingerly, I reached out and touched her arm.

"Mum. I need a break."

It was as if it was the first time she had heard me. "Okay," she said. "Make me a cup of tea. I've got something to do."

She left the kitchen and went out into the passageway by the stairs. There was a communal telephone out on the landing but the neighbours, being too old and frail to make it up three flights of creaking steps, hardly used it, so it became exclusively ours. As I drew the water for the kettle and lit the gas ring, I heard the heavy metal phone dial being turned several times. After a few moments, my mother's voice began but it was like a quiet rumble and I couldn't catch every word.

"Stay out... Vernon won't... life like yours." Suddenly, she hung up and I heard her slippers flip-flap on the lino back towards the kitchen. Her face was tense, as though she was making a supreme effort to store something away without letting me know about it.

"Tea's up," I said, imitating my dad. She walked over to the window and pulled the greying net curtain back.

"All those people down there and not one for me to trust," she said softly and as she spoke I suddenly felt very afraid but in a new way which I could not understand.

"You want something interesting to type?" she said, turning to me. "Sit down. I'll dictate."

"Don't go too fast, mum, or I won't keep up," I advised but she waved her hand dismissively. "I'll wait for you."

Putting the tea aside, I returned to my place at the machine and inserted a fresh piece of paper. My mother began and I typed.

"-urther to our telephone conversation this morning, I wish to remind you to stop

-ucking my husband you -ucking bitch. I- you dont give him up youll be sorry. love isnt like that get your own bloke -ancy piece. I have children dont make them lose their -ather please. I- you are religios woman this is easter Jesus wouldnt like it to take anothers man.

signed the wi-e."

Before I could comprehend what she had made me type out, she had pulled the sheet of paper out of the machine and had stuffed it into an envelope which she put back into the typewriter. Then she pushed me out of my seat and began to type out the address on the business card she'd found that morning. Her speed was furious and fast. Quickly I glanced at the envelope. It was perfectly done.

"I'm going down to post this. You stay here," she ordered. I watched her from the window go over to the letter box on the corner, without waiting to change into her street shoes or put a coat on. Despite her weight, she moved like a woman with a mission and people cleared her path. She'd left the business card on the table and I picked it up.

Gloria Taylor, R.A.D.A. Dip.
24a Pemberton Villas,
Notting Hill.
Tel: Bay 4536
Teacher of Elocution, Speech and Drama

FOUR

They had a row. Dad came home the following evening looking pale and angry. He dashed up the stairs without waiting to say hello to me and flung his briefcase on the bed.

"I want a word with you," he told my mother stiffly. I had never known him speak to her or anyone else in that tone. Meekly, my mother got up and followed him into the bedroom. They closed the door.

I was straining to listen to what they said but there were only flashes of noise like lightning between thunderclaps and then I heard scuffling, furniture being knocked against. My heart thumped heavily in my chest. Who was hitting who? I didn't know if I should run out into the street and fetch help or if I should just sit it out. Rich would be home soon, I hoped, he'll sort it out. They'll stop for him.

In a few minutes the violence subsided and a heavy silence prevailed. Before I could believe that one of them had killed the other, I heard both voices again, this time muted, relaxed, as if all the violence had been drained out of them like a bleed. Quietly, submissively, my mother opened the bedroom door and came in to fetch me. My father's face was dark and fearsome. It was not like him at all. I had never known fear from him but now I felt it burn through me.

"Your father wants to know," my mother began, "who typed the letter today. Tell him."

I looked from her face to his, then back again. My answer seemed important but I felt as if I was being led into something I wouldn't be able to get out of. I said nothing.

"Did you type the letter?" my father asked. I couldn't lie to him, he meant too much to me not to tell him the truth of whatever I did, good or bad.

"Yes."

35

He heaved a sigh which seemed to contain relief, embarrassment and anger at the same time. Then he bit on his lip, as though trying to contain something potent and of which he was very afraid.

"You stupid little girl! What possessed you to do such a thing? Do you know who Miss Taylor is? She's a very respectable woman. I was arranging a very special treat for you — private drama lessons. She was even going to give you some elocution without charging extra as a favour to me."

"Why should she do you favours?" my mother asked suspiciously.

" Her brother Ron was in the army with me. I bumped into him on the Tube last week and he invited me into his sister's place for tea. That's why I was late home that day. I was keeping it as a surprise — the lessons — until my wages came through. And now this!"

"Give her one!" my mother said, suddenly, her eyes alight. "Smack her. She needs discipline. You're always spoiling her."

I was too overwhelmed by the injustice of it all to defend myself. I knew Daddy wouldn't hit me, he'd never laid a finger on me, surely, he wouldn't start now when I was innocent.

"Come here," he said harshly. I obeyed, moving slowly, still believing that what was special between us, how we had always trusted one another, told the truth, would preserve me.

I felt an unexpected strength from my father's arm as he carried me from my waist into the bedroom and threw me onto the bed. I didn't resist because I still couldn't believe anything would happen. He slammed the door shut behind us and began to beat me hard on my legs with the back of his hand. I kept crying, "why, why, I didn't write the letter," but he didn't hear me. He just kept on slapping at my thighs. Through my own tears I saw that he was crying.

"Daddy, daddy, please listen. She told me what to write. I just did what she said. I just wanted to type. She did it. You know she did it. Why are you hitting me? It's her, it's always her! You know it's always her."

He stopped and looked at me, his blue eyes bloodshot and full. "I know, kitten. I know. But she won't have it any other way." And he tore a rip in my tights deliberately to make it look as though he'd done a good job of beating me.

Many, many years later after Dad had died, she too passed away. There were only three mourners at her funeral, a Jewish funeral as we had promised her, Richard, his partner Avi and myself. Neither Rich or I knew any of the ritual or what we were supposed to do. When the rabbi started his graveside chanting, Rich and I looked at each other, embarrassed at our ignorance and wishing it was all over. We were instructed to toss a handful of dirt into the grave and then the rabbi came over to us both,

36

pulled out a small knife and made a small cut in Richard's coat sleeve. Then he came to me and aimed his blade at my jacket.

"No," I said, "Not the jacket. My tights." The old man looked at me, surprised and offended.

"I can't. It's not *halacha* — not modest for me to touch you there."

"Give the knife to me then." He passed the little blade into my hand without touching my skin and I leaned over and cut a tear in my tights in the same place as Dad had done all those years ago. I cut it hard and broke the skin. The blood seeped out and dripped onto the icy ground in a tiny teardrop. The rabbi winced visibly.

"You've hurt yourself," he said.

"No, it doesn't hurt," I replied. "Not any more."

Christmas in Berlin

Elaine Feinstein

It began one cold evening last October when Peter brought his girlfriend, Sophie, home to meet us. Now Peter is the child that looks like me. My daughters take after my husband, Andrew: they are fair, English and very sensible. They are both lawyers and live in Huntingdon near us. Peter writes poems and travels wherever he can scratch a living and I thought I was ready to accept whatever he did until he said Sophie's parents wanted us to visit them for Christmas in Berlin.

"Did you tell them we are Jewish?"

"I told them we aren't anything. Are we?"

In a way he was right. My husband Andrew believes in nothing much and says so. But I was born Karen Goldschmidt, and have to say I'm Jewish. That's my history. It's who I am, and why I left Berlin long ago as a child with one suitcase and a violin. I'd never been back, or wanted to. Still, I accepted the invitation. For Peter.

*

Sophie's father was an Art publisher, and the family had a luxurious flat. I could see Andrew was impressed by the material splendour of it. I liked both parents, though the North German cooking, the apple in the cabbage, and the timbre of the voices disturbed me. After our first meal, Sophie's mother brought out photograph albums so we could see Sophie aged six in the dancing school.

"She's a very pretty girl," I said.

"But stubborn," said her mother. "Like her grandmother. Let me show you."

And she searched for a picture of her mother, where the resemblance was as strong as she said. In the same album were uncles, all in uniform. Once I couldn't help saying, "Isn't that the uniform of the Waffen SS?"

Upstairs, afterwards, Andrew was very angry with me. He wanted me to stop seeing monsters.

"Even when they are real monsters?"

"They are dead monsters," he tried to comfort me. "Sophie's parents were only four and five in the war."

"And the uncles?" I asked.

39

I woke up the next morning very early. It had snowed overnight but not heavily; enough to whiten the street below and cover the parked cars. I lay and remembered the same snowlight and the same city as a child, and my handsome father carrying me on his shoulders to look at the Christmas tree.

When I was dressed, there was no one about. On the music rest of an old Steinway piano lay a piece of Chopin I love, and I lifted the lid and began to play. It was only when I paused to turn the page that I saw Sophie was there listening.

"That's lovely," she said.

"I'm out of practise, you know," I said quickly.

"Peter told me you used to play professionally when he was young. How could you bear to stop?" she asked.

"Well, you know we moved out of London -"

"That's not a reason."

"There were many reasons."

"Can you talk about it?" she asked me.

"Many performers have nerves before concerts. Mine were... just rather worse, I suppose," I said lamely.

"Did you try to get help?"

"Doctors? Yes."

"And a therapist?"

"Yes, of course. He said it was because of my childhood. My lost parents. You see, I don't know what happened to them."

"Who took you to England, then?"

"I travelled on my own. On one of the *kinder-transporten*. When the Germans wouldn't let people emigrate any longer, children were allowed to leave. On their own. My parents arranged it."

"They must have been very frightened to let you go." she said thoughtfully. "Were you angry?"

"Yes — how did you know that?" I asked, surprised. "I blamed my mother."

"What was she like?"

"Remote. Not unfriendly. But bony, determined. A teacher at the Music Hochscule."

"And your father?"

"He worked in the theatre."

"Why have you never tried to find out what happened to them? Your parents, I mean?"

"But I did try. Of course I tried." I said, astonished.

"There are records, aren't there?"

"Yes. The Germans were very methodical. But I could find nothing. It is as if they were just spirited away. As if they had never existed."

"Why didn't you come to look for yourself?"

"At first I had no money. And then... all right, I suppose I was afraid." I admitted, with a flash of irritation. "You really are a very persistent girl."

"I'm sorry." she said. "I thought we might look now. Together."

"Look for what?" I asked.

"All the memories." she said softly. "Perhaps it would put them to rest? If we looked, together."

"Go back and find the flat, you mean? Where we used to live?"

"If it's still standing. Do you know the address?"

"I do." I said.

And, being Sophie, she got her way.

The next day we set out together just after lunch. Peter knew where we were going but I didn't tell Andrew.

It was a brilliant, blue day. There was no snow underfoot but the puddles were frozen and the air was sharp in my throat. When we found the right building, our feet made no noise on the stairs but I heard other footsteps. I could see a child with olive skin and dark eyes coming down wooden stairs with a school satchel. But the flat itself evoked nothing. The present tenant couldn't help us. She didn't even want us to go in to look because her husband, she said, was sick. And when we did get inside, the furniture was so different I could hardly tell it was the same flat. There was no piano. It was just a room. Everything had changed. When I looked out of the window, even the birch trees had gone.

I was disappointed, but what had I been expecting? Had I imagined I would find my parents still there? Absurd. Then, as we began to leave, a woman coming along the landing looked familiar to me.

"Is your name Bloomfield?" I asked hesitantly. "You look like a woman I knew once."

"It was my mother's name. But when did you know her? She has been dead twenty years."

And so it was we found someone prepared to reminisce a little. Proudly, she explained she had been in the same flat all through the war, all through the bombing.

"I remember your father." she said, as she poured coffee. "Such a charmer, my mother used to say, though she didn't approve of him."

"Why was that?"

"Wasn't he an actor?" she said. "At the theatre? My mother was a very strict Lutheran. She always said how sorry she was for your mother. A little woman, wasn't she, your mother? With glasses. A teacher maybe."

41

Of the disappearance of my mother and father, however, she knew nothing.

"You must have known they were Jews." said Sophie, more forthright than I was. "Didn't you wonder at all what had happened to your neighbours?"

"If you want to find out more, go and ask at the theatre. Or ask one of his girlfriends. There were enough of those."

I was silenced by this, but Sophie was not.

"Do you know their names, these girlfriends as you call them?" asked Sophie.

"Well, I know one. Gave herself airs like a Countess. Used to be a famous actress, living on the Ku'damm. Frieda Kellerman. These days she drinks, and looks like an old prostitute."

"I've seen her in silent films!" Sophie said. "She must be in her seventies."

"If she interests you, I can tell you where she lives." The woman laughed spitefully. "Just above the flea market. You know? Where those Turks and Rumanians have their stalls. I saw her there myself. Anyone will tell you."

We had to get to Maybachufer. Over by the canal. Sophie said we should catch the Orient Express, the overhead U-bahn, but I wasn't sure I wanted to confront my father's old mistress.

"We can't give up now, can we? Now we've found someone who knew your father? I just hope she hasn't completely lost her marbles." she said.

"You have a marvellous grasp of English." I said. "And your mother was right — you're a very stubborn girl."

*

Kreuzberg was like a Middle Eastern souk. There were women in veils and the smell of spices and coriander. A stallholder pointed out Frieda Kellerman's card on the wall. And she really did call herself a Countess.

A low, amused voice answered our knock.

"*Mein Gott,* such a banging. What do you want with me?"

When I said I'd come to ask about an actor, and gave my father's name, she looked at me closely.

"Eyes don't change, do they? Whatever time does to the rest of us. Come in."

She led us into a living room which was little more than a storeroom for carpets, and sat us on stools while she examined me.

"Your father had a photograph of you. He pinned it to the wall of my flat. Not this hole, of course, but my grand flat near the Ku'damm."

Then she brought out wine and glasses and told us her story.

"Well, I was a star in those days. It was July 1942."

I was incredulous.

"You mean my father was still in Berlin in 1942?"

"Oh yes. There were still a few thousand Jews in Berlin that year. The deportations only began in October 1941. Didn't you know? There was a special dispensation for useful Jews. Protected musicians. A surgeon or two. Of course, it was only a remission. After the deportations began, there was only hiding."

"Are you saying you hid her father?" asked Sophie.

Frieda offered both of us another glass of wine. It was quite a treat for her, this visit. She was launched on her story now and needed little prompting.

"In 1942 they started to deport Jews district by district. They would telephone first and say, politely, be at home today, and most people were too frightened not to be there. They packed and waited. Well, your father didn't wait for them to find him. And for a time he was lucky. But he didn't have a ration card. Everything had to be bought on the black market. People sold their wedding rings, anything.

One day I was walking along Bayerische-strasse, and I heard his voice calling me. He looked old and sick, but I recognised him by his eyes. And his wonderful smile. From where I was standing I could see two German soldiers. I knew he must have been desperate to take the risk of calling to me."

"You must have been frightened?" said Sophie.

Frieda laughed.

"No, I was too stupid. The soldiers were just boys."

"You could have been shot or sent to the camps."

"I was only eighteen, my dear. I didn't think of those things. Anyway, I brought him home to my flat. I had a cupboard built in the gap between two walls. A walk-in wardrobe. Like they had in the films. Made it as comfortable as I could. And there he was safe, except for the catchers."

"Catchers?"

"One night an officer came to my door. 'Countess?' he said to me, 'we are very sorry to trouble you.' 'Please come in,' I said throwing the door wide. 'Have those vulgar people downstairs been complaining again?' His eyes were very bright and he took no notice of me, and soon his men were searching everywhere. At length he paused before the wardrobe I had put in, in front of your father's hiding place, and took out a revolver. 'Shall I shoot into this?' he asked me, his eyes glinting. I stared back steadily. 'If you wish.' I still hear the shot in my dreams. Then he opened the wardrobe and I saw the hole at the other side. I couldn't know if it had

43

penetrated the part of the wall where your father lay hidden, but inside there were only dresses and shoes. 'Well, we are wrong,' he said. 'I am sorry, Countess. If you will send us a bill for the damage.' And that was that. For a time we could live in peace."

"You make it seem as if he could almost have survived the war." I breathed. "What went wrong?"

"The air-raids, my dear. Hans could not go to the public air shelter. A bomb killed him."

It was Sophie who asked what had happened to my mother.

"She went off in the first year of the war to join her parents in Cologne. Her father had won an Iron Cross and she was sure he could protect her. She was wrong, naturally. They all died together."

*

When we left, I tried to work out how much I believed. It was a freezing night and getting very late but there was neither bus stop nor taxi to be seen in Kreuzberg. And then we heard the noise of feet and drunken singing, and a group of young louts marched round the corner. I knew that song. It was the Horst Wessel.

"Let's get away from here." I said, urgently.

But they had tramped round the next corner, still singing. Then we heard the sound of breaking glass, wild voices and the sirens of fire engines. There was a smell of burning cloth and something sweeter. We both knew something terrible was happening.

It was Sophie who said, "It must be those louts." And she set off running towards the noise, yelling after them, "Swine, swine!'

"Come back, Sophie." I called. "It's not your business to catch them. *Not your business...*" and my voice trailed off.

She returned, completely unafraid, angry only that they had got completely away.

"Sophie." I said, "what did you think you could do if you caught up with them? One girl among so many thugs?"

"I know it wasn't very sensible of me."

"It was very *brave* of you!" I said, shakily. I wondered if I would have shown as much courage all those years ago, or any more than the average German. Let me be more honest. I knew I would not.

I don't remember much about that night. Andrew was very angry with me, I suppose; he always tried so hard to protect me. He didn't believe a word of the Countess story. And I wasn't sure how much I believed either. But something had altered in me.

At a party the following night, I sat down at the piano and played with a group of other people listening, for the first time in years. It was a very small victory. But then, if you've lived like I have, you can't expect grand ones. I've lived timidly, and I don't suppose that will change very much, but my life isn't over yet. And perhaps Sophie has at least given me the courage to make use of it.

Lost Tribe Found

Ellen Galford

Lily and Ben. The Krazy Kousins. My mother calls them "Mr. and Mrs. Weird." They are the word *meshuggeh* made flesh.

Well, yes, they do have their little quirks. Ben finds conspiracies everywhere. Lily sees things. Sees Things. Which is why they moved out of 17, The Avenue two weeks after moving in. Lost a fortune on the transaction. But Lily didn't like what she'd Seen in the spare bedroom. Ben didn't argue.

"They make each other worse," sighs my mother. Who could disagree?

Still, family's family, and when not issuing dire warnings about dangerous coded messages in television commercials, Lily and Ben are perfectly delightful people.

But on this particular afternoon, my mother wants to strangle them.

" 'Two-thirty' " I said. 'No later than two-thirty...' That beautiful roast turkey (Did I tell you how much I paid for that?) is going to shrivel into a piece of shoeleather."

"You don't think maybe something's wrong? God forbid, an accident?" My grandmother. Always looking on the sunny side.

We certainly hope not. Apart from wishing only life's good things to come to Lil and Benny, it would spoil our little party. Grandma's eighty-fifth birthday, a special family lunch.

"We'd have heard," says Uncle Sam. "Ben would ring us on his mobile."

"Not if he's lying dead in a ditch somewhere," mutters Grandma.

There are fourteen hungry people gathered in our sitting room. My mother's sizzling like something on her own kitchen grill. "Should we eat? Should we wait? I'd hate to start serving, and then they walk in halfway through, and you know how touchy Lily can be.."

"Maybe," says Aunt Julia, "they've got the date mixed up."

"Not likely. Lily was on the phone to me only last night to tell me what I shouldn't cook for lunch today if I didn't want to give everybody cancer, piles, and senile dementia....".

Before her unthinking reference to piles can get Sam started on that subject, which is very dear to him, my mother makes an executive decision: "We eat."

Just as well. Grandma's already blown out her single symbolic candle (the cake is inscribed Happy 21 Plus) when Ben and Lily finally appear, rumpled and round-eyed.

47

"To say that we're sorry we're late," Ben announces, "would be, under the circumstances, pathetically banal."

"We've had an experience," breathes Lily, "the likes of which you would never..."

They look at each other, and then back at us.

"No, they probably wouldn't ever..." says Ben, "so there's really no point in even going into it. They just wouldn't believe it. So I suggest we all just get on with the party."

My mother is just angry enough to take him at his word. "Well, that's fine, then. You've missed the meal and the presents and singing Happy Birthday, but you can help us finish up the cake."

Ben waves his hands. "I couldn't eat a thing."

"We couldn't manage a mouthful," Lily intones, "because of the trauma."

"I wonder," whispers Ben, quite audibly, to Lily, "what the long-term effects will be? Nobody just walks away from something like that unscathed. I only thank god we're still alive."

Even my miffed mother pays attention now.

"We were," says Ben, "on the slip road, just coming off the motorway...."

"No, it was after that, sweetheart. At the roundabout..."

"You're crazy," he snaps. "Anyway, suddenly something goes wrong with the car. I have a perfectly firm grip on the wheel, and I don't lose control, and the road surface dry as a bone, so it wasn't a skid, and not another car in sight...but all of a sudden, we're literally pulled sideways."

"It was," Lily breathes, "like being sucked down a drain..."

"Hah!" from Grandma. "I told you they had an accident..."

"It wasn't an accident, Aunt Bessie," Lily murmurs. "I swear to god there was nothing accidental about it."

"We come to a dead stop," says Ben. "We're way off the hard shoulder. In the middle of an empty field. Then the car starts rattling and rocking and bouncing, literally bouncing, up and down."

"So we get out," (from Lily), "not knowing what on earth's going on. And then we, I don't know, black out or something. Both of us. And then suddenly we're awake again. But we're back sitting in the car. Just round the corner from your house."

"We just look at each other," Ben continues. "My head feels like it's whirled round 360 degrees. Then I start remembering things. And so does Lily."

"Like the two men..."

They both go quiet.

"Men, what men?" my mother screams. "Hijackers? Car thieves..."

"No, very nice chaps, very charming. Lovely crinkly smiles. One of them even reminded me a little bit of poor old Uncle Solly, god rest his soul..."

"They took us by the arm," Lily continues, "and led us down into this little dip in the field......you couldn't see it from the road."

"That's where they had it parked," says Ben.

"Had what parked?"

"Their ship. It was long and sort of oval, but flattish on top, and a little bit translucent..."

"Like bone china," Lily explains, "You remember Mama's good wedding china, the set that..."

"Enough about the china already, Lil... Go on..."

"So they invite us in."

"Well, invite isn't the right word, really, since they didn't actually say anything. But you couldn't say they forced us in, either because it wasn't like that, we just..."

"We just found ourselves inside this thing."

"So what was it," sniggers Sam. "The Starship Enterprise?"

Ben stands up. "That's it, Lily. I knew we shouldn't have even started. I'm tired. Let's go home."

He's pushed back down again. Somebody tells Sam to shut up. The tale continues.

"It was big inside. Doors and arches and passageways. They took us into this little place that was like a theatre. A few rows of seats, and a screen on a wall."

"Tell them what else they had, Ben," nudges Lily. "You'll never guess what they had. In that room."

Ben looks puzzled for a minute.

"You know..the..."

"Oh yes. The candles. They had — a menorah."

"A MENORAH?" All our voices, in chorus, making the chandelier shake.

"It was lit, but with these glowy light bulbs, not real flames. They were a funny shade of blue."

"Well the men were sort of blue-ish, too."

"Greenish!" snaps Ben. "Definitely greenish."

"No, blue-ish. Like the silk chiffon I wore to Sheila's boy's Bar Mitzvah..."

"Sha! Anyway, a third one comes in. He's dressed like the others— dark suit, and white shirt, collar and tie, very neat and tidy. Except they're both wearing hats, and he's wearing...a *kippel*."

"A WHAT?" Again, all of us together.

"You know—a skullcap, a *yarmulke*. Black velvet, with little shiny

49

embroidered designs. Oh, and a beard. He had a long silvery beard."

Then Ben falls silent. Looks up at the ceiling for awhile, then down at the floor.

"Go on...so what happened next?"

Lily giggles. "He may not want to say."

We all look at Ben. He's turning magenta, the shade of borscht with just a touch of soured cream.

"Tell them what they did," urges Lily.

"They don't need to know everything," he mutters.

"It's important. Go on..."

"Maybe it didn't really happen to us. Maybe none of this happened..."

"All of a sudden," Lily snaps, "he's ready to deny the evidence of his senses. Well, it happened all right."

"You tell them. I'm going into the garden for a cigarette."

He's out those French windows like time flying.

Lily lowers her voice. "His trousers. They made him take off his trousers."

"Made him?" Horror.

"Nobody forced him. They just smiled, and pointed to his belt buckle, and then his flies, and, very slowly, as if he's hypnotized, in some kind of sleepwalk, he undoes everything. And the next thing you know, his trousers are down and..."

"AND????"

"And the undershorts too. And they stand there —at a very respectful distance, but they all have a good long look."

"Oh my god,"— my mother's about to pass out; it's all too much — "and what did you do?"

"What do I do?" Lily shrugs. "I do nothing. After all, I've seen it before."

"Then what?"

"Then they have him zip himself up again, and they slap him on the back and it's nice friendly handshakes all round. Then half a dozen other chaps come through a door, and the man with the beard opens up a book — except it's not really a book, it's made of some kind of metal — and reads from it, and they all start davening. Ben looks a little confused — after all, this is a man who won't even put his foot in a *schul* on Yom Kippur without a shotgun to his head — and the bearded fellow, he's obviously the one in charge, just smiles and waves, as if to tell him just to go through the motions. So Ben starts bobbing his head up and down, and moving his mouth as if he's praying too."

"A *minyan!*" cries my father. "He was the tenth man! They needed him to make a *minyan*..."

50

The French windows swing open. We all jump sky high. Ben stands there, with his face closed up like a clam.

"It's alright," says Lily. "We're past that bit. Come back and tell them about the prayers."

"Hebrew. Definitely. The accent was strange, and I didn't recognize the actual words, but it was Hebrew all right."

"For somebody who needed to have the rabbi whisper in his ear line by line at his Bar Mitzvah," says Grandma, "that's pretty good going."

"So then," says Lily, "they sit us down and show us a video."

"Big technical expert," sneers Ben. "That wasn't video. God knows what it was..."

Lily overrides him. "Images, anyway. Starting with an ancient king... Assyrian, I think..."

"What makes you think he was Assyrian?" sniggers Sam. "What makes you think he was even royal? How big were his ears?"

"Some people," sniffs Lily, "have no culture. Didn't you ever visit the British Museum?"

"Anyway —" Ben takes over — "next they show us a great battle. Spears and shields, people getting their heads cut off, rows of captives, all that..."

"Then a burning city... Jerusalem. It had to be Jerusalem."

"How do you know?"

"For god's sake, stop asking me how do I know? Because our great-great-great-ancestor Hymie Pippick was running around the battlements pouring down boiling oil. Because his wife was throwing down *matzoh*-balls that looked just like Grandma Goldstein's on the heads of the invaders. Heavy as lead — killed seven Assyrians with a single blow... That's how! You want to hear this story or not?"

We tell him to go on already, and stop expostulating.

"Then all these thousands of people, in ten great long lines, with sacks and bundles loaded onto mules and oxen, all trudging off across a deso-lated landscape, with soldiers with rods and whips pushing them on... Then the ten lines divide, and four groups go one way, towards the desert, and three others go towards mountains, and two get on to reed boats and sail down a river. And the tenth lot, the last bunch of stragglers, stands alone in the middle of a great empty plain. And up from the horizon comes this enormous cloud thing, and it rolls across the ground and swallows up this entire band of refugees. Then they're inside the cloud, but the cloud's rising up through the sky. Then they're in space — the earth's hanging there, far behind them. Then the cloud lands on the surface of some other planet. It looks just like someplace on earth, with green plants and run-ning water. Then the cloud disappears."

51

"So what happens then?"

"So no more pictures. They motion us to get up from our seats, as if the show's over, and it's more handshakes all round. Then they present us with a gift — all wrapped up in thick paper — and everything goes pitch black. The next thing we know, we're back in our car trying to figure out what happened."

There's a long silence. Eventually my mother breaks it.

"I told you, Lily," she says, "that a portable in your bedroom was a big mistake. I think you and Ben spent half last night watching some ridiculous science fiction story. Then you slept in, and that's why you're late for Grandma's party."

"Well then," retorts irate Lily, reaching down into her enormous handbag, "what do you call this?"

She produces a brown paper parcel. We jostle for a better view, as Lily begins, slowly and ceremoniously, to open it. Then, one by one, she lifts out the twelve objects it contains. "You want proof? Here's proof."

They look strangely familiar. Smell strangely familiar, too.

"A dozen assorted bagels — two plain, two salted, two onion, two poppyseed, two sesame, and two garlic," says my father. "Almost like you'd get at Brodsky's."

"Exactly like you'd get at Brodsky's, I'd say," chimes in Uncle Sam, holding one up and scrutinizing it closely. "Do you think, there's maybe a branch of Brodsky's in Outer Space?"

"Mmm, delicious." I grab one, and take a bite. "Tastes exactly like a Brodsky's bagel too."

Lily screams, "No!" and snatches it away from me. "Not that one, for god's sake not that one. Spit it out!"

"So what's wrong with it?" I ask, defiantly swallowing.

"That's the one with the strange little seeds on it.."

"They may be strange to you, Lil," says my mother. "But to me they look like sesame."

"That's what they look like," pronounces Ben, "but I wouldn't be so sure."

"I'd keep an eye on that daughter of yours," says Lily to my mother. "See if she shows any strange symptoms."

"Like seeing little blue-green men?"

Lily and Ben have had enough. They gather up their coats, their dignity, and their eleven remaining extraterrestrial bagels, and depart.

"Mr and Mrs. Weird," sighs my mother. "What ever next?"

"I hope you haven't offended them," says Grandma. "I'd hate for a family feud to spoil my birthday."

But Lily isn't offended. She rings us first thing in the morning.

"I've been thinking," she says. "If that Lost Tribe needed my Ben as the tenth man for a *minyan,* then their population must be declining. That's why they've come back to earth."

"Why's why?" asks my mother, "I don't follow."

"Sometimes I despair of you, Sylvia," sighs Lily. "Don't you ever get the point? They've come back here to breed."

My mother falls silent for a minute, then says, "Okay, okay. Sounds logical to me." Anything to keep the peace.

Lily then enquires after my health. Wonders if I'm beginning to feel just the slightest bit queasy.

Maybe I am. Sesame seeds never did agree with me.

Says Lily, "We'll watch and wait."

A Suburban Tragedy

Jack Gratus

The arrangement had lasted for almost a year.

Once or twice a month—no more—he would visit her small, comfortable flat in a between-wars mansion block. He would walk there—it was only twenty minutes from his own house. She would receive him in a long, pink, silk dressing gown, her short, reddish-black hair softly framing her wide, pleasant face, her plump recently-bathed body wafting Madame Rochas when she walked.

She would take him by the hand and lead him to her living room, a warm, snug place furnished in dark blues and greens. There, by the two-seater sofa, she would leave him and while she went to prepare a tray of coffee and cake, he would either browse through one of the magazines neatly arrayed on a glass table at the side, or sit back, eyes closed, anticipating the pleasures that lay ahead.

From the kitchen would come the alluring sounds of the kettle boiling, the tray being laid out with cups, saucers, plates, spoons and forks. Five minutes later she would return, pushing a trolley across the room, the four small wheels making tracks in the thick, soft carpet. On the trolley was the tray and beside it a sumptuous cake.

"Ah, cheese today," he would announce. "My favourite!" Or mocha or almond or chocolate. Because, in truth, they were all his favourites. Her baking was, indeed, very fine, even better, he had to admit, than his dear wife's. He'd rub his small, strong, bony, liver-spotted hands together in anticipation.

She would smile her quiet, wide, knowing smile and start to cut a slice for him, bending to do so and the folds of her silk dressing gown would part slightly like the lips of a lover about to receive a kiss, revealing the lacy embroidery of her brassiere and the enticing white mounds of her breasts.

Slicing through the cake with the gleaming knife released its bouquet which would merge with the tang of the strong black coffee and her own fragrance to create a perfume that was, by itself, enough to arouse him. To be here, if only for an hour or less was a kind of heaven, a solace, and a refuge. Also, excitement and lust and laughter and exploration and discovery: all that had been missing from his marriage, wonderful though that was.

Outside the warmth of the flat the world was, since the death of his

55

wife, a lonely, menacing place, one of fear and shame. Fear that came to him in the middle of the night when sleep abandoned him to the wretched sense of worthlessness and futility, the widower's fiendish companions. Shame for the demonic thoughts that plagued him, he who had led such an exemplary life, who had raised a family of three, all of them now as respectable as their parents, and every bit as conscious of their position in the community as he and their mother were.

While he was here, he could breathe freely, his joints no longer ached, his bones no longer creaked; his head was clear and he could think about how this woman, no more young, no more firm of body, totally fulfilled his needs in her modest, playful, uncomplicated, undemanding way.

Only when, an hour or so later, he slipped out of her building, would his skin tingle and his cheeks smart with guilt, and he pulled his hat down further over his eyes.

They had met at their local health club which they both attended two or three times a week at a quiet time in the middle of the morning; he at his doctor's insistence that he had to lose the weight that excessive eating — consolation of widowhood — had caused. There, they put their bodies — his older than hers by a good ten years — through the rigorous routine given to them by one of the club's young instructors, forcing their legs to ride exercise bikes that went nowhere, to walk the treadmills to stay in the same place, and to climb hundreds of steps while still remaining firmly on the ground. *Meshugge*, but that's what you did these days to keep healthy.

He had been struck by the self-confident manner in which she carried herself amidst the preponderance of young, lithe women. It was as though she was saying to them: Your muscles may be harder and your flesh more firm than mine, but I have experience, and with that I can get any man.

True. She got him.

At first it was the surreptitious glance, he of her straight back and wide hips undulating encouragingly beneath the unerotic black of her workout tights as she climbed those infernal steps that led to nowhere. Then her of him, curious, amused, challenging. Then the exchange of smiles and the nods of greeting. Then he manoeuvring to ensure that he was walking the treadmill next to her so that he could exchange inconsequential pleasantries with her, about the weather outside, the temperature inside, the loudness of the music that the young instructors insisted on playing, the tunelessness of popular music today.

Which led to first names and gradually, over the next few weeks, with gentle probing from him, the broad outlines of her life. She had been born in Poland, came to England as a young child, and had always lived in Ealing. She had been no more than a girl when she married; her husband had

56

passed away five years ago. Her daughter was married to an American army officer and lived in the States. She seldom saw her. Sad, they agreed, when parents and children drift apart from each other.

He found himself looking forward to his workouts, which he had never done before. He made plans to meet her after their workouts, to invite her for a coffee or even a meal, but always he faltered, partly out of respect for his wife's memory, partly out of shyness. It had been a very long time since he had flirted and he had forgotten the ritual.

Friday nights he dined at his daughter's house, and after his grandchildren had gone to their rooms to play with their computers or telephone their friends, and her husband had disappeared into his study to work on a brief, or, as he suspected, to escape his father-in-law, he broached the subject.

To his delight and relief, his daughter reacted positively.

"Of course you should invite her out. It'll do you good. And knowing you, Dad, I've no doubt she's the very soul of respectability."

He'd assumed she was and said so.

"So, then, do it and good luck!"

A week later, he lay beneath her fragrant sheets and soft duvet, tired, flaccid, and inexpressibly content, reflecting — as she went to fix him a drink — that much as he had loved his wife, something had been missing from their marriage. Their passion had lasted only until the birth of their first child — two years after their wedding. Then two more children followed and their love-making became both desultory and infrequent; and after the hysterectomy it ceased altogether.

When she returned to the bedroom with his drink, she sat opposite him in her pink gown on a pink-upholstered chair, her legs crossed to give him just a peek of thigh, while he remained in bed sybaritically sipping the whisky — a very good one. She began by asking him whether he had enjoyed himself. Enjoy, he told her, was too feeble a word to describe his feelings. After all these years, it was more like a revelation: that his body was still capable of sensations his mind had all but forgotten. She had been gentle, firm, soft, hard, coy, outrageous — introducing him to variations in rapid and dazzling succession. In the time they had spent together she had magically converted a man in his late sixties to a stud in his early twenties. Or so it felt to him.

He said so.

"I'm pleased," she said.

"And you? What about you? Was it..."

She smiled and nodded.

Then she remarked how fortunate he was to own his own house because the landlord of her flat kept putting up the service charge. Surprised by this sudden change in the subject, he agreed that it was iniquitous.

"It's becoming impossible to live," she sighed.

Was there anything he could do to help, he found himself asking. Uncharacteristically, since he knew himself not to be essentially a generous man — other than to the regular charities that called on him. But then, that was expected of a man of his standing in the community. This was different. This was to a stranger, albeit one with whom he had enjoyed the best love-making of his life.

She demurred.

He insisted. Suddenly he felt himself opening up, to the experience, the adventure, the possibility, indeed, of passion.

"A small amount would help to tied me over," she ventured.

He asked her how much she would need, and flinched at the sum mentioned.

"But not all at once," she assured him. "Perhaps you could let me have a little at a time... whenever you visit, perhaps."

And, as she kissed him on the way out, her small, sharp teeth nibbling his lower lip in a way that made him want her again, he agreed to her proposition. Only when he was home again did he fully realise exactly what she had proposed. But by then it was too late. He was hooked.

If he reserved contempt for any other human, it was for the man or woman who did not take life seriously, who failed to consult the map before setting out on the journey. Until then, his business, his marriage had been subjected to his rigorous control. If it could be helped, nothing was left to chance; if it couldn't, he made every effort to prepare for all eventualities. And to ensure that whatever he did would not injure his good name. For that counted most. "A good name is better than great wealth," his father had instilled in him — and he in turn had instilled this in his children. In their turn, they had adopted a rigidity of decorum and a worship of respectability that had astonished even him.

Now, here he was, about to embark on an erotic adventure, the end of which was in the realm of the unknown, flavoured moreover by the most unexpected and not wholly, if the truth be told, unwelcomed spice. For the first time in his life, he would pay for his pleasure.

Though they saw each other regularly each week at the health club, she insisted on restricting his visits to only once or at the most twice a month.

"You'll grow tired of me," was her explanation.

But he found out later that there was another reason. She had other 'visitors', not many, perhaps no more than six or seven: all of them about his age and comfortably off as he was. The information was easy to come by; he asked her and she told him.

"Why should I lie to you? This is how I make my living. If you have objections, you must not come back."

He had, but he knew she meant what she said. If he remonstrated, she would tell him to leave — and he also knew that that, by now, was impossible. It had sneaked up on him surreptitiously, cunningly. He needed her. The routine of his visits was no longer merely a delicious interlude in an otherwise slow-moving sequence of days and nights, a stimulating pause in the monotonous and repetitive procession towards the inevitable. It dominated his thoughts, making anything else he did, even — God forgive him! — the weekly Friday nights with his daughter and grandchildren seem of little consequence. Time spent with his illicit whore — the word itself gave him a thrill of repulsion — was warm and welcoming, and whether that warmth and welcome was genuine or merely a reward, a quid pro quo, mattered not at all to him.

Every time he left the cosy caress of her arms, he sensed the unspoken rebuke of his darling wife. That the man she had been married to for over forty years, the father of three wonderful and successful children, the grandfather of four beautiful grandchildren, the giver of charity, the sayer of Saturday morning prayers, should have come to this — the shame of it! It was as though he were committing adultery, something he'd never done.

Exhausted, emptied, he would fall onto his bed and seek in sleep cessation from the agonies of ambivalence he suffered. But he got no respite. Vacillating between remorse and lust, between joy and despair, he flailed about in tortuous indecision. He wanted her — desperately — but just as desperately he wanted to be rid of her. He wanted to return to the old life, of certainty, boredom, predictability. At the same time, he did not know how he could live without her.

"I'm worried, Dad, you're not looking well," his daughter said, her high forehead — inherited from her mother — creased in a frown of concern.

He assured her he was fine; it was just that he wasn't sleeping.

Then, her eyes glinting wickedly, she asked, "Is there someone keeping you awake?"

He turned away from her saying nothing.

"I want you to see the doctor," she insisted. "For my sake, please."

He said he would.

Truth be told, he was also growing anxious about the exhaustion which shadowed him wherever he went. Morning and night he felt drained, and the little sleep he got seemed to make no difference.

It was that woman, he told himself.

That woman...

The phrase began to take root in his mind and spread its poison throughout his system.

Perhaps that woman was really the devil in disguise, come to impugn his virtue, to challenge the purity of his widowhood.

Things were coming apart. He who used to know what each day would bring, who planned what he would do from the moment he awoke till the moment he slipped into bed, what he would wear, eat for his meals, buy from the supermarket, read, listen to on the radio or watch on television, now faced the daily terror of uncertainty. Indecision opened up before him like a chasm, enticing him to fling himself into its tenebrous depths.

Enough! Something had to be done!

It was time to end their relationship, and soon. On his next visit, he would leave her with a larger cheque than usual, and that would be that. Before that, he went to see his doctor who examined him, pronounced him fitter than a man of fifty, prescribed a mild sedative and suggested he look in again in six months time.

Emerging from the doctor's surgery, he was overwhelmed with relief which was immediately followed by an urgent need to see her. Usually they arranged his next call when, on departing, he gave her his cheque — always a cheque, never cash, that was too demeaning. But now he decided to pay her a surprise visit and rather than walk the few blocks, he hailed a passing cab.

As he climbed into its leathery interior, his stomach gave a lurch and he feared he might humiliate himself by throwing up. The No Smoking sign and advertisements for health insurance and finance companies jumped and jiggled in his blurred vision. He slumped back, wiped the sweat from his face and breathed slowly to calm his palpitating heart.

"Where to, mate?"

He gave her address.

In minutes the taxi pulled up in front of the flats. He got out and as he paid he felt again the thud of his straining heart. Again he blamed her for bringing him to this state; and he wished he had not been so foolish to give in to his necessity for her.

Crossing the threshold of her building normally set off a shiver of anticipation that thrilled his every fibre and he would run up the stairs with a light tread, but not today. Today, he felt very different. His feet dragged and he had to pause at every landing for breath, cursing himself for not taking the lift.

He rang her bell.

No answer.

He rang again, pressing his thumb down hard. He could hear the peal echo forlornly through the flat.

The door swung open. A short, stocky man stood there, bare-chested and hairy. Though he had never seen the man before, he knew him to be another like himself, and the shock of recognition struck him in the chest, dead centre. The stranger's lascivious face was puffy, his eyes were hooded with desire. The smell of coffee, cake, of soft sheets and softer arms — her smell — exuded, preternaturally, from his pores mixed with the sour odour of concupiscence.

He glimpsed her approaching the front door, drawing her pink, silk gown around her white shoulders. He knew that beneath the gown she was naked and that, until he rang at the door, she had been in the stranger's arms, giving the same succour, the same raptures, the same taste of heaven that she had given him.

Gone in that moment was all he had felt about this place; gone the sense of safety, of warmth, of adventure, of pleasure. Lust, jealousy and anger surged within him; loathing — for her, but mostly for himself — pressed painfully against his chest

"Yes? What do you want?" the man demanded.

"I...I..." he started, but got no further. Shame gripped his throat so tightly he could not breathe.

He had to be away from there, as far as his legs would take him. The world must not know his disgrace. As he turned to run, a sharp wrench ripped his ribcage apart. His legs buckled and he struck the tiled floor.

Helpless, he saw her staring down at him. She appeared concerned. He opened his mouth to beg her not to leave him there where his children would find him.

But no words came.

The Circuit

Dan Jacobson

This is how it happens. A door opens. Lights blaze up. There is is an impenetrable blackness beyond. Voices of unseen creatures are raised in a hoarse cry. Life streams through me once again, and with it, terror.

I run.

It is all I can do. The sequence is always the same; yet everything happens at once. There is only one direction I can take. I am hurled towards it with a power much greater than my own. In front of me, towards me, under me, crushed grey cinders fly. Or am I the one who is flying, scudding, streaming? The beasts behind me, their heads lowered, tear at the track with long paws. The sound they make is rending yet pattering too, merciless yet hideously delicate. You would think that the cry which swells out of the blackness, and rises in pitch, would drown it out, but it does not do so. Nor does it overwhelm the other noises at my back: panting, slavering, whimpering, mewing, the snap of teeth. You would think also that the sudden rush of cold air from all that black space would dissipate the stink that follows me. But no, it is always there. Together with the smell of damp cinders, metallic fumes, a choking sweetness I cannot name, my nostrils are filled with the musk of the hounds' bodies, the meatiness of their breath.

That is how it happens every time. I run in a straight line, then in a curve which leads to another straight line, and so over and over again; until, with the same suddennness with which I was jerked out of my den, I am hurled back into it. The beasts vanish, taking their rage with them; the vague roar beyond the doorway subsides. I am safe in the dark stillness. The force that sent me hurtling around the field drains from me instantly.

Sometimes long periods pass and I am left in peace; but there are other occasions when I am hardly back in my den before the door is flung open, the lights burn, and I am running for my life. In one night this can happen six times, ten, a dozen, until it seems to me there will never be an end to it. Or rather, that there can be only one end to it. I will tire, stagger, fail, the beasts will leap, there will be an instant of tangled screaming and tumbling, soaring and tearing, and those claws will have ripped me apart, those teeth will have met inside me. I long to gather myself and spring sideways from the flat, naked course ahead of me, as all hares are born to do; but the bar which is attached to me, which floats alongside me, will

63

not let me do it. The same force that drives me out of my den when I want to remain there, cowering out of sight — that same force holds me rigidly on the path, directly in front of the muzzles pointing at me like needles, boring ever closer to me. Then, just when I think I can go on no longer, when I have almost begun to hope for the incandescent moment of my own extinction, there comes instead the slam of darkness, silence, solitude.

Empty days and nights follow. Anyone looking at me then would think that I am completely comatose, even lifeless, a rag, nothing more than a handful of fur affixed mysteriously to a flat, metal arm. I cannot move, it is true, unless that arm moves me; nevertheless my mind is still active. I try to use these periods to find out why I am compelled to live as I do, in such alternations of frenzied activity and stupor, of terror and idleness. Much depends on the position in which I am flung when the door closes. Since the door to my den does not quite reach the ground, I can see a little way out of it; lying on my side I can actually see more with one eye than I can with both eyes when lying flat on my stomach. In this manner I have been able to gather valuable information about both the beasts who hunt me and the relatively harmless humans who attend to them. The humans, who naturally interest me less than my enemies do, are tall and clumsy: this being the consequence, presumably, of their habit of walking on just two legs. They are the beasts' slaves: they walk tethered to them, they feed them, they fetch water for them, they stroke and brush them like valets, they talk to them in soothing, sycophantic tones, they dress them in little coats with buckles. Such attentions the beasts take for granted, of course, as proper masters should. My suspicion is that the shouting I hear out of the darkness comes from the humans, who are cheering their masters on; like any enslaved caste, like any downtrodden rabble, they want to see someone who is even worse off than they are (i.e. me) humiliated and destroyed.

As for their masters, the hounds, the hunters, it is actually easier for me, given my vantage-point in the den, to see them as wholes, from top to bottom and end to end, than it is to see the humans who are so tall. Like wraiths or devils, they are shadowy, wind-swayed; like predators, they are will and muscle. They walk on tiptoe, on grotesquely mincing legs, their frail rumps raised higher than their heads; from those rumps hang tails that are tucked into the curved, secret hollows behind, with a faintly obscene flourish at the end. Their long backs slope down to necks too emaciated to hold upright their cone-shaped heads; their ribs show like those of starvelings (no wonder they are so eager to get their teeth into me!), and between rear leg and torso there appears on each side a paltry, triangular flap of skin which expands and contracts at every prancing step. Out of their pointed faces, out of their open mouths, over their white teeth, a flat, serpentine tongue lolls and lets drop its spittle.

All this is demonic enough. But there is the effect also of their staring eyes; swept-back ears; polished pelts of grey, shining black, brindle, fawn, white. Not to speak of the macabre farce of the little jackets in bright colours with which they are adorned. When they chase me they wear jackets too; different jackets, embossed with magic numerals. Dressed to kill, they tear at the cinders with their claws. I hear them and run; run and hear them.

*

That is how it has always been. Nothing will change it, I am sure. They will always be what they are and do what they do; I will always behave as I have to. Only, something has happened recently that has made a difference. It is a difference in my mind merely, in my understanding of what is at stake between me and them; it does not show itself outwardly. Yet I now sometimes find myself waiting almost impatiently for that electric jolt of terror to burst through me, for the door to open, for the yell to go up from the crowd. I am still appalled, of course, by what follows; I have to be; I could not run if I were not. But I am curious too.

No, I have not fallen into the complacency of telling myself that because they have not yet caught me, after so many attempts, they will never succeed in doing so. Or rather, if I have begun to think in such terms it is for reasons more complicated than any such bald assertion might suggest. Lying in the dark on my side, looking with an eager eye at my tormentors, I found myself wondering unexpectedly if the time would come when it would be possible for me to recognise and remember them as individuals, from one occasion to the next. Was it always the same hounds who pursued me? Or did they change from time to time? And if they did change, why?

Hard questions. Initially the task of answering them seemed far beyond my capacities. First, there were so many of them. Secondly, the resemblance between them mattered far more to me than any differences I might be able to observe. Thirdly, there was the distraction of the coats they wore — why should I assume that they did not exchange them with one another, and so (perhaps intentionally) manage to confuse the onlooker? Fourthly... But do I need to elaborate on the chief difficulty? The sudden dazzle of light, the terror which possesses me, the speed at which everything takes place, the fatal presences behind me, their heads bent to one aim: in such circumstances who can look for distinctions, who can expect his memory to work effectively, who dare expend energy on anything but trying to get away?

65

Well, I did my best. Obviously it was easier for me to make the necessary discriminations when I lay hidden in my den, but I did try at other times too; even at the most desperate of times. Eventually, after much trying, I began to get results. I learned to tell the brutes from one another not just when they were parading and titupping near my door, but even on that shelterless track, when they were cascading after me in a molten mass. I even learned to know some of them by the names their slaves used in addressing them, and which I had previously taken to be nothing more than interchangeable, honorific titles: Glamour Jack, Flibbertigibbet, Quasimodo, Queen Alexandra, Tony Pandy, Grey Steel, Snapdragon, and the rest. What is more, after intense study and the taking of unprecedented risks as we ran, I began to recognise those among them who presented the greatest threat to me. In other words, I got to know whose teeth were most likely to be snapping at my tail, whose strides covered the most distance at each bound.

Though I did not realise it at the time, a crucial moment or series of moments came once I discovered that I could almost always tell in advance which among a particular group of my enemies was likely to be the wickedest and most dangerous. I remember lying in my den and thinking how rich I would become if only I were able to use my hard-won knowledge by laying bets against others — other hares, hounds, people, whoever you like — as to which of the brutes would outstrip the others. Of course, in my solitary condition this was mere fantasy. In any case the knowledge I was acquiring was to bring me riches enough. Spiritual riches. Gifts of understanding. Power. Again, it took me a long time to realise how this could be so; but I got there in the end.

You see, I learned that none of my enemies managed to hold on indefinitely to a position of leadership among them. I also learned that once a leader lost his pre-eminence, it was gone for good. More than that: if he began to fall back in the troop, the process would go on inexorably. And then? He vanished! No more prancings, no more brushings and fondlings from his slaves, no more pursuits of someone who had never done him any harm. Over now. Gone. Finished.

All this I gleaned either in the relative comfort of my den, or, with eyes rolled back, in the dazzle and darkness of the chase. But its ultimate meaning eluded me until, one day, without forewarning, a thought in the form of three simple words stole into my mind. *They grow old.*

Obvious enough? Yes, I grant you that — now. That is how it always is, with new ideas. Yet it was not until I was once again doing what I was compelled to do, flying, scudding, fleeing for my life, that a further insight came to me. I am one, they are many; I alone am sent out to do this over and over again, a dozen times in a night perhaps, innumerable times

66

every year; yet I feel no older, or slower, no less infused with electric power. And where are those hounds that pursued me a year ago, or two years ago, or five? Old, lame, exhausted, enfeebled, dead possibly. While I, their victim, their prey, the object of their lust, the creature for whom life and terror are one, am still here, racing ahead of their successors, and the successors of their successors.

Bastards! Let them wear themselves out, generation after generation of them, chasing a timorous creature so much smaller than they are. Now I wait with some restlessness for each outing, longing to see which of them has managed to survive the course, what newcomers are among them, how well these newcomers will perform. True, I am as frightened as ever, but fear itself has become a source of exhilaration for me. I dream of one day winning control of the force which controls me, and of using it so that I can dawdle for a moment, and come directly under their noses, and thus drive them even crazier than before, and then whisk myself away from them. Let them scrabble at the cinders behind me, and send their infuriated stink ahead of them; let their eyes burn and their spittle flash: the harder they run this time, next time, the time after, the sooner they will wear themselves out.

Am I the victim, then? Think of their children, as maddened and hungry as they are, as unavailing, heads lowered, necks stretched, mouths open, minds aflame, hearts bursting; and of their children's children; and of me, the electric hare, flying.

Strudelbakers 1951

Zvi Jagendorf

"*Mixgarm* nu," says Onkel Mendl, frowning and licking his pencil stub. The crumpled piece of paper he is reading from is a strip torn off a one-pound bag of sugar. When he finishes there will be a trace of white dust on the square green table where they make their holy strudel.

Mixgarm
Ninedy granshit large
Eidy granshit midyem
Foddyvool blenkit
Nu?

Mendl looks up from his piece of paper to see if I am keeping up.

"Don look in de air. Is nuddink der." His broad thumb presses down on my ruled page as he stares suspiciously at the round entries and the clear but wobbly column of numbers dangling along the margin.

"You didn't say how many, Onkel Mendl."

"How many?"

"Yes, how many *mixgarm*?"

I am trying to keep my mouth in a straight line. It wants to go loose and let the shriek out. I'm not laughing at Onkel Mendl. He has a hard enough time working at Romeo Rags and making his weird English understood by those big Londoners who heap the sacks of clothes in piles and move the stuff onto shelves. No, it's *mixgarm* that sets me off. It is Mendl's best invention and a regular on the Romeo Rags list.

Mendl thinks I'm making fun of his stock keeping at Romeo Rags. How could I do that? It's the best job he ever had. But *mixgarm* sings in my head. I think of army surplus vests and socks peeled off, brown and yellow underwear, green berets and blue caps all tumbling around in a crazy dance. Harry James plays the trumpet and the socks get tied up with the underwear, vests crawl into shirtsleeves and the big heap of musty clothes throbs and trembles on the floor of Romeo Rags while Mendl tries to keep count with his pencil stub.

That's what Mendl needs me for, to keep count of the stock list once a week because he can't really write, not English anyway. And now when business is good and the trucks shunt into the delivery yard near King's Cross Station spilling out the war junk left behind by armies and navies all over the world it has got to be done almost every night.

"How many *mixgarm*, Onkel Mendl?" I repeat. My uncle gets a cunning look in his eye. He is a hunted bear, a soft bear with oval eyes in the forest near Yablonitza where he was born and he's looking out at me from behind the dark green leaves. A shot rings out. A flat crack bounces off the walls of the little room where they do the holy strudel. It's the door downstairs. Tantie Rosa is on the way.

Mendl won't tell me how many *mixgarm* to put down. Not tonight and not tomorrow, because he doesn't know. It's not that he's a bad counter. He's fine. He counts the pennies when he empties the phone box and puts them into exact piles for the bank. He counts the pages when he prays every morning to make sure he's said it all. Onkel Mendl doesn't understand Hebrew. He reads OK but the words are like empty envelopes for him. He puts in them whatever he wants to complain about that day and counts the pages so he knows God's got the lot. But Mendl doesn't have the *mixgarm* number. That's his secret.

In walks Rosa all flush, bones and wetness in her business clothes. She's out all day doing the shoulder pads for Mr. Glick of BeeGee Trimmings and she's very tired.

"The buses," she says very loud "the buses. You can wait till you are dead. Then the wild animal conductor, the antisemite madman, pushes me off and rings the bell. 'No more standing.' A wild animal. Where's Bernard?"

Tantie Rosa is peeling off her nice coat, the one she wears for appointments with "good buyers." She likes flowery scarves and pink and lemon fluffy cardigans and tight skirts that hug her bony legs and show a bit of knee. One of her favourite songs is about the bony legs of Elisabeth, a German woman, I think. She sings it loud in the bath remembering it all from Vienna when she was a girl and going dancing. That was before Mendl.

Wenn die Elizabet
Nicht so grosse beine hat

I keep my eye on that German Elisabeth with the long legs and the fuzz in her armpits. Her horses are black and her bottom bounces in the saddle soft and hard, soft and hard as she rides. I watch her from behind the wall of Opa's timberyard as she gallops along with her friends in the Hitler Youth. I hope they're all dead.

"Where's Bernard?"

"He's over at Heinzy's playing chess."

"So where's his homework? Has he finished his homework that he can go and play *chess*?"

She hisses the word to make it sound like steam sluicing out of the vats in hell.

"We were sent home early because of the fog. Nobody got any home-

70

work today."

I know how to cover up for Bernie though this is getting harder by the minute. Bernie has proved to himself that there is no God and eating kosher is total nonsense and garbage. He's tried to show this to me but I can't follow him. He flips the pages of his barmitzva Bible and gets mad about the fate of the Amalekites and the Hittites.

"How could he have told them to exterminate a whole tribe of bloody people? How could he? And how could they have gone and done it? Just like that? A bunch of spineless fascists."

Bernie says he goes to the toilet and eats a Mars bar after meat meals just to show them. I've seen the Mars bar before and the wrapping after but I don't know if I believe him. I mean, to eat milk things after meat is quite a big step even if you don't believe in God.

Onkel Mendl's attention has wandered from his list. He's not clutching the pencil anymore. I know what he's thinking: soup, potatoes and white cheese with green onions. Supper.

Tantie Rosa has gone up the few stairs to the bedroom and is peeling off her colours and straps and slips and shivering a bit in the cold. She thinks she's a sex pot and makes love to herself in the mirror every day, taking off her glasses to bring her bony nose and thin lips right up to the surface so she can worship her idol. Mendl doesn't look at her much, not in *that* way. He mostly looks at her as if he was inspecting a bundle of *mixgarm* waiting to be counted and sorted and sent out into the world to make money.

Rosa reappears transformed. No legs, fluff, spikes and colours. All gone. She has become a sack, a green sack. Her angles have been swallowed by the housecoat that wraps her up from ankles to neck. Mendl looks at her with more interest. This bundle makes hot food and will stand next to him when they wash dishes and talk in the steamy little kitchen.

"Karpels made an order," Rosa announces. Her English is healthy and confident with bits of Vienna thrown in when she's home or around other refugees.

"He made a big order though he's not sure business improves."

Now Mendl looks at her with astonishment and admiration. When he married her they said she couldn't boil water. She threw herself on the floor and spat blood when he refused to swallow the glue she called goulash. Now in a new country she's selling shoulder pads to the best of them and cooking meals fit for the royal family.

"Why isn't Bernard here already? Why is that boy always making trouble?"

Rosa is standing in the door head cocked to one side like a pigeon.

"That boy is never where he should be. What's he doing? Reading comics?"

71

"I told you Tantie Rosa, he's at Heinzy's playing chess."

I am supposed to be the truth teller in this family because that was my dead mother's character but Rosa doesn't believe me. She's totally suspicious as far as Bernie is concerned and she has a point. He is naturally shifty and he doesn't mean a thing he says. Most of the time even I don't know where he is. When he tells me he's bunking out of Hebrew classes to go to watch football in the park, he's probably gone to the market to see the puppies and canaries. When he says he's doing homework with one of his friends you can bet they've gone down the West End to look at the women in slit skirts outside the strip clubs. Bernie piles Brylcreem on his hair to get the hedgehog out of it and slicks it back over his ears with soft flicks of his comb.

"Der boy is sure mit Heinzy . Yunno he likes to play a long time."

Mendl is defending Bernie not because he believes in him. He needs supper not a row and he doesn't want to see Rosa get in a temper, throw a fit and run to cry on the bed upstairs. When she gets this way he tries to comfort her but his big, hairy, brown hands can't calm her shaking back and he pats her there gingerly with arms stretched out as if she was a dangerous scratching cat.

"Der boy vill come soon. So come and eat."

Rosa gives up and goes into the kitchen. Mendl's face sags with relief as he starts cleaning the table. He hums a little and puts all the Romeo Rags stuff in a pile with my school books. Julius Caesar on top, Mendl's list underneath.

In the middle of soup Bernie walks in. The hot spoon is half in my mouth as he pushes the door open and flips into the chair all in one glide like a wing forward slicing through the defence. Mendl, concentrating on his soup tries not to notice very much. He just points to the bread and says:

"Wash de hands."

Mendl thinks that washing hands is the best way to prevent disease and hold off God's anger. Rosa isn't saying anything which is bad.

She pokes at the peas and carrots with the tip of her spoon. Bernie is enjoying this. He loves danger.

"I washed my hands on the way," he says picking up a piece of bread but not putting it in his mouth yet. Rosa pokes at peas. Mendl has to choose between eating and conducting a violent inquiry about where hands can be washed between Newington Green and Stamford Hill. Bernie, I know, has worked it out in his mind. He's thought up a list of all the possible hand washing stations on the route: Heinzy's house, two public toilets, one a bit of a detour, a yeshiva, a library and the town hall. Mendl feels he is trapped. He's been caught in this kind of game before.

72

"Go get some soup and put a *kappel* on."

Mendl has given in but it's not total surrender. He's got the sacred headwear rule in place and is secretly bargaining with Bernie. A piece of headcover for a plate of soup and a bit of quiet.

This is a hard one for Bernie. For him putting a cap on his head any-time is a sellout and a shame. The tough kids in school never wear them even though it's a rule. They'd rather wipe their bottoms with them and Bernie has got religion to fight against as well.

"No bleeding business of his what I put on my lousy head," is Bernie's opinion and it's got him kicked out of Hebrew school hundreds of times. But at home Bernie is quite unpredictable. Sometimes he'll stick some-thing on his head without a blink as if he was scratching his skull and start eating with his nose in the plate and his eyes half closed. But this time he's not in a giving mood. By the wild look in his eye I figure he's been down the market and got excited by the smell of the animals and the pushing and rubbing of the crowd. He could have started up with one of the girls down there and got her to say she'd meet him near the Regent Cinema on Saturday night. If he had done that and told her stories about his being a boxer or a champ dancer in clubs it would be totally ridiculous for him to stick a piece of black cloth on his head just to please Mendl and God.

Mendl goes one step further. He reaches down below his chair where he keeps old newspapers and fishes out a tiny bit of black cloth. That was the smallest piece of headgear in the house, minute enough to have been put on Bernie's head at his circumcision. Mendl means to say "put this on, who will notice?" But he can't say it out loud. So he goes:

"Dis *kappel* is good. Yetzt eat."

The black scrap of rayon hangs between them like a pirate's flag while Rosa watches through the steam on her glasses and I shuffle my feet under the table.

A curse, a kick of the chair and Bernie is gone. The door bangs, the chair is empty and the *kappel* is shipwrecked on the table between the salt and the bread. Rosa stares at me like the prosecutor at the Nuremberg trials.

"You see what children do to their parents? You see what trouble? Why?"

She bangs her big spoon on the table and it leaves a stain on the cloth. Luckily I don't have to answer, Rosa is asking the world, the shoulder pad buyers, the journalists who write about film stars, the women whose sons are successes, she's asking them all to pity her for being the mother of a boy who never ever gave her *one minute of pleasure* in her entire life.

Mendl sighs not because he's so sad about Bernie but because he's

73

warm and sweaty in the folds of his neck and wants to get on to the next plate.

"You vant lemonade?" he says to me and it almost knocks me off my chair. Lemonade is like champagne in this house. It's served on holy occasions and birthdays only, and that's as strict a rule as wearing hats. Pouring lemonade is a sacred act like making strudel or blessing the wine. It has to be done right with a steady hand while all present look on wearing their best clothes. Mendl needs some ceremony now, in the middle of the week, to get him through the awkward gap between Bernard and the potatoes.

He slips out and is back in a moment with a bottle. Rosa looks angrily at the bubbling drink in our two glasses and at his approaching hand.

"I don't want," she says covering her glass. "I lost my appetite because of that boy."

Mendl keeps the bottle in mid-air and fishes for her eye. He's only trying to make her forget her troubles in the fizz. But the woman is obstinate. Her hand stays over the glass and her nose droops in sorrow over the empty soup plate. Mendl is in trouble. He is watching his meal disappear into a solitary five minutes of chewing and swallowing while Rosa thrashes about in a fit on the bed upstairs.

I have an idea. "I'll go and see if Bernie's still outside. I'll talk to him." I don't wait for Mendl's nod and slip out.

They're not as hard on me as they are on Bernie because of my dead mother which makes me an object of pity or worse an example of righteous suffering for Bernard's education.

"Look Bernard how de boy *nebbich* do his homework and keep his books nice and clean." Mendl's praise only makes Bernie want to spit in my soup. I mean who ever heard of anybody getting marks for having a dead mother? Worst of all is that Yiddish word *nebbich*. It sounds like scummy bathwater going down the drain and it marks you as a loser for life.

So I go into the gloomy dark of the street and no one's hanging around either of the two bus stops. I peer through the gate of St. Ursula's across the road. Bernie sometimes roams around in the garden of the convent looking for French letters. "Bern," I even try a whistle but there's no Bernie, just the threads of fog hanging around the trees and the rumble of a bus up the road somewhere.

When I get back upstairs he is there snug in his seat and all three of them are eating potatoes and white cheese with total concentration. Steam from their dishes is practically swirling over them like a typhoon but they are at rest in the eye of the storm doing the thing that binds them together best — eating. I know better than to say anything and go and get my helping from the kitchen. Bernie has clearly pulled one of his routines. I look at the top of his head. There stuck into the folds of bryl-creemed hair is the flattened out bottom of an ice cream cup. You can see the yellow stain of banana punch round the edges. They're all eating with real fervour because Bernie has covered two inches of his skull with a piece of non-kosher ice cream wrapping. It's a miracle. Everyone is happy. Mendl has got his food, Bernie his laugh and Rosa is excused from rushing upstairs getting her face all smeared with tears.

"Don't let the food get cold," says Mendl to assert his authority over the family altar. I join in and try to ignore Bernie who's made a fool of me and shown me up for a smarmy snot, stumbling about in the dark outside the convent gates. Meanwhile he has helped himself to a full glass of sacred lemonade. That was his talent: first throw a match at the pile of straw then collect a reward for putting the fire out with his pee.

Yet Rosa is still the unpredictable element here. She likes her food as much as anyone but she's not as totally concentrated on getting it inside and she has not given up her fight against Bernie. She went to war with him fifteen years ago in Vienna when he showed insufficient gratitude for being dragged out of her belly by one of the best and most expensive doctors in the city. This time she doesn't confront him with words. She doesn't call him "lazy swindler" or "snake" or "parasite" or "English footballer." She mumbles under her breath, developing an in-throat commentary on Bernie's character. You can't hear anything definite but sounds of aggravation and disssatisfaction well up from her plate in the direction of Bernie who ignores them and Mendl who doesn't hear them. Rosa could still explode. Then plates would fly and Bernie would get hit, first by hands and then by anything, spoons, candlesticks, hairbrushes, rulers, calendars, coal tongs. He never reacted to that. He just went pale and covered his head with his hands while he waited for the fit to pass. He knew her better than she knew him but that didn't mean he forgave her. This time though she quietens herself down and she and Mendl go into the kitchen to wash up, leaving Bernie in the room with me.

He picks up the pile of papers with my Julius Caesar and Mendl's list. "Caesar shags on Romeo's rags, written down by the poor slave and scribe Josephus the Hebrew. What are you getting for it?"

Bernie is probably jealous because Mendl doesn't ask him. Not that he'd do it but he wants to know they need him for something.

He looks at the list.

"Groundsheets and long underwear women! Dirty bastards. Did he give you money?"

Bernie knows Mendl doesn't give me a penny for the list but he's desperate. If he's taking out a girl he needs cash and the telephone money is dead since they put a new lock on the box.

"Have you got any?"

"No."

"Not in your socks?"

"Nothing."

Bernie suspects me of saving pocket money and bus fares. But he's wrong. I've got no money though I have saved *something*. It's my dead mother's gold tooth and I keep it in an old purse of hers with some pictures and a letter in Yiddish from her father. I look at the tooth sometimes but it bothers me to touch it because I think of it set in her mouth and being touched by her tongue when she was alive and talking.

Bernie is fascinated by this tooth and he doesn't mind touching it at all. He says it doesn't make sense to think about dead people as if they were alive, moving, smiling and talking and all that. You've got to think about them as part of the earth.

"Your ma's tooth," he told me once "stopped being part of her when it fell out. It could be anybody's tooth now. It's independent of humanity." But I see my mother trying to smile and holding her hand up by her mouth to cover the gap where her tooth used to be. That tooth is the centre of my mother's face and I can't look at it without hearing her voice which isn't really a voice but a jumble of unclear sounds in a language I've forgotten.

"Will you let me flog it? I'll give you half."

Bernie stops fingering my Latin book and looks me in the eye.

"I need cash and I can't get it anywhere else. Melzer will give us a few quid for it."

My dead mother swims up through the garden window and puts her finger to her lips saying SHUSH and moving her head. I don't know if it's yes or no she's saying or even if it's me she's saying it to.

"What do you care about a bit of gold made in Vienna? It's just like a toenail — only you can sell it."

She isn't there any more and I have no answer for Bernie. He could steal the tooth anytime, I know, and nothing much would happen. I would cry and tell Mendl. Rosa would scream and hit him with her shoe. But he would survive and I needed him to talk to in bed at night. Anyway he's being honest asking me for it because he's secretly sorry about my dead mother even if he pretends not to give a fart for anything THEY want him to care about.

"Clear up de table boys."

Mendl is back flushed from the steam and the animated talk in the kitchen. He needs the table empty for his labour of love — strudel baking.

Mendl is an expert strudel baker. That is, Rosa is the real artist and he's her technical director and stage manager. To make the strudel he needs an empty table and total concentration. No radio, no chatter, no interruptions. Just one table, a man and a woman, the dough and the filling. When we were younger we used to beg them to let us watch while they laid it out. Mendl would bring the dough in, warm and eggy from the kitchen. Then he'd dust some flour onto the smooth green surface of the table and the holy work of thinning and stretching would begin. They would stand opposite each other on either side of the little table and work at the dome of dough moving it over the surface to one side and the other, teasing it out, juggling it, squeezing it, getting it to cover more and more of the green, wheedling it into a thin, perfectly intact wheel without a tear. Mendl thought a hole in the dough was a crime.

When he directed the work of stretching and thinning, getting Rosa to pull a little harder here and a bit softer there, he was like a great conductor reaching over a big sighing orchestra, making it sing to his sway. He was Toscanini and she was his first violin responding to his hands with love and obeying the rhythm of his elbows. But if he saw the first sign of a tear in the dough, even just a trace of a thinning bubble, he brought the music to a halt. He made Rosa sit down while he bent over the wound and mended it with prods of his fingers while his broad lips pouted in concentration.

When the dough was stretched out on the table like the skin of a hunted animal they stood over it and their faces seemed to glow and reflect its whiteness. It was their mirror and it showed them Adam and Eve. Shining into their faces it said "Fill me with apples."

This was Rosa's side of the holy work. She took charge of spreading a snaking line of sour apples and raisins and nuts and orange peel, doling it out on the dough with twists and flicks of her spoon while Mendl watched for any sign of a tear or a weakness in the structure. This was the really tricky part because Rosa had to know how much filling would pack the dough and stuff it nice and fat without spoiling the perfect thin skin that Mendl needed to make him happy. What made it right was the correct weight of soft, tart fruit to the proper resistance of thin, crisp skin. Only Rosa knew the secret of that.

Then when she had finished shaping out the line of filling they bent over the table, both of them together like surgeons over a patient, and began to wrap the dough round the fruit tenderly and in unison, not saying a word, not even looking at each other but completely together as they never were away from this table and the strudel they made on it.

Bernie is jumpy. He wants the tooth and for some strange reason he can't just take it and "fuck you." He drags me upstairs to our bedroom which is really a bit of the posh room partitioned off.

"Take it out, let's have a look."

77

"I don't want to now."

"Come on we'll have a look and talk."

Bernie knows I depend on him for information about girls and techniques of kissing. He keeps me awake all night with his crazy stories. But there's a price to pay. He prods me towards the shelf where I keep my mother's purse.

"You can have it," I say "take it. Go and do what you like with it."

Bernie stands there looking a bit strange.

"I bet your ma was a good dancer. I bet she got dressed up and went out to have a good time."

I don't understand Bernie. We hardly ever talk about my dead mother and when he makes fun of THEM he never mentions her. Even when I go to the clinic for my monthly TB checkup Bernie keeps quiet as if it was the most natural thing in the world.

"She wasn't like THEM. Complain, eat, complain, worry, eat, pray. She liked a laugh. She must have been really popular when she was a girl."

This doesn't sound like my mother. But I begin to see what Bernie's aiming at. He wants to enlist her on his side. She will then make it alright for him to take her gold tooth out of her purse and sell it so that he can go and enjoy himself with a girl.

"Don't bring her into it. Just take the tooth and forget all about it."

I take the tattered maroon purse and open it. Two tiny pictures of me and her. She's looking frightened. I am bundled up. A train ticket. The faded Yiddish letter. The tooth. I can't touch it. It looks like a yellow glass eye glaring at me from inside the dark, accusing me of being a bad son, of not protecting my mother's memory, of letting body snatchers chop her up. I feel sick and dizzy.

"You alright?" says Bernie, scooping up the tooth with a flick of his finger. He was gone without waiting for an answer. I am sitting on the bed with the purse spilled out in front of me. It looks like a dead, rotting bird.

I sit there for a while listening to the noises of the house. The radio goes on and off. Mendl and Rosa have cleared away the baking stuff and are talking quietly while the strudel in the oven bathes in the heat and concentrates its juices.

My mother slides in from behind the curtain. She's not angry, just pale and preoccupied. She's looking for something, perhaps Bernie, perhaps her tooth. She takes in the whole room with her dead eyes and she takes note of everything in it separately. My books, my football souvenirs, my list of girls written in invisible ink, my hidden chewing gum and the holes in the elbows of my school blazer. She misses none of these things and she shows neither approval nor disapproval. She's too busy concentrating on looking and I understand that even though I wish she would look at me.

Then she's gone and Mendl and Rosa are climbing the stairs to their cold bedroom.

Soon the four rooms in which we live will be silent till Bernie sneaks back and wakes me up with his latest story. It is quiet but the silence is crammed full of the spicy smell of the strudel. It fills the cold rooms with the fragrance of fruit and cinnamon and roasted nuts and baked dough. It creeps into the cupboards, under the beds, into the battered suitcases and around the bottles of holy lemonade. It comforts Mendl and Rosa in their bed and mingles with his sweat and the cheap scent of her night time face cream. Soon he will go down and take the strudel out of the oven.

Then its fragrance will draw me down like a spell to the little room with the green table. There cooling off, left to glimmer in the night like a golden trophy will be Mendl and Rosa's perfect child, an object of praise, a source of pleasure and pride, warm, silent and ready to be devoured.

The Hand of God

Gabriel Josipovici

Jews — even the most secular Jews — cannot seem to get rid of the idea of God. He haunts our lives even when we claim never to give him a thought. Take my friend Victor. I vaguely knew that he was Jewish, but had never heard him speak of Jewish matters, attend a synagogue or keep a Jewish festival or fast. I do not know if his wife Hilda was Jewish and their daughter was certainly not brought up to think of herself as such. Yet when the moment of crisis came, there was God in the middle of it all.

There have been many examples, in our modern world, of promising and even very good writers — Rimbaud is of course the most famous — suddenly ceasing to write, giving up abruptly from one day to the next, when nothing in their lives or earlier work could have prepared us for such a move. That is what happened to Victor.

Though only in his early thirties, his career seemed already well-established, his reputation steadily growing. It was not just the quality of what he wrote that drew me to him, but the sheer quantity and variety of it: novels, short stories, poems, articles, stage plays, radio plays, opera libretti — they poured from him in a seemingly endless stream, yet each item, no matter how small or how great, showed the same qualities of craftsmanship, clarity, precision, wit and fantasy. When one leads a dull and humdrum life as I do, but has nevertheless had, now and again, intimations of something else, of values beyond the purely economic and hedonistic, then a friend like Victor is more than a stimulating companion, he is in some sense a living proof that there is something else to life than merely getting on and getting by. Knowing him, I have sometimes thought, must be what knowing a hero or a saint must have been to people of an earlier age.

Not that Victor fitted ones common idea of the artist. He lived an ordered, simple life in Clapham, with his wife and daughter, taught in a local school and, even after the relative success of his second and third novels, never showed the least desire to change his way of life. Indeed he always insisted that he needed the regularity of school-teaching, that he did not want to become dependent on his publishers or ever be forced to write what he did not want to write. Nor did he have a very high opinion of publishers and literary people, never accepting invitations to prize-givings or book launches, his own, of course, excepted.

He was not interested in literature; rather, writing was his life. Enter-

81

ing his study at the top of the cool, high-ceilinged house in Clapham, you felt that this was a living, vibrant space, a place of peace and order and creativity. It is impossible to describe it without sounding sentimental or idealistic, so I will only say that on the few occasions when he invited me up and allowed me to sit there with him for a few minutes, I felt at once that my life had been enhanced, and I went away happier and richer for the experience.

That is why when he stopped writing and turned his study into a lumber-room the shock was devastating.

Outwardly, nothing changed. His life went on as it had always done, teaching, being with his family, occasionally inviting friends over and in turn accepting invitations to visit, and to the outsider it would have been impossible to guess that anything dramatic had occurred. His agent and his publisher, though mildly disappointed, were not particularly put out, since his success had always been more a question of esteem than of large sales, and they had other, more lucrative authors to whom to turn. But for me, as the fact sank in that he really did mean it when he said that he would never write again, it was a blow almost beyond bearing. I felt when he told me — we were sitting in the downstairs drawing-room with the French windows open onto the garden and the sound of birdsong filling the room — I felt then rather as I imagine those clerics must have felt when they were informed that the new science now proved that the earth was not the centre of the universe but only a minor planet orbiting round the sun: it can't be true! Surely someone will arrive soon to say that it is all a mistake! But it was and no-one did.

He was quite open that day about what had happened. It was not that his gifts had suddenly deserted him. It was not that he had come to realise that his ambitions would never be fulfilled. (Such a thought would never have entered his head; his ambitions were not to win prestigious prizes but to write to the best of his ability and perhaps to prove himself worthy of his great heroes, Kleist and Kafka.) No. It was much stranger than that.

This is what he told me.

He had been sitting at his desk at the top of the house, with the window wide open and the big chestnut almost within touching distance, his notebook open on the desk in front of him but his mind far away, when all of a sudden he felt himself falling. He was quite clear about what was happening, he said. He was falling out of the study window and he could measure his descent against the tree. Although he was falling at enormous speed and knew he would hit the earth in a fraction of a second, he said, he was also falling very slowly, and every leaf on the tree and every cobweb on every leaf and every ant crawling about the trunk was clearly visible to him.

He knew it was the end, he said, and he knew that somehow he had been expecting this for a long time. That was important, he said: somehow he had been expecting it and even waiting for it for as long as he could remember. He was not frightened, he said, but on the contrary, calm and lucid and full of a sort of serene acceptance, almost of relief. He reviewed his whole life and concluded that he had done what he could with the gifts and opportunities that he had been given, and had no regrets. And it was at that moment, he said, as he was examining his life and recognising it for what it was, that he felt a hand fold itself round him and in one swift but firm movement pluck him out of the air and thrust him back through the window and into his chair at the desk in his study.

"It was the hand of God," he said. "I had no doubt at all that it was the hand of God. It plucked me out of the air so gently and so firmly, though I was hurtling towards the ground at terrifying speed, and it returned me to where I had been before I began to fall."

"I knew at once that it was the hand of God," he said, "and I knew too that everything was over."

"Everything?" I said stupidly.

"Everything," he said.

"I don't understand," I said.

"I sat there at my desk," he said, "as I had sat only a few minutes, perhaps a few seconds, earlier. I was quite calm, despite all that had just happened to me. But I knew with absolute certainty that there was no longer any point."

"Any point?" I echoed foolishly, for I really did not see what it was he was trying to say.

"The hand of God," he said. "It snatched me up. It plucked me out of the air as I was falling. It prevented my certain death. It returned me to my desk as though nothing had happened. As it always will do. Don't you see?" he said. "It will always snatch me up. Now I am sure of that. However often I fall it will always ensure that I remain unhurt. That is what is unbearable."

"The world," he went on, "has closed in upon me. It is no longer open, as it was before that moment. Now I know that God will always be there ahead of me until the day I die. And without the possibility of falling, how can I live? How can I write?"

I tried to persuade him, of course. I tried to make him see that quite a different construction could be put on those extraordinary events. But he would not have it. Without the possibility of falling, he said, he had lost the possibility of hope. And without the possibility of hope his life, as a man and as a writer, was effectively over.

I changed tack then. Surely, I argued, his experience might have made it necessary, for reasons that I could not fathom, to stop writing temporarily, but there was still life to be lived, still his wife and daughter, his pupils, his friends, and perhaps one day the urge to write would return...

He looked at me in his familiar way and I sensed that I had not really understood a word of what he had been saying to me. At least I know when I am out of my depth, so that when he said firmly — "We will not speak of it again, please. I simply wanted you to know." — when he said that I could only nod in dumb assent. And, indeed, we have never spoken of it again. His life goes on as before, and so does mine. But we both know that it effectively ended that day when the hand of God plucked him out of the air and returned him to the safety of his desk.

The Tale of a Shamos

Robert Lasson

Life. Life is a series of mazes, leading from the womb to the grave. Miss a train, turn left instead of right, pick up a newspaper in the subway, and it can turn the mazes inside out and start you down a completely unexpected path. Not that the end will be different. You'll die, you'll die. Only the drive to the cemetery will be different.

If I had not been on Sixth Avenue that day, I would not have found the five-dollar bill. If I had not found the five-dollar bill, I would not have been in Hector's Cafeteria. If I had not been in Hector's Cafeteria, I would not have picked up a copy of the *Daily Forward*. If I had not picked up *The Forward*, I would not have read the ad. If I had not...

Too fast. Let me back up a little. I am a maniac reader. Everything. Books, magazines, cereal boxes, catsup labels, time tables, subway posters. My battered copy of Maimonides has grease stains on every page. I splashed through The *Managerial Revolution* with root beers and egg creams. If I still had my old Scribner's edition of *Look Homeward, Angel,* I could discourse on every spot: the pale blood-like blob on page 56 — tomato juice from Shaby's, a luncheonette run by two sunny hulks at Stanton and Clinton. That beige dagger-like swath on page 78: someone jostled me while I was holding a pickle at Marty's, 38th and Seventh. Every spot, every stain... I could give you chapter and verse.

I cannot eat unless there is something to read. Same before going to bed. My own private Gehenna will be a well-appointed hotel room completely devoid of the printed word. Not a "This Week in Gotham". Not a brochure about other hotels in the chain. Not even a note tacked to the door: In Case of Fire. Okay. So I'm sitting in Hector's. In front of me, on the table: a dish of "food." With "vegetables." And a cup of coffee. And nothing to read. It had not occurred to me to buy a paper before coming into the restaurant. First of all, I had not eaten for three or four days and reading, I blush to tell you, never entered my mind. Besides, try giving a newsstand Neanderthal a five-dollar bill for a paper.

The food was on the table, as I have said. The aromas were grating their way along my olfactory nerve. My brain, not to mention my shrunken stomach, was screaming, "Eat! Eat!" But how could I eat with nothing to read?

Dilemma. Should I leave the food on the table and dash out for a *Post?* I half rose to do just that when a man two tables away got up to leave. He had been reading a newspaper and I looked at him, muttering, under my breath, "Leave the paper, mister. Please. Leave the paper." And by God, he did. I leapt on it like a ravenous dog — only to discover that (1) it was *The Forward*. (2) It was yesterday's *Forward*. So what? you ask. A paper is a paper. A salvation. Yes and no. You see, I had not looked at a Yiddish word for 12 years.

It occurs to me that this doesn't really tell you very much. After all, who reads Yiddish these days?

Aha! Now I have forced myself to play my ace. (This writing business. It's so easy to lie — "The figures in this poll are 45% accurate 12% of the time" — but who in the world can believe it? My ace, then: 12, no 13 years ago I was one of the luminaries at the Yeshiva. I dazzled them with my insights. When I talked about the Books, the Mishnah, the Rashi, the professors would cock their heads and predict great things for me. The Brooklyner Gaon. So what happened? Why am I not ensconced in some fancy *shul* designed by Frank Lloyd Weiss that looks like Mount Moriah? Why do I not have by my side a skinny *rebbetsin* with a bad complexion who will walk with me, my faithful partner, down life's stormy road, dressed in gold lamé toreador pants? Why? Why this? Why that?

Because I lost it. It, Him, you know what I mean. I wish I could tell you how or why. I can't. It wasn't even a gradual thing: a twinge that grew into doubt that burgeoned into disbelief that raged into apostasy. None of that. I simply awoke one day and It was gone. Flown. Empty. In the treasury, not a penny. Godrupt.

It was the most horrible day of my life. I couldn't face anyone. I thought perhaps it was a temporary thing, a fluke, a "bad day." I ran out of my room, bought an armful of newspapers and magazines and rode the subway all day. I made no effort to think, to "evaluate." I just rode, man. Marlon Brando on the IRT wearing a *tallis kut'n* under my shirt. (You know, that thing with fringes that Zero Mostel sported in "Fiddler on the Roof.")

I got home at three in the morning and found under my door a few notes from my classmates. I undressed and went to bed. Maybe in the morning...

But morning came and with it, the feeling of the day before...that awful sense of loss, of emptiness, of amputation.

By 7:30 I dressed and fled from my room, carrying nothing. Not a shirt, not a book, not a toothbrush. New and naked. If this were a movie, we would now have a montage. A calendar page marked 1969 is torn off a pad. Superimposed over this is footage of me walking the streets. Then 1970. I am thinner, still walking the streets. 1971, a little fatter now, pushing a garment truck on Seventh Avenue. And so on. Thirteen years of odd jobs. Messenger, plumber's helper, movie usher, temp clerk, you name it.

And now, back to Hector's. I'm sitting there with my platter — and my newspaper. My yesterday's *Forward*. Cautiously, I open it up. I read. My lips move as I read the letters, the words. I read about an election in California and now tears are falling off my streaked beard into the carrots. I'm weeping, my shoulders are hunching. The words, the letters, those crazy letters that were first pounded into stone by some dirty band of desert wanderers — they destroy me.

Ah, you're thinking: he's home. He's got it made. Touching. Wonderful. Shmuck!

Wouldn't *you* weep if you saw your mother and father on the street after they had been dead for 13 years? Do not misunderstand me too quickly.

So there I am, reading, eating and crying. I turn the page and see a pathetic little corner of classified ads: introduction service, marriage broker, books. Then I see the ad. My ad:

SHAMOS
Orthodox Synagogue. Experienced Bal Tfilah. Bal Koreh.
Under 50 years of age. Salary: $225 week. Congregation B —
J —. Houston, Texas.

I read it once, with amusement. Then I read it again. The third time I knew it was my baby. I would get that job.

But first I had to make an important decision: who was I?

An ex-diamond from the Yeshiva fallen on slim days? On 13 years, on 4,800 slim days? No, that wouldn't do.

I would have to re-create myself to fit the job. But who? What? Whence?

Tucking *The Forward* under my arm, I fled Hector's and went to the Library on 42nd Street, where I had been spending many of my days. But this time, not to read. Only to be warm, and to think.

The phrases of the ad kept echoing in my head like chords. $225 a week. Texas. Orthodox. *Bal Tfilah:* Leader of Prayer Service. *Bal Koreh:* Master of Reading. Texas. Under 50. Orthodox.

Yes, I would do it. But who?

The research I did in the Library. Later, as the tattooist etched the number on my wrist, he asked, "What the hell is this? This ain't a Social Security number."

"It is for me," I told him.

A word about tattooing. "The Lord spake unto Moses: Ye shall not make any cuttings in your flesh for the dead, nor imprint any marks upon you." *(Leviticus 19:28.)*

It's funny. I didn't feel a twinge of revulsion about it. On the contrary, for the first time in my life I felt the dreadful power, the authority of the first line of a song I had sung thousands of times without understanding its meaning: *Eem ayn ani li, mi li?* If I am not for myself, who is for me? I even responded, with a quiver, to the last line: And if not now, when? The middle line — And if I am only for myself, what am I — this would have to be borne out by history.

Who was I, the new me? Bruno Rosenzweig. Born in Vienna. Middle-class background — family-owned department store. Studied in Poland and Lithuania. Graduate of Auschwitz. Came to America only three years ago via England and France. Speaks English with a slight European accent, which will eventually disappear. Refuses to speak a word of German. Refuses to speak of the Unspeakable. (I had read Frankl and Bettelheim. The first, I remember, had three horseradish stains on the third page, evenly spaced like pawnbroker balls. The second was almost virginal, save for a spattering of brownish specks on the end papers which would, under so-called "anti-human precipitin" and "absorption inhibition" tests, turn out to be human blood, Type A. My own, from a sudden nosebleed.)

Here I must speak of morality. And while I'm in a confessing mood, I might as well tell you that when I was really down — it happened three or four times — I could make enough for a cheap night's lodging by filching things... transistor radios, electric shavers, compact little goodies... from department stores. Only the poor know Macy's.

All right. Tattooing, lying, stealing — no problem. But what can you think of a man who uses — uses — the most hideous event of modern times to — to what? To get a job!

What if I whine that this was an "agonizing decision?" That after I settled on it, I gnashed my teeth and wept in one of those chill marble cubicles in the men's room at 42nd Street? Even if I tell you this, and it happens to be true, would that make any difference? Of course not. I have more respect for your intelligence, your sensitivity, to even mention it. Strike it from the record!

So how and why did I do it?

If I did it to come out of the cold, then I'm a lousy pariah.

If I did it only to get a job, then I'm a worthless scoundrel.

If I did it to see if I could bring it off, then I'm an actor.

So why?

I did it because I had to do it. Remember: I did it because I had to do it.

So what happened? What I expected. That night, on a rented typewriter, I wrote a brilliant letter, complete with statements and references that could not be checked *(Alles kaput)*. In three days I received a letter with a round-trip airline ticket to Houston. For the "first interview."

I hit the electric shavers hard for two days, bought myself a second-hand suit and, clothed in humility, strode through the glass lobbies of Kennedy Airport. Luggage: 30 magazines in a shopping bag.

What can I tell you? I was a hit. The answer to Congregation B —— J ——'s prayer. They took to me like a missing maverick. And the teas, the buffets, the informal dinners! Those Jewish Texas ducks, Niemaned and Marcused to the toenails, who call me, despite my modest protestations, "Rab-bah"— I love them. (Affairs? Marriage? Life? Who knows?)

I myself have begun to speak with a Texas accent. I have been approached to tutor Bar Mitzvah dropouts. I'm acting out the world's oldest gag: I'm teaching Hebrew on the side.

Every Saturday, when I read from the Torah, I pack them in like Thomashevsky. They've never heard anything like it. I was amazed at how easy it was to get back into harness. They unroll the Torah, that marvelous scroll of sheepskin. I look at those familiar hand-lettered heiroglyphs, and a shiver starts along my spine.

I point with the silver finger where I am to commence, and I close my eyes and open my throat, and the singsong chant flies up into the Texas air as though it were freed from a dungeon. It wafts through the synagogue, caresses the mink stoles and strokes the $300 shoes. It creeps through the cracks around the windows and mingles in the open heat with the stench of oil and affluence.

And if, one steamy Texas day, God grabs me by the lapels as I walk out of Meyer Brothers, who will be less surprised than I?

Shoes

Shaun Levin

Imagine. Smooth red leather shoes with thin shining gold threads hugging the tips. Stretching along the sides. And circling the slim heels. And so soft. Soft and smooth like the skin of a peach. The touch you can feel without touching. So I've stopped. My nose up against the cool window, watching the shoes reach out towards me. So elegant and inviting. Waiting for me to slide my feet in. One at a time. Slowly and lusciously like a knife into summer butter. The heels lift me off the ground. I am floating. My palms are sweating against the glass. A circle of mist has formed around my nostrils. And my feet are so tired. And heavy. Like lead in these flat heels. The day began months ago, and I need to rest. How I long to walk into the shop and buy the shoes. For a split second I can picture myself. I can see myself parting the doors like swinging saloon doors. I'm here. I've made it.

But I can't. Not any more. People know me now.

The last time I could buy shoes like these was back in high school. In the days when I could hide from the world behind family. I'd take the bus into the big city where the buildings and the streets and the hot smells were so beautiful and the people were all strangers to me. It was safe then. I could tell the salesman they were for my sister, please, or for my mother.

"Should I wrap them, then?" he'd say.

"Oh, yes please," I'd say.

And I'd watch him cover the box with wrapping paper and ribbons. And I'd sit with the box on my lap, rubbing against me to the gentle vibrations of the bus-ride home. I'd get rid of the packet and the wrapping and the box before I went inside, and conceal the shoes beneath my jacket, under my armpits, and go straight up to my room.

Buy anything? my mother might ask. Just walked around, I'd say. And stuff the shoes into the back of my cupboard, covering them with the spare mohair blanket I kept in there. Each night I was surprised to find the treasure beneath the yellow and faded blanket. Each night I'd rediscover the shoes, safely stashed away like stolen goods. My first pair were. Imagine. Black platforms with thick perspex heels with golden stars set inside them. Always a man of extremes, my mother would say.

I'd sit at my desk, right leg over left, feeling the gentle weight of the shoe as I swayed my leg up and down. Up and down. Impatiently waiting.

For something. For something to happen. I would file my nails with the emery-boards I hid in my desk drawer, or stroke my long straight hair with the ivory brush. Eyeing myself in the mirror. I would run the tips of my fingers along my legs, down to the shoes, caressing the leather that pressed safely against my toes. And hugged the sides of my feet. And I'd hold the heel in the palm of my hand. That cool transparent texture. Ah. Like glass. Like glass it was.

Then I'd walk slowly across the room, keeping to the carpet, careful not to let the loud heels touch the floor. With heels like these you can't walk too slowly. And if you don't keep moving, you lose your balance. Stop pacing up and down, my father might shout from downstairs. I'm doing my homework, I'd say. So just do it then, he'd say.

I only stop now at windows with shoes for men and for women. With my face gazing at the rough cowboy boots and the indelicate Italian shoes, I let my eyes feast on the long shining black boots and the thin heels on the slim blue or white or orange shoes. Not shoes. There should be another word for them. They have these tiny silver studs or. Imagine. They have gold-tipped points. I've got used to doing this. Facing one way, and looking the other. If the winds change I'll probably remain this way, squinting to the side, my face to the front, for the rest of my life. Never make faces, my mother would say. You can never know.

I now have my shoes made for me. I can no longer walk into a store, buy the shoes, and take the nice and easy breezy route home. The route that's green and tree-lined and no one sits on park benches and calls out to you. Hey! Those beautiful high-school boys you want to look like, but cannot, will shout. They point and jeer. The sound of their beer bottles ringing as they smack them together and cheer *le'chaim*. Throwing their heads back to laugh and drink warm beer. Their thick hair shining in the sunlight and the tight skin. Clinging to their bodies. Like a lover. Cannot be touched. You see nothing. You hold your hands tightly at your sides. Your insides tightly in your hands. Just walk, you tell yourself. Don't worry, I'm walking, I'm walking.

It's a sunny day. Imagine. The sky is blue and the sidewalks are clean. I walk into the store and the salesman, nice jacket, shirt, pants and, ooh, bulge, approaches me, respectfully.

"Sir," he'd say. "May I help you."

"Those there," I'd say.

"They're you," he'd say, and smile. "Care to try them on?"

"Ooh, yes," I'd say. "Thank you."

That's how it would happen. Nice and easy. Just like I said. Sometimes it's not enough to do what you want in the safety of your own home. You want to take it with you onto the street. Sometimes you become so afraid of an open door you stop the thoughts from venturing out. And chase away the voices wanting to come in. Sometimes I think that pacing up and down in the green boots that cover my knees and point towards my crotch, and the pair of tight shorts with the threads around the cut-off seams from endless spins in the washing machine, are not real if no-one can see them. I stroke myself in front of the mirror. I knead my chest, pushing on the muscles, pressing against my nipples. I pull my stomach in. And hold my head back to feel my hair tickling my spine. And it's just me looking at me.

I wanted the shoes. I wanted them like a man who wants a man cannot live without a deep voice so close to him he can breathe its soothing sound. I wanted them like the cynic longs for beauty and the joker longs for candour. Ah. Standing on the tip of a mountain singing out to the world. High-heeled shoes carry you to places so warm and strong, you cannot but long to go there. I reach inside and touch those places. Stroke them, lean on them. I pull on my black tights and that light silk blouse, so thin only skin can see it. The blouse that tickles the calloused and sensitive tips of my nipples and makes that rustling sound as it rubs against the stubble on my chest. I swing my hands and move my hips to a rhythm only high heels and silk dresses can dictate. Then I am happy.

I have memories. Nice childhood memories from a childhood I prefer to forget. My mother's dressing room with tall oak cupboards and a thick cream carpet. And the vanity table with the square mirror and perfumes and light pink powder with the soft brush. And the wine-red thin and narrow Lancôme case with rectangles of blue, green and brown eye-shadow. When she was out, the room was mine. I could try on anything I liked. The tennis skirt with the pastel sunflowers and the skin-colored stockings that stroked my cock. I was in a void of evening gowns and soft shoes that were too big. And just right. For me. I would step out of the dressing room into the bedroom, throwing the skirt to the sides and spinning around to make it whirl around me. And the mink stole that even in summer was so cold I wanted to rub my cheek in it forever. I would wrap it around my shoulders and stand before the mirror. All dressed up.

At the vanity table I'd brush my cheeks gently with rouge and paint my eyes with blue shadow. I would screw the lipstick from its tube, careful to stay within the lines of my lips. I'd make an "O", painting first the bottom then the upper lip. And rub them together, back and forth, spreading the colour evenly. I'd kiss the tissue between my lips. And the taste. The flavour that can't be compared to anything in the world. Sweet and silky and artificial.

Memories like these become immortal. That's when dead things stay alive inside. But like the dead, they haunt you. They come back to trouble

93

you with unfinished business. They take you through labyrinths of mysteriously connected threads. Everything is joined to everything: the rouge to the mirror to the white skirt to the shoes in the window. And back to Michelle and the ballet classes I wanted to be a part of, and to her brother Wayne I loved so much I wanted to be Michelle.

So? Buy the shoes, for God's sake! Easier dreamt than done. Believe me. It's not a question of money. And it's not a question of whether Leo would frown or not. He encourages me. I know he does. He brought me back a satin nightgown from his last trip to London. That's proof enough. He's a nice guy. My boyfriend. Leo. You'd like him. Imagine. Tall and dark with a beautiful chest, and a thick pair of hands with long, slim fingers. From the moment we met. Well, after the first few times. I told him, this is what I like. You like it, stay, you don't, don't. He said, you look good in that. Let's see you walk across the room. Mmm.

I try, as I must, to memorize their shape so I can tell Olga. Give me specifics, she'd say. Or else you'll never get what you want. So I must remember the things that count. The size of the heel and the shape of the tip and whether the leather is smooth or shiny. I like the heels to be high enough so the ground seems not too hard. And the points must be round. Olga says the rounder the tip the kinder the step. More subtle. The philosophy of footwear, she calls it.

As for herself. She says if only she looked different she'd make her own shoes. What's the point, she says. If a person's fat and ugly, she says, who cares what they wear. No one notices. Unless they dress like thin people. Fat people who dress like thin people are different.

"Come in," she says.

Imagine. The Palace at Versailles boiled down to fit into one room. She likes things to look that way. Her house is like her figure. Loud to the eyes and soft to the touch.

"Tell it to me," she says.

"Imagine," I say, and tell it to her.

I sit across from her on the red velvet chaise longue with the heavy wooden frame. And one soft lace cushion. She pours tea from her samovar, and we suck on sugar crystals. Olga sits in her chair with the high back. She strokes her Pekinese ball of fluff and sketches what I tell her.

I see the strips of gold on the shoe. I have them imprinted on my memory, so I can tell her where to put them. These things are important to remember. I have learnt not to take the small details for granted. In the beginning I would say to Olga, put the glittery stars on this side of the heel, and make a rounded point. And back at the window the glitter would be on that side of the heel, and the point much pointier. And I would be disappointed. I've learnt to pay attention to what I must remember.

I have no choice, as it's not that simple to walk into a shoe store, dressed in a three-piece suit, pin-striped shirt, paisley tie and leather briefcase, and ask the mouth with the wad of bubble gum, do you. Excuse me, do you have those red leather shoes. Ahem. The ones in the window with the gold strips. In a size forty-four. The shop assistant shoots a string of sharp cracks of gum from the back of her mouth, accompanying her tune with a furrowed brow. Whooz it for? Her nose becomes a raisin, and her eyes — narrow slits of suspicion.

People do that here. They don't mind asking who it's for, how much you earn, how much rent you pay, or what is it exactly the two of you do in bed? I just can't imagine! It's not that I mind, they smile, it's just I can't think how you people can enjoy yourselves. If you want to fuck, they say, why not fuck the real thing. This is the real thing. If they only knew.

Leo and I get our kicks from imagining how the couple at the next table. The couple with the steady jobs and the baby-sitter. Will react when they see us at home. Never mind in bed, just walking around the house. Me in my tight skirt, skin-colored stockings, and high-heeled shoes. Leo in his Levi's, white from wear around his beautiful thick cock with the dark blue vein running up the underside and his heavy hair-covered balls, and his brown cowboy boots. And that white vest that hugs his wide chest tighter than I can. They'd flip. And if they came on Thursday nights, they wouldn't know what to do.

I love Thursday nights. Thursday is shaving day. Leo shaves me on the bathroom floor. He lathers me slowly, icing my chest like a birthday cake. His beautiful muscular hands over my body. He then takes the razor and goes gently across my skin. Removing the bristles from my chest. Circling my nipples. Stopping to pinch them with the tips of his fingers. And like a magician, uncovers me. He then does my arms and my legs, taking care not to touch the sensitive flesh. Thoughts of his hands so close get me hard. I turn over. He shaves around my arsehole. I am so hot. I am ready to come. Leo blows me, drains me, leaves me limp and smooth. I'll never leave you, he breathes. I know, I can say, because I know he will. Then it's time for dessert. Dessert is nice. Dessert is me.

Leo lines my hole with Johnson's baby lotion, straight from the pink plastic container, and then tickles the insides with the tips of his fingers. First one finger then two and then three, four five. Opening me up wider and then wider and I want to take in as much as I can to take into me that beautiful strong muscular hand that is all mine. He then takes his fist from my arse and lies down on top of me. Now that my arse is open he can jam his beautiful cock all the way in. Slide it in. My muscles slowly contract to hold onto his cock and he goes in and out and in and out. He is on top of me and I push myself up onto all fours and he is holding his arms across my chest and kissing my neck and pulling at my nipples and he lets his hands wander across my smooth chest down down down to my cock and he plays with it and I can't tell anymore where the sensation is coming from nor what the sensation is and I want to forget myself. But I can't. Because there are no words in that place of nothingness, in that void of pure pleasure. And I must pound my arse against his waist and take in as much of his cock as I can, and I can feel I am about to come and I push harder and harder, longing to be taken away. To disappear into his beautiful body and his strength. And then I am full.

And other times. Yes, other times I lie in bed and feel this thing between my legs, and it's a dead piece of flesh tied to my waist. I play with it, pull at it and hit it around. Numb. A useless piece of meat. And sometimes it gets big and hard and wants to be held. I tighten a cock-ring around my cock and balls. And I play with it, running my fist along the hard shaft. I imagine Leo and me and the shoes and the flesh and the hair and the water and the cum.

When Leo comes home, I walk around for him in my high heels and stroke the long straight hair that runs down my hard back, and make him want me. Get him to look my way and whistle or smile or pant. Want me, I say to him, tell me that you want me. Tell me that you'll fucking-well die if you don't get your cock into me. And he does, because he does.

That's how we met. I was the one who did the seducing. At a Purim party two years ago. I wore a chiffon evening gown with an open back and a slit down the side. I wasn't shaving my legs then, so I had on my black stockings and the shoes I'd picked up that morning from Olga. I was feeling like a million dollars. I was standing at the drinks table smoking a joint and pouring myself another Harvey Wallbanger. It's the Galliano bottle, I say to myself. You're right, I say.

He came from across the room. I had noticed him before, but kept the image of him to myself. He was the only one not in fancy dress. There were Queen Esthers and Hamans filling the place with screeching rattles. There was a pirate and her damsel in distress. His green eyes were close to mine. I could smell the sweet taste of alcohol on his breath. A drink, I asked. Whisky, he said. Ooh, I thought.

We talked a little. He said he didn't really have a job at the moment. He painted houses, he said. We danced together. He had his hands on my skin. I could feel his rough palms moving up my back and folding over my shoulders. Let's go, he said.

I walk away from the window. Fixing my hard-on in my underpants. I could spit on the sidewalk if I wanted to. But no. I just keep walking. I have a picture in my mind and I take it to Olga. I walk along the sidewalk, feeling lighter now, smiling at the memory of how Leo and I met. There have been several others like him. So I know it will not last forever. But I know that when it passes, the memory of it all will remain. The feeling, that is. And that in itself is enough.

Seder

Deena Linett

Molly Greenblatt, a professor of philosophy, was not a very observant Jew but she valued tradition, and all the memories of the seders of her childhood were filled with light. The flight from Egypt had contemporary resonances: she thought of it often when she read news of refugees from this country or that — from everywhere it sometimes seemed. And since childhood she had loved the celebration of freedom from slavery.

This would be the first year since she and Richard had divorced that none of the children would be home. Andrew and Philip, the twins, had been at their respective schools for three years, but then Lila had been here. Now she too was gone, and Molly wanted to mark the holiday, but couldn't think how. She found herself scrubbing the same section of kitchen counter again and again. Then, on a whim, she picked up the telephone and dialled the Reform synagogue she sometimes went to for High Holy Day services. She was thinking about abundance as she was connected to the rabbi.

"Molly!" he said, "How are you?"

She told him her idea, which shaped itself as she said it.

"That's lovely. I can think of. . . Let's see, there's Hymie Rodriguez..."

"Rodriguez! How do you spell Hymie?" she asked, considering Jaime, and Chiam.

"The usual way. He's a refugee from Cuba."

Cuba too, she thought.

"And Estrellita Chu, from the Philippines..."

"A mini-U.N.," she said.

"You said people who don't have anybody."

"Yes, oh yes..." Awkward at giving, she nevertheless told herself, let's get on with it.

"There's one more person, poor old thing lost his daughter in that awful Turnpike pile-up down near Fairview last fall. Sam Krebs."

"I'll take them."

"Wait, I'll get you the phone numbers."

So she called them, Mr. Rodriguez, Mrs. Chu, Mr. Krebs. It got easier after the first call, which she made with trembling hands as the light poured in through her newly-washed windows and gleamed on the immaculate counter-tops. She could have invited students, but she saw students all the time and it was a *mitzvah* to have these older, lonely people.

"Mrs. Chu? My name is Molly Greenblatt. I was just talking to the rabbi, and... Would you be willing to join me for Seder?"

*

"There was a little mistrust," she told Philip when he called the next evening to say hello. "But I think it'll work out."

"Great, Mom. I'm proud of you."

"Let's wait and see how great it is," she laughed.

Michael Walsh, the man she'd been seeing for nearly a year, was intrigued. "What made you do it?"

"I'm not sure." For years she had tried to understand her attachment to the old traditions. "It's a festival of freedom," she told him.

"Harvest, I thought."

"They're all essentially harvest or planting festivals, but this one celebrates the Exodus. From slavery. Want to come? You'll be the youngest person there," she teased. Michael was her age, fifty-three.

"No thanks. I've got to take Cath," he said of his daughter, "For her Easter outfit."

"Little clash of cultures, eh?" Molly said, soft. "You don't have to take a sixteen-year-old for her Easter dress at night."

"You found me out," Michael admitted. "Frankly, I don't feature eating dinner with a lot of old people with ferocious table manners."

"Mi-chael!"

"So I'm not such a great guy after all."

She sighed. "You don't want to."

"Isn't that what I just said?"

"I'm sorry."

"I am too," he said.

"It gets pretty complicated," she murmured.

*

Over the next several days she ironed the heavy white tablecloth and napkins, bought food and candles and wine. And cooked.

She polished the silver; she loved handling the intricately carved old silver. She had simplified her life so that there were almost no curves in it, she thought as she rubbed a soft cloth over the ornate patterns of intertwined leaves and medallions, curlicues and furbelows. This silver was the only thing she had that had belonged to Grandma Sophie, who had carried it in potato sacks when she came from Russia.

As a girl Molly used to imagine her grandmother young, buxom and red-cheeked, hiding the forks, knives and deep-bowled spoons in a root-cellar under piles of potatoes and onions when the Russian inspectors came. Older she had imagined her grandmother's plump shoulder and arm, the inside of her wrist with its blue veins; she imagined a inspector dazzled by that white arm, the curve of forearm. And later, when she immersed herself in the literature of the war years, her mother would say, "Why do you insist on torturing yourself?"

Molly, filled with disdain, would think, "This isn't torture..." It had taken a dozen years and becoming a mother herself to understand that her mother had wanted to shield her from suffering.

The reading changed the nature of her imaginings. Now she thought she had romanticized her grandmother's youth, and her mind filled with new pictures: the shadow of a big man at a loudly flung-open door, the shadows of others behind him.

She would be sitting at Seder with all the aunts and uncles, Aunt Sarah and Uncle Jacob, and Aunt Bess — and always there were others, friends of relatives, distant cousins. The first retarded person she had ever met turned up at seder once, Debby, the cousin of a cousin. Customarily there were lots of people at the table, and they were dear to each other. Then the intruders at the door. Noise and sharp movements and cries. Candles overthrown, shards of broken china, the clatter of falling silver. Blood and wine on the tablecloth.

The image reappeared after a long absence, when she and Richard were parents. Andrew and Philip were about eight, and Lila five. It all came back, the sequence like a dream, immediately recalled, precise and freshly astonishing. She had gasped.

"What?" Richard said, as three young faces turned.

"What's the matter with Mommy?" Andrew asked. Sensitive Andrew, he always read her face. Philip had come to stand at her side. With his skinny eight-year-old little body he would protect her from dragons and fire-engines and strange dogs and whatever was scaring her now.

"It's nothing," she told them, patting Philip's little behind. "Go and sit down, sweetheart."

"Seder means order," Richard said. "Does anybody know why?"

"Because we eat things in a certain order," Andrew said.

"Because we can't eat anything after the *afikomen*," Lila said, carefully pronouncing the Greek word, glancing quickly at her brothers to see if they would heap scorn on her little head. It must have looked safe, because she grinned and piped, "That's an order!"

"That's right, honey," Richard nodded, "And because we say the prayers in a certain order. This is a service, like in synagogue, but we do it at home."

In the quiet moments of seders for years and years, as the children ran, then older, walked, and finally resisted altogether the ceremonial opening of the door for the Prophet Elijah, Molly saw the desecration of her white table: spilled wine, overturned dishes, shattered water-goblets, the menace of strangers forcing their way through her door.

She was rolling *knadles* and dropping them into boiling water when Michael called. "I haven't seen you lately."

"I'm making Seder — cooking! I'm having such a good time." She wiped at the sticky mixture on her hands with a paper towel and looked at the clock. You had to time these just right or they turned out like rocks.

"I thought you didn't much like cooking."

"This is different. I love making Seder."

"How are they getting there?"

"Someone's bringing them — the rabbi arranged it. I'll take them home."

"I hope it goes well," he said.

"Why shouldn't it?"

But afterward she thought, What if they don't like it? What if they don't like me? The notion was daunting, as if a shadow lay across the kettle where the knadles bubbled. She actually looked to the window to see where the sun had gone.

*

Five o'clock. She put the finishing touches on the table, ran a dustcloth over the coffee-table — again — and checked to make sure there was enough water in the low bowl of crocuses in the middle of the table. In the living room next to Passover candies, sliced fruit-jellies dusted with sugar, she had put a tall white stoneware vase filled with yellow daffodils. And under the lamp at the end of the sofa there was a flat Irish crystal dish with the candies she had loved as a child, hard sweets with soft chewy centers. They wore wrappings of white paper with minute colored drawings of fruit, and each had a little opaque lining, so you had to wait till you opened both to see whether you got the really good ones or not. Sometimes in the old days she could wrangle a trade with her cousin Mary, but usually she loved the jewel of sweetness that unfolded in her palm.

Her father had had a series of rabbis in his family. That's how she used to think of them, a series: men robed in black stretching back into antiquity. It made her laugh now. She remembered one of her father's favourite stories. When the Children of Israel left Egypt, the watchdogs didn't bark.

Awash with memories and tiredness, she stood in the doorway to the dining room and looked. Her heart lifted. As she went upstairs to do her makeup and change into a new white dress, she heard, from what seemed a great distance, the sound of her own voice, singing.

*

The doorbell rang at seven exactly. On the stove four pots simmered. The oven was full, and smells of cooking chicken filled the house; it smelled safe, like the houses of her childhood. She opened the door.

There they stood, refugees from the whole world.

She wanted to gather them.

"Hello, hello," she murmured drawing them into her house. Mr. Rodriguez had bought a new jacket for the occasion. She noticed the little white ticket with its control number on his sleeve. If she mentioned it, she would embarrass him.

Mrs. Chu looked around, smiling, assessing. She had defined her mouth with '40's blood-red lipstick, and her thin dyed hair had been pulled back severely from a wrinkled brown-skinned face. She was tall. Molly thought, Aren't Philippinos small people? But this woman was a Jew, so who knew where her people might've come from. She dressed like a woman who was accustomed to think herself beautiful. Molly found herself smiling at the shade of some other life that hovered around the dark head.

Mr. Krebs's eyes filled, Molly saw, and then the tears disappeared, though all evening she never saw him wipe them away.

They came into her living room, saying how pretty and bright the house was, and where did she get the flowers? and how good it all smelled. Mr. Rodriguez handed her a package wrapped in tinfoil. *"Kugel,"* he said. "I made it. My wife taught me. It has raisins in it, a tropical *kugel,"* he smiled.

She nodded thanks, urging them to sit while she went to the kitchen to put the *kugel* into the already-crowded oven. When she came back carrying the heavy glass tray with the chopped liver garnished with egg, Mrs. Chu said, "Oh dear. I should have told you. I'm allergic to eggs." She held out the bottle of wine she had brought, and as Molly thanked her, she wondered at the woman's accent — it was like no European or Russian accent she had ever heard — and toted up the ingredients of everything: eggs, eggs, eggs.

The men ate the chopped liver, saying, "This is very good," and "Too bad you can't try some, Mrs. Chu," and "May I have a little seltzer?" Mr. Krebs asked, "If it wouldn't be too much of a trouble?"

As they entered her dining room breathing their appreciative ooohs and ahhhhs, the teacher took over; the mother. She showed each where to sit

103

and helped Mrs. Chu move her chair over the heavy carpet.

She picked up the stack of five slender volumes which contained the order of the service, saying, "We all come from different traditions. I hope you will like this *Haggadah,* it's very dear to me."

"Fine by me," Mr. Krebs said.

"Traditions," nodded Mrs. Chu. "What difference it makes? We're all Jews."

Mr. Rodriguez smiled. She distributed the books, wondering briefly why she had put out five, shook her head a little and took her seat at the head (or the foot, depending), nearest the kitchen doorway. When Mr. Rodriguez brought his water glass to his mouth, his hand trembled. How could she not have thought of this? She would have to lead the Seder. The men might take offence.

She drew a deep breath, grinned, opened the book, and began.

Mr. Krebs took one pair of glasses off and felt in his jacket pocket for another pair. Molly had put her own reading glasses beside her plate. As she put them on, she attempted a smile of fellow-feeling with Mr. Krebs, but he was carefully refitting the first pair into their red plastic case and didn't notice. There were dark spots on the backs of his hands, which had long slender white fingers and hairless wrists. Her eyes stung.

She held the Seder plate with its symbolic foods aloft.

"This is the symbol of the Passover," she quoted, and, holding up the *matzoh,* "And this unleavened bread is the bread of affliction which our ancestors ate in the land of Egypt. For we were slaves unto Pharaoh in Egypt. . ." She could have recited the entire service by heart. "We don't ask why the Holy One, Blessed be He (or she, she thought with a secret little grin) set them free from bondage, but we must behave as if every one of us was personally redeemed. . ."

"Because if the Holy One Blessed be He did not freed our ancestorias," Mrs. Chu offered, "We would still be in slaves!" She sat back, smiling, proud to contribute.

Mr. Krebs's eyes swam. Molly looked down into her book. This was harder than she'd imagined.

*

Then, without her being aware of it, it got easier: she was in it, doing it, and she could feel their pleasure. They participated, they told little stories about their families. She thought, They have brought their histories with them to my table.

Mr. Krebs had come to Great Barrington to be in the "shoes business" with his father-in-law, and Mr. Rodriguez told about Havana in its heyday. He said every Passover his father used to tell him and his brothers the story of the redemption from Egypt: "When the Children of Israel left Egypt, all the dogs were silent." Molly was astonished. All these years she'd thought it was her family's story. Mr. Rodriguez paused and they all stopped to look at him. "Imagine!" Mr. Rodriguez said, "Not a one of the watchdogs was watching..." He laughed and laughed. Molly imagined a wife's pleasure in this story. She wondered what their marriage had been. How many moments of glory and pain people carried around with them. It's a wonder we can walk, she thought, images of people bent beneath refugees' burdens filling her. Mr. Rodriguez was seized by a fit of coughing. Molly got up to refill his water glass. "Ahhhh," he said, nodding at her, sipping. "Thank you."

Then he talked about fishing, and Mrs. Chu put in, "We had some fishes! *Pating*," she said, "Was like those fish you had in Cuba. We used to go in the little boats, and you could see them, the *pating*..."

"What's the word for that?" Mr. Rodriguez said.

"Sharks? I think was sharks," she said, satisfied, nodding. "With the big teeth, they eat anything."

"Yes," Mr. Rodriguez nodded, "Sharks. Those Jaws fishes."

"Right! That's the ones."

It was time for the soup.

"Ah!" they chorused when she brought in the heavy tureen filled with fragrant soup. Her hands trembled with its weight. There was a flurry of moving things so she could set it down.

She lifted the lid. Her *knadles* bobbed in the sea of golden chicken broth. "No sharks," Mr. Krebs smiled. She laughed.

"A *michel*," Mr. Krebs nodded.

Michael? she thought, for the moment confused.

"What means that word?" Mrs. Chu asked.

"Something deeply pleasing, I think," Molly said. She was exhausted, she realized, from the effort to make them happy. She watched the meticulous way Mr. Krebs wiped the corner of his mustache with his napkin after every spoonful of soup, and thought, Michael, you were wrong.

They all exclaimed over the dinner, heaping praise upon praise until she felt heavy with it all.

*

Now the table was covered with *matzoh* crumbs, there was a red horseradish stain near Mr. Krebs's plate, and Mrs. Chu had spilled some wine. Bits of fish and chicken dotted the cloth. Still, the candles flickered and the flowers hadn't yet faded. The unused silver, scattered this way and that, shone. It was nearly ten. She had sung the Four Questions, embarrassed, at her age, to be the youngest person in the room.

They had made Seder. All that was left was to break the *afikomen* and

105

eat it. Then they would sing a few songs and she would take them home. "Oh!" she exclaimed, "How could I have forgotten?" She held up the *matzoh* and began, "For years we have eaten our dinners in freedom..." predictably filling with the ancient grief, she went on, "While our brothers and sisters in what was the Soviet Union and elsewhere did not have the freedom to do what they liked... Now they too can celebrate this festival in freedom. May their freedom last..." She could not go on.

"You really take this freedom stuff seriously," Richard used to say, but it was all right, because he had too. She brushed at her eyes with her napkin, avoiding looking at them. The table had fallen silent. She hadn't finished her compote. She was so tired. All the scrubbing and polishing and grinding and grating and chopping had collected in her arms and legs. If anyone were to come, she would not be able to move.

If anyone were to come.

Mr. Krebs had opened the door for Elijah without selfconsciousness, and she had not had her vision. The intruders would not be coming.

*

When the phone rang, she smiled, thinking, The children, and wondering which of them it would be. She rose, excusing herself, and went to stand in the doorway between the kitchen and dining room. Lila's voice. "Happy Passover, Mama. I miss you."

"Oh my dear girl," she began, glancing at Mr. Krebs, who had lost his daughter. In the periphery of her vision she saw Mr. Rodriguez slide a dessert spoon into the pocket of his new jacket. It was a brown tweed jacket with tiny dots of red and orange, green, blue. I did not see that, she thought, her mind at once clear, an inner voice crisp. She spoke to Lila for a few minutes, her back turned now to the company, who sat making small-talk.

Grandma Sophie's silver.

She gently rebuffed their attempts to help clean up, and made ready to take them home. She glanced back at the table as they left the dining room. Part of her wished Michael were coming tonight, but there was something comforting about having all that work to come back to.

At the door she hesitated. Then she said it. Very softly: "I think you have a spoon of mine."

Mr. Rodriguez's hand slapped reflexively at the pocket.

Behind her, Mr. Krebs was helping Mrs. Chu with her coat, a worn reddish-brown fake-fur.

"May I have it?" Molly whispered.

"I don't. . ." He trembled. "I'm sorry, Ma'am."

106

She winced.

He extracted the spoon from his pocket. She palmed it, surprising herself with her dexterity and capacity for subterfuge, and went to put it on the table. "I have to put out the candles before we leave," she said.

Years before, helping her cousin Mary clean up after a seder, she had been scraping dishes into the garbage when Mary asked, "Did you count the silver?"

"I didn't think to," Molly had said, looking up, feeling responsible.

She never counted the silver.

They trooped out into the night, a small fragile flock. It was only a spoon. "Be careful," she warned, of the place where tree-roots had caused the sidewalk to heave and crack.

She looked up. There were a million million stars. It was chilly, but nice to be outdoors and all the neighborhood dogs were silent.

Cappuccino Express

M. López-Levi

Getting up requires not consulting my mind. Swing my legs off the side of the bed, wake them as the soles of my feet make contact with the wood. Eyes still stuck, I stumble to the shower and eventually I begin to feel my torso, my arms... Finally my head admits to being part of my body, and in the end my eyes open, though focussing is a problem.

I already know what to wear, the collarless shirt I bought yesterday, silk so lovingly managed it feels like heaven, matt, smooth to feel loved by its touch, with the necessary frisson when you run your fingers over it. Black Calvin Kleins and my usual jacket, and by now I feel good enough to walk to the kitchen counter to choose the form of mind wake up call. I ignore the cafetière, its produce too weak for the occasion. The expresso machine is too fiddly and the percolator takes too long, so it will have to be my Spanish coffee-kettle, with a look of having been designed in the sixties to look like the year 2000, coffee armour with a waist. I fill the filter full, ease it over the bottom with water, set it on the fire and allow my eyes to unfocus again, and idly pursue the dreams I must have had in the night but cannot remember.

The day begins as I feel my nerve ends shiver, jolted into feeling, ready to take on the front door. As it shuts behind me and I bound down the steps to the pavement I look into the office panorama in my mind. Editorial meeting first thing, have to find a way to take the Phoenix conference over, I wonder if anyone noticed that I have been in touch with Ken over it for weeks, got the damn prima donna to interview — again! What will happen about poor Joe, maybe I can take Annie out for lunch and ask...

The obstruction on the pavement drags me out, a woman with a double pram and another two kids trailing either side, I wish people would realise some of us are in a hurry, can't she take them out later, and anyway what is she doing with so many brats? Some people just don't want to have a life. I try to get back into the planning but I'm at the newstand, so I pick up my bunch, immerse myself in the tube frenzy, mentally clear a space directly in front of me all the way to the train.

I fight for my corner, on the right carriage to jump out at the exit at my stop, glare at a tourist (What the heck are they doing up so early on their holiday?) so I can wedge between door and partition, open my paper and shut myself off. I'm off at my stop, up the stairs easy, time on the escalator for checking out the talent coming down. Automatic pilot gets ready

109

to cross at the lights, eyes straying to the coffee shop to see if anyone is having breakfast before work, but instead I notice that they have coffee making machines, and pots, on display. I promise myself a good look later and dash.

Work happens. There is the excitement of some phone call, the power play in the meeting, but otherwise, it goes. And lunch comes, with good company, Jo from the office next door, who I am intermittently flirting with. We go to the coffee shop at my suggestion and I manage to keep my social mind on the gossip and the latest film while my eye takes in the intricate plethora of coffee making equipment. There are outsized cups standing next to the miniature cafetières, complicated looking combinations of metal and glass and hard plastic in shapes so twisted that they must surely defy usefulness. While she goes to the toilet I give them my undivided attention and find, almost hidden in the variety of brewing containers, a perfectly formed, miniature, one cup only, cappuccino machine. Jo comes back, we talk of going to see a film later, we arrange to meet for dinner and do it tonight. She is smiling at me now, looking satisfied, but also ironic; she has a sharp tongue on her and has caught me unawares before, when her sweet exterior has split for a second to reveal a pointed mind. Usually pointed at some unthinking not very astute remark of mine.

I spend the afternoon seemingly editing Colin's article, in fact daydreaming of the perfect cappuccino. In the morning? Too fussy. In the afternoon, on a Sunday, with the papers and the thought of a walk in the park. At night, after a good dinner — I could invite Jo to dinner — or maybe for an afternoon of cake and cappuccino. I suddenly want the cappuccino machine with the passion I usually reserve for a newly discovered dish, or an unknown attractive face in the office.

I make up an appointment and leave slightly early, to catch the coffee shop open. I walk towards the tube and find the CLOSED sign facing me, the lights out and the machine firmly on the other side of the glass. My want at first sight is beyond my reach for the night. I enter the tube station feeling disorientated, lost, wondering where I am going, feeling blank about the rest of the day. The imposition of change in my plans has thrown me to a limbo where making the smallest decisions — this platform or that, the ticket in which pocket — takes up all my mind. Once on the train I remember my date with Jo. I was going to come to her office at leaving time. I resolve to call her and arrange to meet in town. Meanwhile, I head into the centre, buy the weeklies that must be read, and find a coffee shop, which without a display of machinery in the window, looks naked, and settle to read until Jo arrives. I order a cappuccino, just because I can't think of anything else when they come to take my order.

110

When the articles become boring, not far after the third paragraph, and when all the magazines read like each other, after the second, I feel myself lost in reverie. I could put the cappuccino machine in that corner of the counter, the one with the single malt whiskies, it would dominate the kitchenscape, draw the eye. I wonder if I will need any special kind of coffee, whether now I will be able to go to the coffee counter at Sainsbury's and buy an exclusive cappuccino label. Or better still, will a specialist coffee grinding shop provide a consistency particular to cappuccino, in those dearly old fashioned paper bags. It would impress Jessica — my ex — who once accused me of drinking anything with caffeine in it. She wouldn't be able to say so of course, she would make a softly disparaging comment and I would see her eyes darting for another look when she thought I would not notice.

Ah, so much happiness for so little outlay. None of the coffee contraptions in that window had a price tag attached, but I imagine it would only be double figures, at the most. I am awash with the warmth of knowing I can have what I want, no one can stop me, I have earned the right by having my work. Interesting, stimulating work, with a degree of prestige attached, a good salary. Although it never goes far, the big city swallows money so that I only have to see some friends, treat myself to the odd home improvement, like the cappuccino machine, and it's all gone from my account. I never understand it. I am earning twice as much as my father ever did yearly. I'm careful, I don't have a drug habit, not even alcohol, I get high and drink only with friends, I am not excessively vain, I just enjoy myself. And it all goes. But I will be paid at the beginning of next week, so a tiny dip in the red won't do me any harm.

Jo turns up and asks after my meeting, I invent some daring comment and a successful conclusion. During dinner I lose myself in Jo, the conversation is becoming scented with the heavy alluring perfume of possible passion. Or at least sex. We wind our way to the film, a new epic Hollywood with a social conscience but also with long fast cars and glamour. The end is shot in a hot desert, marvellous colours, the dusty hugeness impresses me. We head for a drink, I am about to suggest my place and Jo decides to go home, on her own, without explanation. With nothing explicit I can hardly appeal as I am doing in my head and I walk her to her bus stop.

I wander home disappointed but relaxed, it's been an interesting day in all, I'm sure Jo will come round eventually. Home feels cosy after the city lights, I am glad for the umpteenth time to have my own place. I sit in the dark in my comfortable chair and find myself lighting some candles in the window and losing myself in their spell. Grandmother always lit the candles while I grew up and they remind me of quiet companionship. Friday

111

night in the city and the sound of sighing, the week over. Time for oneself now, to go shopping, do chores, absorb the news of the week, catch up on the videoed programmes. A nightcap and late night telly see me off to sleep, no alarm clock tomorrow. My mind jumbled with images of cappuccino and Jo smiling, and then I drift, half formed sentences from the articles I was reading while I waited for her swirling. What was it about? It seemed important, relevant...

Waking up on Saturday takes a long time, and I love it. Even when the sirens push their way into my room from the street, too early, and bring me back to the world, I don't mind, as I can lie here in that perfect in-between state of dreamy awakeness. Awake enough to enjoy that I am still asleep. My mind is tickled by the scraps of a real dream, which I don't have often. I follow the images, they're golden, and they become the still of the desert. The colours are vivid and the expanse goes to the horizon, unmarked, in all directions. I don't feel lost, I know where I am going.

There is a promised land waiting for me in the direction of the rising sun. I am walking, and I am not alone, there are many with us, although sometimes I can't see them, and then suddenly I am in the middle of a crowd. We are listening to the man with the smooth voice and the clever eyes. He is telling us that we have been saved so we can see the promised land — I don't understand why he is trying so hard to convince us — we know, we are all going towards it, we all know how much better life will be once we get there. He doesn't need to tell us, it's our choice.

We begin the day walking, all of us together, and we compete with each other to get through the desert as fast as we can, claiming landmarks as our own. There is no end to the desert, even though we know the promised land must be very near. We talk of the riches of the promised land, the valleys full of fruit and the river beds made of gold pebbles, and the wine from the grapes, and spices from the gardens. We know we will be happy once we get there.

But the wind, suddenly, from being a breeze, became a wailing, turned into a desert storm, reached a crescendo of noise, raising dust and shouting in our ears: where are you going? You are lost, looooost. There is no promised land, he lies, he lies...

The images become thinner and are gone, and I have trouble hanging on to the order. Only the vivid colours remain, although as I drift in and out of sleep I remember vignettes. What was it about? It seemed important, urgent and it left me feeling vacant and anxious.

I lay in the warmth, stretching under the covers, trying to recover my Saturday feeling. I could wear casual clothes and nip to the shop. What I actually need is a proper supermarket trip, but can I bring myself to do it? There is always tomorrow, now that Sundays are open for business, at last

112

there isn't a dead day in the week when nothing can be done. I contemplate the thought of making coffee, using the percolator so the aroma will spread around the flat, and it will stay hot while I potter and read the paper. In the end needing to piss gets me out of bed, as usual.

Having nothing particular to do until the evening, and the day is clear, I decide to call Ben and some of the other boys to arrange a game in the park. We get a majority to agree on the early afternoon, and as I fearfully look out the window to see if the weather will hold I wonder what to do for a few hours. I remember yesterday and my quest, and set off for the coffee shop near work — while I am at it I can drop in and look industrious to our main man who is bound to be there slogging — he has shares in the business. The shop is open now and the Cappuccino Express, as the German makers have called it, is there, and I chat wittily with the waitress, though I know she is a lesbian, and buy it.

I pop into the office, Alan is there, as I'd thought, so I go to my desk and rearrange some papers, make a couple of phonecalls — the boys I hadn't caught earlier — and make a fuss of putting some work into my bag, and go off again. I am eager to take my new toy out of its tidy box and play with all the bits, the ones which are removable, the ones that only lift, all as the instructions show me, as I read them on the tube home. Off the tube and on the way home, I realise that I need the right kind of coffee for the machine, so I do a detour to the supermarket and stock up from the colourful supply — although it is hard to choose, so I take one of each of the packets marked cappuccino.

I am bounding now, in a flurry of bags, dying to get home and set it all in motion. I unload energetically and get to it. First I remove the machine from the box, and take off the layers of plastic and packing tissue, then place it right on the counter. I already know the instructions by heart, so I proceed to fill the filter with special coffee, and find a real jug — a Christmas present from Mother — to put the milk in. The coffee had a sachet of powdered cocoa with it and I put it aside for the final flourish. The cup in place, the milk frothed, all together, the cocoa sprinkled — and there it is, my first, beautiful cappuccino.

I take it to the window, put some music on, savour my success. I know this will be different from my expresso machine, which I have only ever used once.

114

The Egg Baby

Sonja Lyndon

Are you reading me? Good. Then I'll begin. In the beginning there was birth. I was born out of agony. German screams bounced off English antiseptic walls. And no-one came. My father? But this was 1946. Fathers were excused in those days, so he was footing it back to the damp basement in Swiss Cottage, a bundle of my mother's foreign clothes under his arm. And somewhere on the way he dropped a pair of cami-knickers, flesh-pink, artificial silk. They swished down onto the pavement — swish! And at that moment, I was born.

Still reading me? I think you are. Though I can tell this is going to be a one-sided affair. I'm clearly the one that's going to do all the talking, all the revealing. You'll just absorb what I have to say in your usual silent, mask-like way. Occasionally your face may crease into a smile or a finger may reach into the corner of your eye to stem a tear. All these things you have been known to do. But for the most part, I know, you'll just sit there, impassive. I realise you're not used to having the spotlight turned on you, but I'm not going to ignore you like all the rest, I'm going to count you in. If you don't like it you can always silence me in the time-honoured way. Shut me up between the covers. Put me away somewhere, tightly closed, refuse to enter me any more. But of course you know that's just fiction. The reality is I would go on existing, I and my story and you, long after you had tried to resist me. Part of me is already inside you. I am lodged inside you, now and forever, whether you like it or not. And the rest of me will lie screaming silently between the covers. I will not cease to exist because you refuse to cast your eyes over my spotted white sheets. Oh no, I and my story and you live on, whether you take note of me or not.

Still with me? You see, as far as I'm concerned you're part of this. Oh yes. Can you deny that you saw those silk knickers parachuting silently onto the pavement? Of course not, you saw the whole thing, which means you were there. You hesitated, not sure whether to call out to my father. But you are such a silent creature, that you hardly considered that an option. It was you though, who picked up the flimsy garment, when you thought no-one was looking. You picked up my mother's pink cami-knicks and just managed to stop yourself passing them under your nose. Then you hurriedly tucked them into your breast pocket. Didn't you.

And all this a stone's throw from the tiled room of my birth. As you stoop to finger the pink silk on the grey pavement, I am being placed at my mother's breast, tightly swaddled, a wine-red face, and a hairless egg-shaped head. In a few days' time they will try and hand me over to another mother and it's only the shape of my head that will make my own mother insist that the baby they have substituted for me is not hers. The other mother is not sure. She likes the look of me. She's never paid much attention to detail, so all this frenzied talk of egg shapes is beyond her, especially when delivered in a shrill German accent. The war is freshly over, but Nazi fifth columnists still lurk in unexpected places, even in English maternity hospitals. The egg baby is snatched back by its German mother, and dispatched smartly home to continental Swiss Cottage.

That's how I came into the world, wine-red and egg-shaped. I've come a long way from that of course. Or have I? The egg shape is barely discernible now, under a helmet of dark brown hair. But wine-red is the colour of my face as I write these pages, and wine red is increasingly my colour as I sip through the early evenings and into the night. Claret, you see, has entered my life in an important way in the last few months. Nightly it appears at my elbow, preferably in a long-stemmed glass, though at times even a mug and once a restraining egg cup served. As for Swiss Cottage, well, life being what it is, an unending series of loops and spirals, of links in a chain, this year I have found myself back in residence, after all those years. So here I sit, contemplating the mystic chain of life, in communion with you.

I've started something in you, haven't I. You stiffened just now, I could tell, and your palms have turned the faintest bit moist. Your thoughts have gone back to your own beginnings. And now I am entering your past. Are there knickers to be salvaged from dark pavements? Shall I stoop and bend and retrieve a pair for you? Maybe not. But something happened, didn't it. Your birth was marked in some way. You can't deny it. Trumpets may not have blown, but you did not come into the world unheralded, I stake my life on that. You're shrinking back now. I can feel the tension in your body, it's affected your grip on my pages.

Where was I? Ah yes. The agony of my birth, followed by my swaddling in Swiss Cottage. Well, of course, after birth comes life — you know all about that, don't you. It starts out small and uncomplicated, then grows in fits and starts, till suddenly, in your middle years, you find it has endowed you with a thousand limbs, all flailing in different directions. You know what I'm saying, don't you. Of course you do. Intelligence is something I know I can credit you with. I'm talking about the ravelled, knotted, tangled life we metropolitans lead.

Take you for example. Your life is so complicated, it's taken you days to even open this book. And now you find yourself on this white sheet with me, four limbs finally at rest, while the remaining nine hundred and

116

ninety-six attempt to pull you in all directions. For we ~~we~~
metropolis have finally mutated into beasts of such comp.
wasted bodies now have to support a forest of trunk-like
tapering to a nostril of startling hypersensitivity. Even as yo
one of your trunks is elongating towards your kitchen, slinking
tap, bottle or cafetière, while another is reaching out for the kn
radio, and others are straining towards fax machine, video recorder,
processor, c.d.rom and all the other electronic toys you surround you
with. As for the remaining forest, it is waving about, sending out ar.
receiving a myriad signals, in an air of general distraction. You're a mass
of agitation for which there is only one solution — amputation. Oh yes.
You and me both: we're in sore need of severance. Steady! I'm not talking
knives or axes. A litre of red is all I need. Liquid works well for me, as I
mentioned before. Cuts me off a treat. For you likewise perhaps; if not
there's the weed, or acid, any number of chemical compounds — they're
all knife substitutes. They cause those extra limbs to fall off in their
dozens, sometimes leaving you with the essential four, sometimes with
only two. My aim is to eradicate them all tonight. To aim for nirvana. And
to take you with me.

Snap. You hurt me then. No doubt it'll be a while before you dare to slip
between my covers again. But I can wait. It'll only take one limb to reach
out for me, which will happen, in time. Meanwhile I'll carry on with my
story. There'll be time for you to catch up. You need a little break from all
this now. An interval away from the spotlight.

What can I tell you? The oval-headed baby grew into an oval-headed
woman. She led a womanly life: she menstruated, ovulated, got impreg-
nated, gave birth. She dusted, sorted, folded, cleared, cooked, washed and
wiped. She listened, watched, recorded, notated, abstracted, regurgitated,
simulated. She smiled, nodded, paused, questioned, responded, cocked an
ear. She did all these things. She aimed to please. It was a goal she had
imbibed with her mother's milk. For her mother had displeased — with
her tainted blood and heavy features, she had given great displeasure. She
had paid a heavy price for that: expulsion from the land of forests and
woodcutters, the land of smoked, cured ham and beer and pretzels. She
could have paid with her life as many of her friends and family did. But
instead she was forced into exile, where she bore me and trained me to
please, as though this would prevent me incurring a similar fate to hers.

Ah, you're back. I sense a shaft of light and a rush of air. I told you it
wouldn't be long. You're intrigued, aren't you, and not a little resentful.
You thought I'd be easy. You saw I was thinner than the others and you
said to yourself: I can do her in bed. You thought I'd be delicate and fragile and that you'd get through me in no time, like a knife through foam.

n minutes, then lights out and oblivion.

Well, others might be satisfied with that treatment. But not me. My ecades of appeasement are over. One day I started to shout. I ceased to address people in quiet, modulated tones; I argued, I gesticulated, I stamped my foot and answered back. I refused to agree. They came for me in the end. I roared. They removed my anger with a syringe. I slumped. Then a voice in my head rang out. I sank down on my knees and sobbed. You are not your mother's child it said. And I thought back to the time of my birth.

When my mother came to see me, I placed my hands on her head. I felt it all over. It was not oval-shaped. I had been duped. I sent her away and felt the dark weight of the century lift. I ran the words *soap* and *camp* and *shower* and *oven* around my tongue to confirm my new innocence.

I left the hospital and looked for a room in Swiss Cottage. I wanted to start again. To begin at the beginning. I call it My Thinking Room. I fight to block out my former mother's German voice, calling it my Sinking Room. I write everything down. I live alone. I have to be alone to find out who I am. My life till now has been one long fabrication. In a vacuum I can be pure essence of *moi*. And that's where you come in. I'm not quite alone in the world; I've got you. Every time you smooth back my sheets, you enter my story. Like now... I've made you part of it. I made you pick up those pink knickers. I made you into a thief and a pervert. This much power I now have. I can make you into anything I like.

I frightened you, I'm sorry. That was foolish of me. Please don't close me up! I need you a bit longer. I think we're almost there. As I write this I feel the crush of papers under my feet; my floor is strewn with a thousand stories, all inventions, from my head. None of them work for long. I need a real life to slip into, now that I've written mine off. The invented life does not sustain. I need a ready-made one.

I know what you're thinking — the other baby has got my life, try and get it back, a straight swap. That's what I sometimes think in the dark of the night. But how do you convince someone they've led the wrong life? It wouldn't be easy.

My former mother is at the door. She comes here frequently. I can't let her in. She wants to snatch me away, wants me back as her child, so that she can pass on her legacy. I don't want it I scream I don't want your tarnished bits of silver, your moth-eaten rugs, your sad plastic lampshades. Lampshades. My tongue is furred. It balls up in my mouth. Sticks and stones I know break bones, but I thought those words could no longer hurt me.

My ex-brother comes knocking, his mother cowering behind. She wants me to feel his head. I do. It's oval-shaped. Her glinty eyes are triumphant.

118

I don't know what to think. They're trying to ensnare me in a genetic trap. Papa, God rest his soul, was the same. I play it cool. But underneath I'm shaken. Could it be a trick? Can you do plastic surgery on skulls?

I shoo them out of my room. When they're gone, I hurl paper balls of my screwed up stories at the door of their exit and I sit down and weep. I reach for the liquid knife, red and glistening in the dying sunlight and let it pass through my throat. I sob at my failed attempts to invent a new life. But I've closed down the only one I ever had and there's no going back. Nirvana or nothing. Are they one and the same?

Which brings me to you. Make of me what you will, but give me a life: dress me in lamé or coat me in tweed, see me in stilettoes or sandals or brogues, give me a waist that is thick or thin, a deep voice or a light trill, make me plain or ugly, the possibilities are endless. But make me wholesome, make me whole. Give me a long line of ancestors whose graves I can visit in verdant graveyards with whispering trees and creaking gates, set against a Constable landscape and a scudding sky. Write me into the book of life, shroud me in sheets of English prose. This is my living, dying, lying wish. Amen.

The Silence of Dishes

Carole Malkin

Crumpled newspapers littered the Miami airport. Young men in under-shirts, clearly not travelers, hung about an arcade of jangling pinball machines. I overheard a frantic woman saying her plane was delayed two hours because officials were searching the crew for drugs smuggled from South America. The filth, the air of lawless disorder surprised me. Those years after my mother's death when I lived with Ruchel, I had absorbed her paradisiacal vision of Miami. More affluent schoolmates had returned from Christmas vacations transformed by golden tans. We heard talk of ballrooms, chandeliers and fountains. But I could see that Miami had fallen from its previous glory, and the change made me feel as if I were walking on a slippery surface.

I had come only because Ruchel's daughter-in-law Brenda wrote, "She's old and she'll die soon. You better come." So I booked a flight from San Francisco for the same week Ruchel's youngest son Simon and his wife Janet were flying from New York.

The cab driver who picked me up at the airport, a former Iranian general, reminisced as he drove about the drivers he had had, of his long black limousine with flags streaming above the fenders and how a lengthy entourage followed. The only entourage now were senile drivers oblivious to all rules, who tailgated and cut in front of us.

"Where's the Bass Museum?" I asked. In my purse was a newspaper article about the Jewish Legacy exhibit, a collection of torahs, silver candelabras and other booty plundered by the Nazis. I figured if Ruchel could spare me, I'd make a side-trip to the museum.

As we turned onto Collins Avenue, I noticed an old woman totter and fall on the sidewalk. I wanted to help her, but my driver said, "Do you want to stop on every street?" Ambulance sirens shrieked, the noise twisting above the scruffy palm trees and dilapidated buildings.

We passed small bodegas and a store called Torah Treasures. A heavy-set, white-bearded man with skullcap lounged in the doorway. Old people, as if on ship deck, sat in front of the small hotels. We pulled up in front of the SeaBreeze, a narrow three-story building. Pink flamingos and palm trees adorned its plate glass front. There was no verandah. The residents sat on folding chairs directly on the sidewalk. Just a glance at the men in their straw panama hats and the women in sun dresses and rolled stockings, and I knew they were Eastern European immigrants like my aunt.

The general palmed the fare and shook my hand as if we were friends and he had driven me as a favour. Then he drove off and left me to face the line-up. A dozen old people turned to me in one perfect, synchronized motion of expectation as I made my way into the lobby. I wondered if Ruchel had any friends among them. Thirty years ago when I was ten, I had gone to live with her. I stayed seven years, and during that time no friend ever phoned or visited her.

Hers was on the third-floor, a corner room. She had written to me in her broken English of her scheming and waiting to get this new room and gain the advantage of two windows. Shortly after this, she had stopped writing completely, and I couldn't phone her because she was too hard of hearing. Finally, Brenda had responded to my unanswered letters with her summons. I went up in the tiny elevator and knocked on the door of 307. Simon had told me she had two paid companions, both Haitian boat people who were illegal immigrants. One of these black women answered my knock. She smiled and whispered, "Ruchel is tired. Couldn't stay up."

Behind her I glimpsed the small room stuffed to the brim with twin beds, a sink, tiny formica table, television, dresser and metal utility cabinet. These were the remnants of Aunt Ruchel's life, the kosher dishes and pots and pans, the photographs and knick-knacks, and she herself was a kind of remnant. The eldest of four sisters, she had outlived everyone despite constant complaints about her health. After my mother's death, she was always promising the drama of hers.

I remembered her waking up early mornings and over lumpy oatmeal, telling me, "I almost died last night." Yet here she was ninety-two years old, shrunken, stiff, barely able to walk, her no-neck head like a turtle's emerging from a shell, her skin deeply lined. It startled me to see her small as a child as she lay asleep beneath her cover. She hardly seemed the person who used to rage at me. Now she looked pathetic and my brave plans to confront her with the past disappeared. "Tell her I was here, and that I'll come back in the morning," I whispered and ran out.

The woman at the desk gave me a key to a room on the floor below my aunt's. Like Ruchel's, this room was crowded with twin beds, a dresser and tiny table, and against one wall a counter with a built-in refrigerator, burner and sink. All that was missing were the family photographs, but the nails on which they had hung still studded the discolored green walls. It was such a cramped, dismal room that the pink plastic wastebasket decorated with a Mickey Mouse decal struck the only cheerful note. A loudspeaker was shouting out numbers outside, "twenty-six, five, thirteen." The bingo game in the adjoining hotel was already in full swing.

Restless, I went out and walked the few blocks to the flat, monotonous beach, so different from the craggy cliffs that met the Pacific in Califor-

122

nia. Even the gray ocean lay dead and listless. I meandered along a wooden boardwalk sunk into the sand and tried to untangle, one more time, why I had come. I wished I wasn't here, but knew I had to see Ruchel again one final time. My father, who had deserted my mother and me, was no more to me than a speck of sand. It was Ruchel who gave me a home.

But when she took me in, it was as a servant. The sight of the kosher dishes brought it all back, the endless dishes I had to wash, the poorer food I was served, the stingier servings, and the lectures I received as I ate. "You don't deserve," my aunt pronounced, taking the joy out of any good fortune which came my way. I was accused of having broken a chair, a stepladder, the television; on other occasions, of having stolen missing photographs, a handkerchief, her corset, chocolates. "I didn't," I cried, and Ruchel spurted out, "So you're a liar too!" Hers was a niggling assault, a slow paring away of who I was, until I learned to sit with hanging head as her accusations sharpened to the final knife to the heart, "If you weren't such a spoiled brat your mother never would have died."

The sea looked thick, viscous, as if suddenly it could erupt and spill into the streets, bringing along a flood of sharp rocks, a force cutting down everyone in its way, and I wanted it to, the way I had wanted destruction thirty years before. I still felt the same despair. If my mother had lived I would have been a different person. I yearned for this other mysterious self with all the grief of a mother mourning a dead infant. Seeking lights and noise to distract me from my thoughts, I fled the isolated beach.

"Twenty dollars," a young Cuban on Collins Avenue shouted to me. He was sitting on a stoop with his friends, but at my approach jumped up and swaggered half way across the street to me. I saw this was a performance for the other boys and speeded up. Another dark-eyed boy who looked no older than thirteen, smiled ingratiatingly. His approach confused me, but I automatically shook my head and walked further along By the time a third boy called out mockingly, "twenty dollars," with a gasp I understood. Did I look that desperate? that old and undesirable?. Although I had scarcely been gone a day, I felt stripped of my identity and missed my family. I ran back to the SeaBreeze where the desk clerk rebuked me for leaving a track of black oil which had stuck to my shoes from the beach. I had to take them off and walk along in stockinged feet like a mourner. There was no phone in my room, and I called from a suffocating booth.

"I miss you," I told my husband, and then not wanting to worry Jim, recovered myself enough to banter, "Not much to do here but play bingo."

"Did you see Ruchel?"

"Yes and no. She was sleeping. Tomorrow's the big reunion."

"It's good you went. She's the last of a generation."

123

"Yes, yes."

"Susan, you can handle it."

"Of course, of course. How are the girls?"

"I picked Joanie up at nursery school and she called me, 'Mommy.' She went around telling everyone I was 'Mommy.' "

"Did she? The little devil."

I spun the conversation out for as long as I could. As long as I held Jim on the phone, I was part of the ordered, reassuring life I had with him, and my violently confused attachment to my aunt dimmed. But we said good-bye. Then I phoned the Holiday Inn to see if my cousin Simon and his wife had arrived yet from New York.

Simon, the youngest of Ruchel's five children, was the one I liked best. I remembered terrible scenes between the three eldest sons, particularly one at the cemetery with Ruchel trying to reconcile them at their father's grave. The Goldstein family possessed a flair for drama. While the sons exchanged insults and nearly came to blows, Ruchel wrung her hands and her daughter Marilyn raced among the headstones shrieking, "Look what you're doing to mother."

As the receptionist rang Simon's room, I twisted around and saw the elderly hotel residents gathering in the lobby. The television hung from the ceiling the way it would have in a hospital room. "Susan? Is that you," came Simon's deep voice. "Do you want to meet for a drink? Janet went to bed early. Just wait where you are and I'll come get you."

With a quarter of an hour to spare before Simon would come and nothing else to do, I phoned Ruchel's eldest son, Sam. He spoke to me briefly and then put Brenda on. We had not seen each other in years, but I remembered this twenty-years-older cousin as a bleached blonde wearing a long chiffon scarf and rhinestone studded wooden platform shoes who urged me to follow her example and have a nose job. Within seconds she was criticizing Sam's brothers and Marilyn for trying to foist Ruchel off on Sam and herself. "I didn't retire to Miami to take care of my mother-in-law." When I put down the receiver I felt drained. Brenda had worked herself into such a state of indignation that there hadn't been even a word of getting together.

A pale blue Ford drew up in front of the SeaBreeze. I jumped into Simon's rental car and he took me to a hotel bar, a dark place of chrome and black marble which made me realize that not all of Miami was run down. A decade older than I, Simon lacked the self-pity and bitterness I detected in his brothers. He'd gained a few extra pounds but remained resilient as ever. Everything about him bristled with alertness. His kinky gray hair formed a halo about his head. He gazed at me and demanded, "Whadya' want?"

124

He was having a Bloody Mary and I asked for plain tomato juice. Turning to the waitress, he said, "And a Virgin Mary" and gave his snorting-through-the-nose laugh. She retreated to the bar and Simon peppered me with rapid-fire questions. "Now give me the run-down. How's Jim? How's Dana? The other kid? Any pictures?" I asked him about his two grown children and his factory. He manufactured tractors and sold them all over the world. "Good, everything's good. We're trying to break into the Eastern Europe market."

When our drinks arrived, he asked the waitress, "How about a few extra cocktail onions?"

She was middle-aged with a ruddled face. "Sorry. They don't like giving extras."

"Oh come on. I know you can pull it off. Just for me. OK?"

She trotted off, and when she returned it wasn't with just one or two for the drink but a whole plateful of onions.

"Now that's terrific." He popped one into his mouth and sucked on it with enjoyment. "Mom's very excited about your coming. She can't believe it. I can't believe I'm seeing you either. How long has it been? It must be ten years."

His voice was loud and commanding. He used to frighten me as a little girl. "My motto's live with dignity and die with dignity," Simon announced as he sipped his second drink. "Sam's right here in Miami, and he could take some trouble with Mom, but Brenda won't let him. For every little thing now, the doctor throws Mom in the hospital. He can't take any risks. A month ago she got diarrhoea. Sam was furious he had to sign her into the hospital and check her out. If he and Brenda helped, it would be a different thing. Meanwhile, Marilyn can't do much, she's so far away. Harry was ready to warehouse Mom fifteen years ago. Ernie doesn't care where she goes, just so long as he doesn't have to put out any effort. If Mom was willing to come back to New York I could look after her, but she hates the cold weather."

Listening to him discuss Aunt Ruchel's fate, I remembered when he and his family had argued mine. No one wanted Ruchel to take me in except for Simon He told the others, "Oh, come off it. It's not going to cost any of you anything. Aunt Stella left some insurance. It will take care of Susan's expenses." Then he turned to his mother and teasingly asked, "Look Mrs. Goldstein, you're not going to put her out on the street, are you? What will the neighbours think? Here's your chance to be a saint."

Simon told me matter-of-factly, "The upshot is Sam refuses to help any more. If she has to go into the hospital again, he won't sign her in. I have to put her in a home. I want you to come look at the places with Janet and me, and persuade her this is the best thing for her."

Ruchel had five children, but Simon was alone in his concern and grabbed the only branch nearby. "All right," I said, smiling and hoping I didn't show my disappointment at being involved. The black oil stuck to my shoes.

*

A thin, young black woman answered Ruchel's door, the other Haitian immigrant who looked after her. She had short frizzy hair pulled back in a ponytail and wore rubber thonged zoris and shorts and a white t-shirt decorated with streamers of sewed-on pink ribbons. "Susan," Aunt Ruchel cried. When I hugged her, she grabbed my hands and kissed them. It was a self-abasing, feudal gesture. I could not keep from pulling away. Slyly observing the effect on me, she told her companion, "This is my daughter." I flinched at this pretence and wondered if I could make myself stay in the room.

The attendant gazed at me curiously. "I didn't know Ruchel had two daughters." She spoke with a Creole accent; the 't' sounds made tiny explosions. Her name was Angelina Ostah, but Ruchel had taken to calling her Esther. She told me, "Esther's better than the other one who comes at night. Esther's very good to me." Angelina sat on the edge of a straight back chair, feet together, hands primly folded on her lap. "Yes, Ruchel," she said indulgently.

"Did you eat breakfast?" Ruchel asked. I'd gotten up early and gone for a run along the ocean. The smell of breakfast sweet rolls had drifted tantalizingly from the hotels lining the beach. Now I was hungry. Angelina rose to make tea and brought out a tin of biscuits.

It was odd for me to be waited upon as Ruchel's guest of honor. I could see the Passover dishes in the cabinet, pink-tinted glass dairy and pale yellow meat dishes with forget-me-nots painted on the rims. The night before the seder I would carry cartons up from the basement and spend all night unwrapping dishes from their newspaper coverings. The next day the guests arrived. Once the meal began I was exiled to the kitchen. Ruchel and her family feasted at the dining-room table, while I stood washing course after course of dishes and longing for the Passovers I had spent with my mother. Only Simon's wife, Janet, had looked in on me.

"All my life I kept kosher. Not a bite of *treif* passed my lips," Ruchel said, proud she had kept this faith amid other confusions. "My girl knows how to do it right. I don't have to worry," she nodded towards Angelina who gave her a cup of steaming tea. Ruchel held the handle with her little finger extended, a refinement clouded by the stains down the front of her dress.

126

I told her about my children. Mischievous Joanie and serious Dana, only nine, but practicing her violin with fervour. She longed to wear nylons and put on jewelry. We looked through Ruchel's albums and I begged for photos of Sara, the first sister to die, the aunt I had never met. She was tall and blonde, a big-boned woman. Although it was a black-and-white photo I could tell her eyes were a very pale blue. Her son was ten when like me he lost his mother. He had been sent to an orphanage.

"What happened to Barry?" I asked.

"I don't know. I never heard from him. He just forgot everybody."

"What was he like?"

"Such a temper. After my sister died, I sewed a jacket for him. He came in and grabbed it and ran out."

The room was like a ship becalmed. We soon sat silently. I sipped my tea and nibbled on a cookie. My sweat stained dress stuck to my sides, and in the wall mirror I saw my thin face, so much like my mother's with its high cheekbones, dark hair and the uneven nose that Brenda had wanted put to the knife. Outside I could hear the roar of traffic on Collins Avenue and the ever-present ambulance sirens. "Maybe you'd like to nap," I suggested. The remark hurt Ruchel. "I'll sleep at night," she answered.

Angelina rescued the moment with, "Ruchel, your television programme." She turned on the set and Aunt Ruchel laughed and enjoyed herself watching a man talking to an old woman puppet, white-haired and bejeweled, but full of Punch and Judy mischief. Angelina sat painting her nails red and laughed with my aunt at the puppet's triumphant antics.

When the programme was over, Angelina snapped it off and turned to my aunt. "Ruchel, time to do your nails. Come. Sit by the light." Gently, she helped her over to a chair by the window. Angelina slowly rubbed off the previous day's polish with a cotton ball soaked in sharp-smelling remover. I watched, fascinated by her smile and my aunt's responding delight. The sunlight illuminated the white and black heads and surrounded them with a private penumbra. "It's hot today," Angelina said. Her face glistened with sweat. She blew on my aunt's nails and asked tenderly, "Would you like a bath?" "Yes, Esther," my Aunt replied with a child's simplicity.

I felt left out. I couldn't keep away from those familiar dishes and picked up a plate which was faintly veined like a Chinese Ming vase. As Angelina ran the bath I was remembering how, as I ate, Ruchel would count the chits she received for each collar she had sewed at the local clothing factory. *"Eynsz, tzvey, dray, fier, finef, zex..."* My mouth used to grow dry knowing she'd soon count herself into, "You didn't cry enough after your mother died. You never loved her."

For the first time I understood she was talking about herself, not my mother. It was a vicious circle, Ruchel punishing me for not loving her and turning me further against her. Angelina was more her daughter than I was.

*

"Susan! When was the last time we met?" Janet, tall and slender, her straight hair in a smooth pageboy, was dressed in a tailored skirt and beige blouse. She sat in the back of Simon's car. I was carefully helping Ruchel in beside the driver's seat. After I loaded her walker in the trunk, I squeezed in the back next to Janet while Simon drove off to the first residence home. On the other side of Janet sat her mother, Gertrude, a pretty woman with thick spectacles perched on a tiny turned-up nose. She was all pink and ruffled. Her frilly sun umbrella made me feel as if the packed car was a steam boat with paddle wheels and that we were drifting down the Mississippi.

After Simon parked in front of a tall brick building, we made slow progress — Ruchel with her walker and nearly blind Gertrude needing to be led — into a luxurious lounge with chandeliers, red and black rugs and soft leather armchairs. A woman in her forties, wearing a powder-blue suit had been waiting for us. She whisked us up to an elegantly furnished model apartment. Each room had a wall cord that Ruchel could pull for help. Janet whispered to me, "If she's sprawled on the floor, how will she reach the string on the wall?" Downstairs we viewed a spacious dining room. The tables were covered with stiff damask cloths and bore vases of fresh flowers.

Then, while the rest of us were left sunk in the deep chairs of the lounge, Simon proceeded to the manager's office to talk about "business details." The four of us attracted attention, and several of the elderly residents gathered around, discussing us in loud voices.

A sunken-cheeked man in plaid trousers called out, "Which one wants to come here?" I nodded towards Ruchel. "That one! Who does she think she is?"

A wave of anger passed through the residents. "You have to be able to walk to come here. They won't let her in with a walker," a plump, heavily made-up woman said in a spiteful voice. Another woman cried, "How old is she anyway?" Stooped and deeply wrinkled, she must have been in her eighties herself but was indignant to hear Ruchel was a nonagenarian.

Strange how much of life is about who is in and who is out, whether it was myself as an orphan, Angelina as an illegal immigrant or Ruchel in her helplessness. Hard of hearing, Ruchel only smiled as she was dis-

128

cussed, and soon Simon returned with a jaunty air and led us away. Janet accompanied her mother and I helped Ruchel. At a snail's pace we moved past the plaid-trousered man and his cronies. As we got into the car Ruchel complained, "My tooth hurts. It hurt me last night. Now it hurts worse."

The next residence was smaller, but here the residents got more care. We walked under a navy awning into a one-story building, down a long blue hall, past blue rooms, to a windowed lounge looking out onto the blueness of a canal and sky. Here and there, nursing aides asked who wanted Cokes.

The manager, a short, pot-bellied man with thick eyebrows, discretely indicated a senator's mother, who wandered about with an aide following after her. "She just keeps pacing. Even at night. She has to be watched every second or she'll walk out and get lost."

He took Simon and Janet away and I was left on a couch sandwiched between Ruchel and Gertrude. Nearby, a short woman with a broad face and protuberant eyes kept flipping her skirt up and down, and another resident, a thin, neatly dressed woman looked very pained.

I asked, "How long have you been here?"

"Three months. They sold my daughter a bushel of hay, and I'm the horse."

Simon and Janet returned saying, "This is the place. What do you think Mom?" Ruchel smiled weakly. "My tooth hurts." As we left, I noticed a room with a few tables. An aide was setting up for the next meal, putting out the plastic cutlery and paper plates to which Ruchel would have to accustom herself.

*

Later that afternoon, I promised Simon I would take his mother to the dentist. When I phoned, the receptionist said Ruchel would have to get there by five on the dot or else the office would be closed. It was four thirty when I tried to hail a cab in front of the SeaBreeze. There just did not seem to be any. I wasted a precious five minutes peering into the traffic and praying for my Iranian General to come along. Finally, since the dentist was only a few blocks away, we decided to walk. Angelina proved a poor guide. "I think... I think this way," she said, and leading Aunt Ruchel with her walker, we inched along following Angelina's vague navigation.

At five minutes to five we arrived at the office but had to manoeuvre Ruchel up a flight of steps. Groaning and giggling we took the stairs. It was a great triumph to enter the office at the stroke of five. Ruchel went into the treatment room where she took out her dental plates. The dentist decided he would pull her last remaining tooth.

In the waiting room, I flipped through the *Miami Herald*. Angelina fidgeted beside me. She tapped her foot and cleared her throat. As I was about to turn the page, the brush of her hand on my wrist stopped me. I looked up.

"I have a three-year-old boy. He's in Haiti."

"Who is he with now?"

"My sister..." She paused, unable to speak, but then went on. "No good there. I want him with me in Miami."

Her eyes were wide and she had the look of an animal caught in a trap. Run-down Miami was paradise after Haiti if only she could get her little boy back. She didn't ask me to help but it was clear she wanted me to get involved. I had been only ten when I was foisted on an unwilling aunt, but Angelina's son was much younger.

For a dizzying moment I considered hiring lawyers and fighting the immigration service, and then it seemed a mad thing to do. Bringing Angelina to the attention of the authorities might just get her deported. I knew nothing about these matters and very little about her. Not only that, but at home a husband and small children awaited me, and I was leaving the next day. "I'm sorry," I told her and fumbled in my purse for a twenty-dollar bill which I pressed into her hand. It was better than doing nothing.

The dentist called me into the cubicle where he had been working on Aunt Ruchel. She was still sitting in the dental chair with a paper bib on. "Are you in pain?" She shook her head. Without her dental plates her mouth was collapsed over her gums and it was difficult for her to speak. The dentist, a tall gray-haired man, stood at his work counter. "With patients this age," he lowered his voice, "they die, or move suddenly and it turns out I don't get paid. I have to take precautions. Will you write a cheque now?"

"I think her son..."

He raised his voice and addressed Ruchel, "Didn't you say this was your daughter?"

"I'll take care of it," I snapped and wrote out the cheque. "Can I have a receipt?"

"Yes, yes, I'll do it myself. My receptionist's already gone home." He went off and Ruchel tried to say something to me. Her numbed mouth was so stiff that it took a while to get the words out. "Should I move? Is it the right thing?"

I thought she and Angelina ought to be together. Now at the end of her life, my Aunt had found a friend who made her happy. But Sam and

Brenda weren't going to act as back-ups and so it was impossible for Ruchel to remain at the SeaBreeze. I answered vaguely, "It's a big decision."

Earlier I had asked Simon, "Does Angelina know she's going to lose her job?" "She can guess," he answered. His attention was on his mother and he had no concern to spare for Angelina. "Could Angelina get a job at the retirement home? It would mean a lot to your mother." "My mother would like it, but I doubt it. She doesn't have a green card." Angelina would probably find another employer at the SeaBreeze. The SeaBreeze was a free zone. Angelina and Ruchel could not get into the posher places. Not together.

I glanced outside the dentist's window to see the street with its little shops was dark already and the street lamps on. How much I owed other people was ambiguous, as hard to decipher as the shadowed alleys below.

"Here you are." The dentist popped into the room and handed me the receipt. "Let her take some aspirin when she gets home. She might not want to wear her dentures for a day or two." He gave me his instructions briskly, removed Ruchel's paper bib, and then disappeared. Ruchel struggled out of the dental chair and I stretched my hand out to help her. "Should I do it? Should I go in the Home?" she asked again.

I wasn't going to move to Miami and sign her in and out of hospitals. Nor would I invite her to come live with me in California, begrudging her a place as she had done to me. I didn't know how to help either her or Angelina. She trusted me and I couldn't look at her when I said, "yes."

"I'll have to throw my things away. Do you want anything?" She was speaking more easily now as we moved down a long hallway towards the waiting room where Angelina sat. "Take my dishes."

"No," I said more firmly than I needed to, and then in a softer tone, "I don't need them."

"I'll give to the girl."

"Yes, do that."

At the door to the waiting room, she stopped short, grabbed my hand and squeezed it. Tears filmed her eyes. There was a long pause and then to my amazement, she told me something which must have percolated into her mind during those long afternoons with Angelina, "Those things I said to you when you lived with me. I didn't mean them."

I glanced away from her. My heart was pounding. It was as if she had put her hand deep inside me and touched all the soft, vulnerable organs. Angelina looked up with curiosity. "We can go," I cried. The bright sound of my voice surprised me. Angelina reached for the folded walker, but I grabbed it, saying, "You help Ruchel on the steps." The walker was heavy, but I strained my arms to keep it aloft and raced down ahead of them. I

131

needed a few moments alone to compose myself. Outside, it had begun to drizzle. People ran into doorways. Cars glided by. Like church bells rung to summon the faithful, I heard the ring of ambulance sirens. "Didn't mean them... didn't mean them... didn't," she said of the poison she had dripped in my ears.

Across the street I saw the blinking neon sign of another Bingo parlor. The night before, I lay awake listening to the numbers echoing over the adjacent hotel's loudspeaker. I hadn't expected to win the jackpot. The payoff had come late and much devalued but better than nothing.

*

In the morning while Janet and Simon packed Ruchel's belongings, I managed to steal a visit to the Bass Museum for the Jewish Legacy exhibit. The crowd wandering from room to room was hushed and reverent. Elaborately embroidered velvet torah curtains hung in high ceilinged, dimly lit rooms. I felt like I was stepping into a synagogue. In one chamber there was a table set with mourning dishes, white platters with black trim used for the meals of lentils and hard-boiled eggs served following a funeral.

I thought of Angelina making her meal that night and perhaps eating on Aunt Ruchel's dishes. Maybe she would preserve those dishes for the time when her son came. Or maybe she would politely accept them, walk out the door and dump them one by one into the first garbage pail she came across. I couldn't blame her if she did. Who wanted to eat off someone else's plate?

Afterlife

Sylvia Paskin

A slant of light through the french windows seemed to land somewhere near my right foot and for a few seconds I distracted myself putting my shoe in and out of the area it illuminated on the Persian carpet. It was the day of my grandfather's funeral and the mourners had greeted us, commiserated and eaten biscuits with equal gusto. Now most of them had gone. I caught my mother's disapproving eye and stopped my game. I got up and went over to the windows. I stood tracing my name on the moist glass. Outside the trees flung themselves around in a late October tango. Suddenly the sun went out like a light and the world looked desolate and unpeopled. He had been dead only twelve hours. I felt a surge of pain around my own heart. I missed him. Then the phone rang on the hall table. I turned round and watched my family behaving as if this sort of apparatus had just been invented and some elaborate protocol was required to answer it. I looked towards where my grandmother sat, her stern grief intimidating to us all. Her eyebrow lifted very slightly in my direction and I knew it was I who should answer.

I was startled to hear Steiner on the other end of the line. My grandfather's agent was calling from Amsterdam. After some soft words of sympathy, he came to the point. There was in his possession a painting lying crated up in his warehouse — something my grandfather had acquired recently in his native Prague and wanted sent to London. I interrupted him, explaining that this was not the moment to discuss business. I said I would ring him later on in the week.

Two days later, Steiner rang and woke me up. Once again he asked me what he should do with the painting. I asked if my grandfather had bought it for the gallery or for a particular client. No said Steiner, it was for his private collection. I was surprised for my grandfather had not bought anything for himself for over thirty years. What mystified me even more was Steiner's subsequent remark. This was a painting about which my grandfather was very passionate and rather secretive. Apparently he had been most insistent that I should see it first — I had worked as his assistant for several years and I would now take over the gallery. I told Steiner to make the usual arrangements and send the painting to me in London. I knew Steiner was obsessive about prompt payment and enjoyed a small moment of triumph by mentioning the invoice before he did.

Some ten days later on a late Thursday afternoon I was showing Amer-

133

ican clients some of our latest acquisitions. They were not in a buying mood and I made no effort to sell them anything. The shop door rang and I saw the blue ArtiMoves van parked outside. The driver handed me a grimy docket and a brown paper package trussed with string and emblazoned with customs declarations. I went back to my clients who announced they were returning to New York rather earlier than expected and would drop by next time they were in London. I was relieved to see them disappear into the dusk. I put "closed" on the door, switched off most of the gallery lights and went into the windowless back office. I sank back into my grandfather's leather armchair and remembered how we had sat there together every day after six talking through events that had occurred in our own domain and in the outside world. He would pour us both a very large, very dry sherry, a taste he had acquired in deference to the English since he arrived on these shores fifty years ago.. He was a tiny, fine-boned man with a bald head and an immaculate silver beard. Everyday a red silk handkerchief with a discreet polka dot graced his top pocket. After lunch he would go into this refuge, close the door, take a few puffs of his pungent Davidoff cigar, place the handkerchief across his face like Badger and snooze gently for precisely twenty minutes. That was how they had found him two weeks ago. Now I sat in his chair looking across at my own empty space and wished he had not left us.

Then I reminded myself of the painting. I went back into the gallery put on some lights and undid the package. The last piece of bubble wrap unfurled and revealed a small dark oil painting with a very ornate gold frame. The image eluded me in the semi-darkness. I took the painting under a light and took it in very slowly. It was the portrait of a young woman wearing a black velvet robe done up close to her neck. She wore a creamy gauze turban that was folded assiduously around her head. It then fell in a swathe and framed one side of her pale oval face. She had a soft coral mouth, the lips slightly open is if to impart a sigh or a kiss but when I looked more closely I could see her mouth was slightly more apart than I had first imagined and it looked more as if she was speaking or had just spoken... She appeared to be moving as if up a staircase of some kind. She held aloft two, huge torches, alive with blood-red flames each with a melting yellow heart. There seemed to be something very strange about the painting — a striking contrast between the menace in the warlike, triumphal torches and the rapture of her dreamy curving mouth. Who was she or indeed what was she? I could think of many mythological figures but she fitted with none of them. There was no signature and nothing written on the back of the painting either. I thought it was early nineteenth century. Certainly it was from Eastern Europe. Steiner had mentioned Prague and my grandfather had been there a few weeks before his sudden death.. I held it up for some time marvelling at its sombre yet intense mood. I wondered why my grandfather had been so fascinated by it and had so desired it for himself.

My family now took it in turns to visit my grandmother and keep her company. Sunday afternoons was my designated slot. She lived in a sumptuous apartment overlooking a Kensington square. She answered the door looking elegant and self-possessed and proffered first her right and the her left cheek making sure each time that I could not actually touch either. We went into the lounge and I answered various searching questions about different members of the family and then about the gallery and the forthcoming exhibition of nineteenth century American landscape paintings. She went to make coffee. I knew the mise en scène that would await me and how long it would take to create it. I would be called to the dining room in ten minutes. There would be her Dresden china set, hand-painted with curlicues of fruit and flowers and rimmed with gold leaf. There would be strong Viennese coffee smelling faintly of figs, in the silver Austro-Hungarian pot, whipped cream laced with cognac in a blue glass dish and a freshly-baked mohnstrudel. Whilst she was in the kitchen, I walked through to my grandfather's study. The room was lined with pale green Chinese silk and dominated by his black desk with carved lions' heads on each of its doors that had so frightened me as a child. Now I traced the heavy carving on their manes without fear. I sat down at his desk and touched the last things he had touched, feeling the tissue writing paper spread over the pink blotting paper, filling his crystal inkpots and lighting the desk lamp. His red morocco-bound diary was lying closed on the desk. It had his monogram on it — J. S. My grandmother called and I went and had coffee with her and promised to call back the following Sunday.

When I arrived the following week I could see something was wrong. She appeared very shaken and said she wanted to sit down. I offered to make the coffee although it filled me with trepidation. As I muddled my way around the immaculate kitchen, I heard an odd gasping noise and rushed to the lounge thinking she had collapsed. She sat on the sofa clasping his diary and moaning softly. I could see tears running down her cheeks. I had never seen her cry not even at the funeral and my mother had always said she was incapable of it since the war. Now she was distraught and I imagined it was delayed shock. I tried to comfort her but she pushed me away and thrust the open diary at me and urged me to read the last ten pages. Scattered amongst his appointments there were a few written entries. "I have found her..." "He won't part with her..." "I must have her..."

What had come over my grandfather, an old man married for sixty years — had he fallen in love? My grandmother snatched the diary back

135

and held it to her, keening over it and repeating his name over and over again. Finally she left the room and I picked up the diary and read further. "At last, he has agreed I can have her..." "I can set her free" There was a gap of a few days and then the last entry of all read "what time has concealed, time has revealed..." My grandmother came back into the room and I tried to reassure her that what she imagined could not possibly be true. There had to be another explanation but the basilisk veil had been drawn again. She had shown herself to be vulnerable and refused to discuss it further. We fell to talking about other things.

The next day I arrived at the gallery early and went into the back office where the portrait was propped against the wall. I picked it up and examined it very closely and once again the strange contrast in it took possession of me. This time the woman's eyes seemed to engage directly with mine. And her mouth seemed to be saying something more boldly than last time. I ran my fingers very gently over the swirls of oil and varnish around her mouth willing her to speak.

I spent most of the day proofing the catalogue and it was nearly seven by the time I had finished. I poured myself a sherry and started making a list of what I had to do the following morning. At one point I looked up and saw a smudge on the floor in front of the portrait.. When I went over to the painting I could see a large flake of yellow paint had fallen from the centre of one of the flames on the canvas. The painting had obviously been slightly damaged in transit. But as I looked more closely I could see that where the fragment had been there was a a dash of opalescent white. Perhaps the artist had re-touched the work or was there something else... underneath the flames? On an impulse I phoned Jacinthe and asked if she could do a very quick job for me, an x-ray photo. She reluctantly agreed and I arranged delivery of the portrait to her studio in Holland Park. A few days later the photo arrived back. Now I could see beneath the flames the woman was carrying two blurred pentimenti. I phoned Jacinthe again and asked her to restore the painting to its original state.

Several months later I took delivery of the painting. True, the woman was still modestly dressed, her turban was in place covering most of her head but it allowed some of her long black hair to escape onto one velvet shoulder. But what she carried had indeed changed. Now there two delicately carved silver candlesticks with candles bearing elongated pearls of light that lent a slight glow to the charming hesitancy of the expression on her face. The candles appeared to have been burning for some time and she was using them to make her way though the shadows that surrounded her. Her stride was calm and confident and the mood of the painting had changed to one of meditation and engagement. I gazed at her and thought of how my grandfather with his intuitive understanding and without the benefit of science had let the woman possess him and then sought to possess her.

The following Sunday I went to my grandmother's as usual. I took the painting with me but kept it under wraps. When we had finished coffee, I asked her to step back into the lounge and I uncovered the portrait. I wanted to show my grandmother she had no rival — well not flesh and blood — this that grandfather had loved was a work of art. I told her everything that had happened but added that I had no idea who the subject was or why the artist had painted over the candlesticks. My grandmother stood for some time both her hands over her mouth gazing at the portrait... at last she spoke.

Apparently for many years in the old community in Prague people had talked about a mysterious woman artist called Lily. Her life was circumscribed by convention, duty and restraint. She moved with grace and ease amongst her family and obeyed every rule except one. At night when they lay sleeping she made her way from her bed-chamber to the top of the house, to another room no one ever went into. She would take a canvas from behind a dresser and prop it up on a wooden stool and paint the stories from the Old Testament — Ruth and Boaz, Jacob and his dreams, Cain and Abel fighting, Lot and his lascivious daughters. But everything she painted she destroyed Everything she painted was forbidden. None of her work was believed to have survived. Except this one... maybe this time she went back and took the Sabbath candles from the table and made her way up the stone staircase to that room... she took a mirror and started to paint herself... like this... then ...a sudden gust of wind, the candles guttered.

She was in the dark.. She saw her folly in moving the Sabbath candles willing them to burn long enough to create her own image in their light. Perhaps they flickered again and she could see herself on the canvas and she was moved to destroy once again what she had created. But she hesitated in thrall just this once to herself. So she put something in the painting they could not blame her for, these exultant torches. When she had finished she took the painting and turned its face to the wall behind the dresser...

We sat for some time in the lounge looking at Lily and spinning wilder tales together. At last I could see she was getting tired and I got up to go. As I reached the front door, she tapped me lightly on the shoulder. I turned. She kissed me and then gave me the portrait.

137

Maza Zoftig

Rozanne Rabinowitz

Working full-time and unpaid for a radical women's newspaper is not all toil and self-sacrifice. There's a few perks that come with the job. To start with, there's press tickets to events and gigs. Then you can get review copies of all the lesbian trash you wouldn't think of buying but can't resist reading.

And of course, the most important fringe benefit was meeting Tanja.

It was 1992. I was writing an article about anti-war activism in former Yugoslavia. I'd already interviewed one woman from Belgrade, a professor who gave me a lot of useful information but banged on a lot about 'civil society', a term beloved by East European academics. I didn't like the idea myself because I've often been regarded as an uncivil person and don't see the point of having a society that is civil. It sounded like everyone would sit around drinking tea in china cups, pinkies out, saying 'how do you do'.

At the end of the interview, the woman said "I am really a writer, not an acitivist. I'll give you a phone number for someone who was involved with many actions."

I arranged to meet Tanja, the activist, on the next Saturday afternoon. But the night before I went out with some friends, got very pissed, and only managed to pull myself out of bed at 1:00 in the afternoon. As I was swilling my coffee I remembered that I was meant to be interviewing Tanja.

I was tempted not to bother. Is this interview really necessary? I've already got a lot of information. Do I need yet more tapes to transcribe, more notes to make sense of? The issue's due out in only a few weeks. perhaps I should start writing the article already. Or perhaps I should go back to bed. Well, first I'll ring this woman to say I'll be late. If she's like the first one, she'll tell me she's got another appointment that day and we'll just cancel or postpone it.

A groggy voice answered. "Late? That's OK. I just woke up myself."

That was a good sign. Another one was the very strong coffee she made. "I really like the paper," she said. "When I saw it in a shop I was amazed that something as good as that even exists. It's just what I'm looking for! I thought I'd like to get involved in it myself. Then when Raja rang me and said you wanted to interview me I was very excited!"

Well, it was worth coming all the way to Kilburn to be flattered like this! I got embarrassed though when Tanja recognised me from the cover photo montage, which showed several women wrecking the Houses of Parliament. I was the one with the drill. I thought I disguised myself effectively with sunglasses and scarf. "Oh, I can tell from the hair. I think you looked very good in the photo." Tanja said. And I noticed that Tanja had very nice hair herself, long and curly and reddish-brown.

I turned on the cassette and we got down to business. Tanja told me about anti-conscription actions: "We hid people, then the mothers of soldiers requested that army leaders release their sons. They broke into Parliament and made a big mess inside. They were shouting, screaming, ripping up papers and fighting. I understood that only if you make a mess, you can do something!"

So much for civil society.

Then she talked about the occupation of Belgrade University. "We wanted the president to resign and the wars against Croatia and Bosnia to end. We had discussions and also made parties. Some said this showed people we weren't serious, but we said that's not true — we were having a serious farewell party to Milosevic!"

"Here's some pictures from the demos." said Tanja. One showed five women with a banner 'throw the war out of history'. Tanja quickly enlightened me on some other history — who'd slept with who in the picture. She'd been with two of them.

The interview proceeded, then turned into an exchange of jokes and international gossip. I began to notice other things about Tanja — that she was very tall and beautifully *zoftig*. But it was later that we came up with the names for what I was noticing.

*

Several weeks later Tanja was teaching me some Serbo-Croat in bed. "What are these?" I asked and touched her breasts.

"Sise."

"And this."

"Gouza."

The word sounded just like what it was: a very fine bottom. It sounded rounded, luxurious, luscious. What needs to be caressed and appreciated. Something you could fill your hands with.

"In Yiddish it is called a *tuches*."

She asked me to repeat the word, making the "ch" sound deep in my throat. "And its also called 'tush' or 'tushy' — I suppose that's the New York version."

"Tush!" Tanja patted and lightly pinched mine. I pondered the differ-

140

ence. *Tuches* and *tush* were more playful words. So when is it a *tush* and when is it a *gouza*? Guess it depends what mood you're in.

"And these..." I smoothed my hand over and up and down her long thighs. "These are *pulkas*. And what is this?" I asked as I drew my finger from her inner thighs — surely among the softest parts of a women's body — to the warm dark hair between them.

"That is *pitchka*."

"What a nice name for it!" *Pitchka*.

"Yes, I like it too." said Tanja. "It has often been used as a degrading word, and some of the Belgrade feminists didn't like me to use it. But just in itself, I like the sound of it. It sounds affectionate. It depends how you use it."

Unfortunately, I did not know the Yiddish for cunt. And I doubted if my mum would know either. "Tell me some more words."

She reached to touch my *pulkas*. "See this, this is what we call *mekana*."

"What, the word for *pulkas*?"

"No-o-o. Your *pulkas* are *mekana*, but it isn't just them. Mekanosity is all over. Here is mekanosity" — she touched the curve between my arm and breast, the inside of my arm where my cheek was pressed. "There is *gouza* mekanosity... and *sise* mekanosity ... And here is mekanosity." She touched my cheek. "*Mekana* means very smooth, very soft, warm and full."

Tanja has broad, high fleshy cheeks that positively expand when something pleasurable is happening to her. They make me think of peaches. Sometimes I suck them. "This is a very special place for Jewish aunties." I pinched one firmly between my thumb and forefinger, as mine used to do. "And when they do this, they say '*bubbelah, bubbelah*, what a *bubbelah*!'"

"And what does *bubbelah* mean? It sounds like something very special."

"It is, and I can't translate it really. Perhaps it means little sweetie, little precious one, something like that, but much more. It can be someone you want to cuddle and caress."

"Oh yes, we have a word like that, it is *chitsa*. Or really, it is my word. It isn't proper Serbo-Croat."

*

In the morning we continued this discussion. "You are so soft, so *mekana*! How come you're so *mekana*? How?" Tanja demanded when I woke up. "All night I couldn't stop cuddling you because you're so *mekana*. I need to know why!"

"We-e-ell, I'll tell you how. From sleeping late. From drinking coffee and eating nice food. From sleeping with you."

We decided over a breakfast of fresh crusty French bread, creamy wedges of avocado, thick garlicky hummous, red onions and mushrooms that certain things are good for mekanosity. The food we were eating and the strong sweet coffee we were drinking: wine and dark tasty beer... and of course, playing our favourite music very loud. *"makes straight girls wish they were dykes...."* sang L7 as we sampled our breakfast and all the different kinds of mekanosity we found in each other. *Sise* mekanosity, *gouza* mekanosity, *pulka* mekanosity... and *pitchka* mekanosity.

"When you were drinking wine last night I noticed how your *bubbelah* parts got very rosy." She gave me that smile that expanded her own *bubbelah* parts to their full splendor. "I think that most of the things that are good for mekanosity make rosy *bubbelah* parts."

"Y'know, I just realised that there's a word in Yiddish for *mekana*. It is *zoftig*. It means soft, smooth, round, luscious, fleshy, abundant."

"And that is you! You are ultra-*zoftig*!" She smoothed the hair off my face, and I snuggled in as close as I could under her arm. "Look at you," she exclaimed, "you are such a *maza*."

"And what is that, *bubbelah*?"

"A *maza* is someone who likes to be cuddled all the time. And more — not simply a preference to be cuddled, but she must be cuddled. Her skin grows warmer and smoother when it is touched. It's essential to her mekanosity to be cuddled. If she's not cuddled, a *maza* gets very sad. Cuddling and stroking is like food to a *maza*."

"But I'm not usually like that," I said. For I'm the sort who hides in the loo when it comes time for kissy-kissy bye byes. I'd keep an ear out until the cessation of squealing lets me know it was safe to emerge and make a hasty exit.

"That surprises me."

"But I hate reallly touchy-feely stuff," I explained. "you know when people are being hippies and insist you've got to hug them all the time. Or you know the way dykes are. I've even thought about writing an article about it called "Compulsory Kissing: The Curse of Lesbian Existence".

"Oh but being a *maza* is nothing to do with all that. That is just false. It's such a cruel world for *mazas,* so very often we must hide it, and it gets lost. And then it comes out at the right time, just like now. Look at you, you're always available for a cuddle!"

And then I thought again. While hiding from the fond farewells I would often stroke my arm, especially if I was stoned. I liked the touch of skin under my fingertips, and the touch upon my skin. I like summer evening breezes on bare arms and legs, up my skirt. I fight with my cats over the best place in front of the gas fire. Yes, under the right circumstances, I'm always available for a cuddle.

We sunk into a fragranced foaming bath feeding each other biscuits, sweet and cakey with a chocolate coating and an inner centre of honey. "In Serbo-Croat these biscuits are called *'medeno srce'* or heart of honey."

'Medeno srce' I tried to pronounce, not getting the rolled 'r' sound quite right. But when I did, I was rewarded with a big honey-flavoured kiss. "Does *medeno* mean 'honey'?"

"Yes! you are learning!"

"So, could we say *'medeno pitchka'*?"

"Oh yes! Now you are learning very well."

"In Yiddish honey is *'mandel'*." If only I knew how to say pitchka in Yiddish. Suddenly it seemed such an important thing to know. I wondered where I could find out. But until then... I slipped my hand along a slippery and smooth *pulka*. "Medeno pitchka, mandel pitchka... I'm sure there is one here."

"And here is Maza Zoftig. That is you!"

Going Back

Frederic Raphael

Christine said, "Are you really sure we want to do this?"

"We're not telling them anything about us," Russell said.

"So what's the point of this pilgrimage again?"

"People die," Russell said. "We'll be sorry if we don't see them before they do, *if* they already haven't. Detour really, not pilgrimage."

"You really want to see *her*. Miriam. You really do? I'm not sure I even remember her."

"She was a great cook," Russell said. "She made great *lutkas*. Don't you remember her *lutkas*. I certainly do. You don't remember her because, at the time, you wished she didn't exist."

"Casimir has to be eighty. I never wished that."

"Eight-five possibly. And she's no younger. You wished it because you wanted the guy for yourself."

"I never *wanted* Casimir. I wanted you."

"Second best *was* best. You told me you did."

"He was — Jesus! — forty-five, fifty years old."

"But he *was* Jesus."

"Never miss one, do you? An opportunity."

"Only if it's important. He was my age. *Jesus*. Younger!"

"They're probably both dead," Christine said.

"Shall I turn around? My letter never came back. You're not *crying*, are you? Let's spill the milk first. They're not dead."

"You have to be funny. When they write your epitaph, know what it'll be? *That*'s what it'll be: He had to be funny."

"I'll hire another writer to say different," Russ said. "This is the Campus turn off. Do we do it or don't we?"

"We're going to do it," Christine said, "and you know we're going to do it. Your letter never came back. Hence... do it."

"Is it all coming back? And do we want it to? Look at that diner: Frankie's. Is that what it was called in sixty-eight, Frankie's? Wasn't it 'Frankie and Johnny's' then...? I guess they broke up. Everyone does, right?"

"I'm not about to remember *anything*," Christine said. "I start remembering things, I'll be a wreck in no time. If not sooner."

"*She* had to be funny too, sometimes," Russell Seymour said. "Try getting a chisel round *that*. They've done some building around here. Oh

Jesus, look at that, Chrissie, will you? 'Hanging Gardens Road'. Who in hell thought to call it that?"

"Some fancy professor from Babylon, Louisiana. Nostalgic for the hometown ziggurat."

"I remember why I fell in love with you now. The slight droop of the right eye after you say something a little bit...smart."

"You remember why you fell *out* of it at all?"

"I didn't. I didn't. Was I the one started talking about divorce? *Conversationally*. Conversationally!"

"You were the one started *thinking* about it. Why lie? You used to call me Chrissie all the time."

"Why lie? Why live?"

"Terrific," she said. "Great heart-warming answer."

"I still do," he said, "call you Chrissie. Sometimes."

They drove for a while and then he said, "Think Caz'll have the smallest idea who we are?"

She said, "You wrote you said."

"So I wrote. Christine and Russell Seymour. Near as dammit thirty years. We must be crazy. How good a teacher was he really?"

"He was great," she said. "He was the only professor ever meant a thing to me. I can't even remember anyone else's *names*."

"Henderson. Dr Henderson? The one Amy Bradshaw took her shirt off at?"

"You had a heck of a good look."

"And I'd've had a heck of a good feel given half a chance. Aren't I terrible though? So what can you remember about French and German literature? Name me one book we did with Caz."

"You bastard," she said.

"I don't remember that one."

"*The Magic Mountain*. We studied *The Magic Mountain*. We studied *Madame Bovary*. That's two titles. Can I get off the treadmill now?"

"Transgression and Bourgeois Society. I have the notes someplace. He favoured the one and not the second, do I recall correctly?"

"Don't ask me questions you know the answers to. Montherlant. 'The Boys'. '*Les Garcons*.' One of them was called Souplier."

"Christine, why are we doing this?"

"What constitutes 'this' exactly?"

"Almost thirty years," Russell said, "and we're fucking strangers."

"You fuck your stranger and I'll fuck mine," Christine said.

"Easy pickings," Russell said. "Easy fucking pickings. Do we swing right here?"

"You swang right years ago," she said. "We voted for *Reagan*? Hard right. So go ahead. Do it again."

"We're here to get his permission is why we're here and you know it. Caz's. We're not going to mention it, but he's going to *know* and if he says it's OK, then it's OK, is about the size of it. So who was he, your stranger?"

"I used the future tense," she said. "As in 'I'll fuck mine'."

"He says we should stick together, will that convince you?"

"We're going to be nice to an old man."

"And an old woman," Russell said, "don't forget Miriam. Why not let's snow them? Why not let's be happy together? It's a little bit sneaky, isn't it, to turn up and make him into the guy who sits in judgment on a marriage?"

"*Madame Bovary, c'est moi,*" Christine said. "There's many a true word, isn't there?"

"But today you have to hunt," Russell said.

"Know what keeps us together? We're both in one of your damn comedy scripts. You don't write them, they write you."

"Got it," Russell said. "Right between the eyes. I remember when you actually *laughed* when I crossed them like that."

"Total recall," she said. "What a drag it can sometimes be!"

Casimir always offered a glass of wine to his class. That was why Russell had brought up two bottles of Château Cissac from the cellar he had had built (he had brought up one and then he had thought about it and then he had gone back for the second). He looked at the label as they stopped outside 131, Taft Street, and saw "*Cru Bourgeois*" and smiled at Christine. She did not smile back.

Casimir came onto the porch as if it were a coincidence. He seemed to be looking for something. He was: it was a book, of course, which he leaned down to pick up, one hand on the swing-seat and a foot swinging up in the air.

Christine said, "Hi, Casimir."

He was old, but he was not decrepit. He was wearing grey pants and a collarless striped shirt and a brown knitted vest, which hung open. There were things in the pockets. He looked at her and took enough time recognising them to seem to have recognised them right away and to be playing at not. "Can it be?" he said. "I've changed so little and you've changed so much."

That was when she embraced him and held him and he looked over her shoulder at Russell.

Russell said, "Maybe I should leave you two to it."

"It's taken him this long," Casimir said. "And even then he says 'maybe'. Come in. Nice of you to warn me ahead of time."

147

"We thought you'd maybe run away."

It was still Casimir's house: the books, the records — there were the old L.P.s in their chapped sleeves, under the compacts, in the canted shelf under the floppy, even yellower French books. The German were above that. The green and red-wrapped Loebs had the library steps still up to them (oh how Casimir would stop everything to go and find a quote no one in the class could understand!). The books explained why he needed such a big place.

"I told her she should marry you," Casimir said, "and yet she comes to see me. *Et dona ferens.*"

"The *dona* are his," she said. "How's...ah...Miriam? Is she...?"

"She's...out," Casimir said.

"I hope she left something for supper," Russell said. "We didn't come here just to see *you*, you know."

Casimir seemed not so much to *be* older as to *act* older. He mocked his age by exaggerating his submission to it. As he fussed to re-arrange the chairs by the fireplace, he was playing the aged professor, but with a measure of exaggeration. His wary nimbleness promised that he lied about his years, or his years about him. "I never *wanted* you to marry him, Christina. I only *said* that."

"So she'd admit she was in love with you, Casimir, right?"

"What was the good?" Christine said. "When I knew he'd never dump Miriam for *anybody*!"

There was a small foreign car in the street and then it was up behind the Chevvy in the carport and a young woman was getting out with tall brown bags of groceries and coming past the windows, not looking in, and up the porch steps.

Christine had time to say, "What's this? Professor Emeritus Michaelstadt now has a *housekeeper*. Or is it a housekeeper-*masseuse*? Or *what*?"

The old man looked at her with eyes that were younger, and colder. Christine watched the young woman bend her knees to lower her packages on the hall-stand. She was fair and in her thirties and her eyes were the same colour as Christine's, that pale blue. Her smooth skin aged Christine.

Casimir said, "I don't believe you've met my wife. Terri this is...Christine and..."

Christine was damned if she would help him.

"...Russell." He remembered without her. "Seymour. I told you about Christine, I'm sure. The favourite student I waited and waited for. Until another one came along. Terri with an 'i'."

Terri said, "I hope you're going to stay? We're expecting you to stay."

"Isn't there still a Holiday Inn? Sure there is. Dinner is imposition enough."

"Everyone stays," Terri said. "He likes them to."

"You feel so great when they finally, finally go, am I right, Caz?"

"Have I corrected you?"

Christine said, "I'm sure there's something I can do to help."

When the women had gone out together, as if they were friends now, Casimir said, "Are you ashamed of me, Russell?"

"I don't know what you're talking about. What did you do?"

"*Actes gratuits*," Casimir said. "Do you remember what those were?"

"They were *gratuites*, according to me," Russ said, "until you corrected me in front of the whole class."

"You're embarrassed," Casimir said, "because of Terri. I'm sorry about that."

Russell smiled. After all these years in America, Casimir still *almost* said "zat". "Embarrassed. You flatter me, Caz. I'm through embarrassment. Great looking woman. Congratulations."

"Because of Miriam. I saved her life, you probably remember that. I didn't talk about it, I hope, but people did."

Russell noticed that Casimir also still said "people" *almost* as if it were "pipple"; affection and condescension were close with Russell. He was a tall man. "I remember that character — it wasn't Olga was it? — stuck a knife through her hand in some novel or other. To prove she was really free. Or was it someone else who was? Maybe it was Boris."

"Fifty some years ago, I saved Miriam from...whatever maybe wouldn't've happened to her. 1944. The beautiful Jewess and the smitten interpreter. You should write that sometimes."

"I only do comedy."

"So laugh at us. What I was smitten with above all was my own vanity, isn't it? Does that mean I owe her forever? To make a woman who wouldn't otherwise maybe have looked at me feel ...gratitude, *unworthiness*. Comedy of a kind, Russell."

"But not for the Network," Russell said.

"You make a lot of money?"

"I make some money," Russell said. "Enough to send the kids through college and leave enough for gas to come see you. Miriam: what...happened?"

"When I told her the two big things I liked about Terri. She said just one word. Guess which."

Christine was coming into the living room, with a swirl of *guacamole* and a glass dish of *nachos*. "That border sure does move steadily north these days. Hispanic Ohio? It'll probably happen."

"He wants to know what Miriam said to me when I told her how Terri

149

and I... One word. Guess which. He can't."

Christine said, *"Enfin."*

"Your wife is a genius, Russell."

"That has to be why she's probably leaving me."

"At last she was free. You *are* shocked, Christina, aren't you? Respect an old man's hopes. Please don't take this in your stride. Other people's acts can free people too."

"Know something, Caz? You're the only person ever called me Christina."

"I hope so."

"Where is she now then? Miriam."

"I didn't kill her, if that's what you're hoping. What do you think of...?"

"Terri? I hate her, of course," Christine said. "With a big 'I'."

"Anything to make her old professor happy," Casimir said. "You're meant to. Bosnia, can you tell? She came from originally. A Muslim already. She doesn't know what that does for me."

"If she doesn't, nobody should," Russell said. "I'll go see if there's anything I can do. I can still lay a table at least."

"It's done," Christine said.

"Christine, OK. Can't you recognise tact? You and Caz have so many things to say to each other."

"And so few we can do," Casimir said. "So how are you, Christina. Grandmother yet?"

"Not that they've told me." She looked at him with eyes that announced a new subject. "I'm going to go back and teach," she said, *"and* study. I'm going to be an analyst. At least I *think* I am."

"I think therefore I'm not?"

"Bad idea?"

"Never too late to do something useless with your life. Teach what?"

"French was my major. They need somebody in our local High School. You used to say I had a *très bon accent.*"

"You also had those black silk legs. Did a lot for your pronunciation. Did that pattern go all the way up? The faculty frequently speculated."

Christine said, "Should we maybe go in and...?"

"You disapprove," he said, "don't you? Of me and Terri. Me too. Me too."

"You were always so proud of your marriage."

"I exchanged pride for...what? All right: greed. Know the difference? Greed has the tits."

"That's terrible. I seriously hate that. What happened to Miriam finally?"

Casimir looked at her and then at a floral pitcher on the end of the man-

150

telpiece. He took it in both hands and looked at it fondly and then opened his hands and let it crash onto the floor. There was time for Terri to put her head round the door before Christine started picking up pieces.

"It's all right, Terri," Casimir said. "I'm only teaching."

Christine was angry and confused: she wanted to cry and she wanted not to cry. "I *remembered* that pitcher. I remembered it."

"Did you love it?" Casimir said. "Did you give a damn about it? Did *I*? Was it valuable? What's valuable? I had it for years. It's broken. Do you miss it or do you want me to miss it?"

When Terri came back into the kitchen, Russell was taking the corn out of the skillet, "How long've you been...with him?"

"I'm married to him," she said. "Three years."

"Oh, this is quite recent then."

"For you; not for me."

"What does it mean to you, may I ask, marrying him?"

"Casals married a girl of twenty when he was eighty. Pablo Casals. The great cellist."

"I guessed who you meant from just Casals," Russ said.

"It means I get his house and his money. We're *eating*. You don't like me for saying that. I don't necessarily like you for thinking it."

"They had a son," Russell said. "What about him?"

"He went to Israel." Casimir was cleaning the *guacamole* dish with his finger as he came into the kitchen ahead of Christine. He sucked it as he indicated to sit in the chairs at the round table in the window. "Please! He manufactures plastic packaging materials for the grapefruit and pineapple trade. He makes a fortune and never has to read a book. It's what I always dreamed for him to do."

"Casimir," Christine said. "You know what you are?"

"I know what I am," he said. "Sit down. Be comfortable. I'm a shit. It was always my secret ambition and now I've realised it. Isn't it most men's? Russell, isn't it?"

"It undoubtedly gets a high share," Russell said.

"*Enfin*," Casimir said.

Christine looked at Russell a lot as they ate dinner and watched the shadows grow longer and then fainter and lights prick the new darkness. They talked as they ate and yet there was this silence, and these looks, between Christine and Russell. They seemed both to talk *and* to be silent. It was as if they were overhearing their own voices and resented each other's cheerfulness.

They ate the corn and then there was stuffed cabbage with butter beans and a salad and then there was an apple *strudel*, whose excellence came as a surprise. Casimir watched their slightly reluctant pleasure as if it were a small, sweet victory over them, which it was. The front door bell wheezed as they were finishing their second helpings. It was an academic couple who joined them for coffee and some of that *strudel*; the wife had been in school with Christine, Rose Anne Hyman, now Pollock; she was a social anthropologist and was recently back from Chiapas, researching the Zapatistas. It was one of those things that agrarian revolts *never* succeeded, she said. It was pretty well *a priori*: politics belonged to the city and the city always won out. Even when the rural population supplied successful foot soldiers, their leaders would finally sell them out. If they lost, they lost right away; if they won, they lost eventually.

The register of Rose Anne's eloquence suggested that everyone in the room was disagreeing with her, and that she was prevailing against odds, even though hardly anyone else spoke. There might have been other people, invisible to Russ and Christine, whose doubts were being allayed, or refuted. Rose Anne's husband was a mathematician who did a lot of marathons and also triathlons.

It was an evening full of talk, much of it informative and lively, that might — *mas o menos* — have been frozen in the Sixties and kept for just such an occasion. It was adult and progressive and very *bright*, but it seemed to be a substitute for some other conversation which someone — was it Casimir, or the Seymours themselves? — either wanted or decidedly did *not* want to have.

Rose Anne and her husband asked if the Seymours were staying over, because they would love to see them again and have them enjoy some of the material from Chiapas (she had slides, she had documentation, she had fascinating tapes), but Christine said that they had promised to get to Chicago the next night, so...

The guest room was a room they had been in before, when it had not been so pretty. The quilt was the same though, wasn't it? From the Ozarks, where Cas had taught before he came to Ohio.

"Funny meal," Christine said.

"Funny evening. Funny day."

"That ghastly stuffing — pork! — and then that great *strudel*."

"*Uneven* meal," Russ said. "Your friend Rose Anne has turned out pretty formidable."

"I don't know about the pretty part. *Or* the friend."

"We're back in this room," Russ said. "I hadn't figured on that."

"He was pretty nice to us, wasn't he?"

"But you don't like him as much as you remembered, do you?"

"He's much the same. And maybe we're much different."

"Casimir with a child bride. Not quite what the script called for."

"You're a little bit pleased. As if he'd done something to me and not to you."

"And hasn't he? He hasn't done anything to me."

"Except maybe liberated you a little bit. Your imagination at least."

"I'm a little disgusted, just like you."

"Is that what I am?"

They got into the bed, which seemed narrower than when Casimir first loaned them its use. Back in the 60s, he used to go away for weekends sometimes, with Miriam; favoured students were invited to house-sit for him.

"Imagine," she said, "I left my virginity in this very room."

"I don't remember getting this far."

"You maybe didn't; it did."

"We shouldn't have done this, should we? Come here."

"In the first place or...?"

"You know what I'm saying."

"The things you shouldn't do, aren't those sometimes the ones you should?"

"I bet you he's fucking her tonight. I bet you he's making a point of it. Because we're here."

"I hope he is," she said.

"Against us," Russ said.

"Goodnight, Russell."

He woke in the night and she was breathing steadily, against *him*, he thought. He lay there listening to the calm rhythm of his sleeping wife and he was touched and infuriated by the untroubled independence of her life from his. Was he so thirsty that he had to get up, or did he get up because thirst gave him an excuse she could not deny? He went out onto the landing and along the gallery above the hall to where the stairs went down. The house was one of the oldest on the campus and, in the blueish moonlight, it seemed as dated as the kind of black and white pictures in which people lived unthreatened lives in an unthreatening America where the Hayes code applied as much to people in real life as it did to what they did in the movies. Was that why he had voted for Ronald Reagan? Because he wanted life back in black and white?

He went downstairs as if there was something in the house that he wanted to grab back, his serious youthful self maybe, slung like an old coat on the back of a chair, a coat that could still slip easily back over his shoulders and still had all kinds of things in the pockets that seemed to have been lost forever. He went into the kitchen and there was the table in the window where the grown-ups had talked about Mexico and politics and it was as if they were still there, himself included, and they had no idea that their talk was talk talk and they did not really care whether the

Zapatistas got licked or got lucky. No, they wanted them licked; they were good people who wanted the good causes to go down, because that way no one could be blamed for not doing enough to support them.

Russ went to the big Mountain Stream water-dispenser and drew a paper cup of water and stood, barefoot, looking at the bruise-dark shadows of the maple trees and the frosty whiteness of the moonlit sky and sipped the water he did not want all that much. Was there anything he did want very much? It made him sick to think of Christine leaving him, or being about to leave him. But then he thought of Terri, those bouncy tits, that stupid pouty mouth, those eyes that said "yes" because — maybe — they had seen things, back in Bosnia, that made yes or no in Ohio not too important. The terrible thing was, you envied people the terrible things that had happened to them more than you were grateful to have been spared them. You tried to be glad to be who you were, but were you?

He took another cup of water, in case Christine was awake and wanted one when he went back upstairs. But he didn't go back upstairs: he went into the living room, imagining that there was something there that he wanted to take: OK, to steal actually. He had no idea what and he had no intention of really taking it. He wanted to have had the chance, only he didn't know what of.

There was a ladder-backed chair at the desk under the front window and someone in a high-collared robe was sitting in it, with her back to Russ as he came into the room. The collar was up around her ears, as if she were pretending that the June night was colder than it was.

"Terri?"

The woman did not turn. She leaned her head against the top rung of the laddered chair and braced her neck and the way she did it denied, with a sort of humour, that she was Terri in any way whatsoever. "Hullo, Russell," Miriam said.

Russell said, "OK. Now I get it."

"What do you get, Russell?"

"The *strudel*. Now I get why it was so good. What the hell is going on around here?"

"He's a funny man," she said. "Not a bad one. But..."

"Funny," Russell said. "Not the word I might have chosen."

"He was good to me. Why shouldn't he do what he wanted to do?"

"Do you want a glass of water?"

"No. I don't want a thing. Not a thing."

"Do you...do you still *live here*?"

"Are you shocked?"

"Shocked? No."

"Disgusted. *Disturbed*?"

"How come you didn't...have dinner with us?"

"I'm here; I'm not here. I don't need to explain; you know why not. I'm old. I'm tired. I'm bored with Mexico and stuff. When he and...she, when they first...got together, I went away. I went to Israel as a matter of fact. Which I had waited all my life to do, I thought. Let me tell you something, Russell: what people waited all their lives to do, they should maybe never rush into. I went and I thought it was exactly what I wanted. It wasn't; so I came back. I'm a citizen. He found it...surprising."

"I bet he did."

"She didn't. She was nice to me. She is nice, Terri, which is not at all her name of course. She said I should stay; I stayed. It's a big house. I wouldn't be in the way. I'm not in the way. I never see them. I'm not lonely because all the time, I have this little purpose in life, never to see them, never to talk to them, never to cross them."

"So when did you make the *strudel*?"

"In the night. I do a lot at night. I listen to the radio and then, in the day, I sleep very often. I take walks. I'm not a ghost. I have my life all to myself."

"You literally never see him?"

"Why would I see him?"

"Doesn't he check to see how you are?"

"You think he should. Why should he? I think it's very kind of Casimir finally, to let me bury myself in his house, don't you?"

He went back upstairs with the glass of water, but Christine was still asleep. In the morning, Casimir made scrambled eggs and bacon and fresh coffee. Terri said to leave the sheets on the bed; she would take care of it, no problem whatever. She had all day.

Russell enjoyed not telling Christine about his meeting with Miriam. He enjoyed it all the way to Chicago. He thought that he just might enjoy it for the rest of their time together, however long that turned out to be.

Great Men

Nessa Rapoport

I was the one who persuaded my friends to go hear him speak on a Saturday night last November. I had been reading about him in the *Times*, but this was long before he had become the name you heard every day. No one really argued with me, though. My friends are good people and good friends to me. If there was a slight sense of indulgence in their agreement, I let it pass. The point was that I had someone to go with. Even in my fascination I'm not sure I would have gone myself.

He didn't look as I'd expected. More square, more block-like, with a thick accent, he read from a prepared speech that was haunting in its way but not so extraordinarily different from other moving testimonies that I could tell you now exactly what he said. What I do remember was this: At one point near the end he looked up from his papers and said, "Every day as you go about your daily affairs, remember that in illegal prisons all over the world Jews are being tortured for the crime of being Jews."

The audience, mostly Jewish I would guess, had enthusiastically applauded. Who could not applaud this man? He had been tortured for his convictions and lived to tell the tale. I applauded, too, as long as I could without embarrassment, but there was a quality of despair to my enthusiasm. Not only did I see in his quieting shrug a sentence that read, "I've spoken of this fact so many times; how many more well-fed audiences will I have to entertain on a Saturday night while people in my country are disappearing," but I was already in despair for myself. How many times had I been roused by fervent speakers like him, impassioned witnesses, how many times had I left the hall to swear that I would do something, anything, to combat the evil I'd heard about that night, only to find that after living with the raw stripped-away feeling for a day or two, for the length of one conversation with a friend, after finding my midtown work frivolous, my friends' talk trivial, I had lapsed into my daily life without a backward glance. Not that I considered myself a bad person. It was just that it was possible to live a decent life without doing anything about the catastrophes that were being inflicted on various people everywhere.

Of course, some would not call that a decent life. I would not. And it was because I do not that I walked out of the building on that November evening already burdened with a sense of future shame. I wanted to remember every day that people were being tortured in illegal prisons, not because my remembering would in itself do them any good, but because if

157

once again I did not remember, of what use was it to care about these things, to have gone to hear him in the first place?

I had gone to hear him because I had followed his case in the paper with unusual avidity. "After the age of twenty-five, you start to think of history," my friend Daniel had told me. I was twenty-three at the time and never read the news. He was ten years older, and although I didn't know what he was talking about, I remembered his saying it because I respected him. I can't say it happened the day of my twenty-fifth birthday, but somewhere in that year the news began to matter. I no longer thought it was a virtue not to know what was going on, and to the astonishment of those who'd known me in my once oblivious life, I'd subscribed to the *Times* and read it with care every day.

At first I would not have been able to say why his story held me, why the headlines with his name or the name of his country began to leap off the page. All I knew was that this was a man who, as far as I could tell, had been uncompromising in speaking the truth as he saw it, in the face of threats to his livelihood, his family, and finally his life. He was a journalist, I was now a budding journalist, he was a Zionist, and my friend Daniel had just surprised me by actually doing what he'd said for years he'd do and going to live in Israel. I read about the house arrest, I read about the grim war of nerves played against him and his wife by the secret police, I read how he said that if he were ever freed he would move to Israel, and finally I saw that in one hasty day he was deported to that country, where, I read in the same article, he did indeed intend to stay. For some reasons this moved me very much, although I had never been to Israel and was not particularly interested in going at the time. It's one thing to say you'll go to Israel when you're living in inhuman circumstances with only idealism to sustain you; it's another to do it when the whole free world lies before you.

That was when I read that he was coming from Tel Aviv to lecture in New York. I'd insisted that we go, without even knowing what he'd say or if he'd be interesting. I knew that it was important to hear how he talked, to see what he looked like, because there were so few heroes in the world that the word itself felt strange on my tongue. I had probably not said it aloud since I was a child. It was feeling my own awkwardness in using the word to my friends that got me thinking about greatness, and why I could think of no living figure to whom the idea applied.

I work in a lowly capacity for a newspaper, where the names of the current great appear all the time. I began working there some time after I began reading the news, mostly because I was spending so much of my day on it that I figured I might as well try to get paid for it. I'm not paid much, but it is considered by the higher-ups that I have a future. Of that I have no doubt — everyone alive has a future of some sort — although whether it's in the newspaper business I'm not sure. The problem with the news is that it's only part of the news. The more you know, the more you find out that what you know is only an aspect of the whole story, which nobody knows. You try to piece it together as best you can, but it is always an imperfect and partial tale that results. I was frequently despondent after reading the next day's advance editorial pages, where often two columnists of opposing points of view would articulate their positions, to my confusion. The one thing you had to be able to do if you worked on this paper was to take a stand, and it was in that area rather than in my talent for writing that my doubts about my ability lay.

At any rate, I had no doubts about the story I was now following. I knew that what I'd heard was true, not only that what he said had happened to him actually had, but that he was right to call attention to it as he did and right in naming it evil.

The rarity of such sureness on my part only reinforced my commitment. I watched with increasing horror as his character was maligned and his arguments skewed. Why I should have expected that he be immune from the criticism that afflicts other men I do not know. "America loves to destroy its heroes," my friend Daniel wrote to me. I couldn't use the word "hero" at work without getting laughed at and I didn't try. But I began to think about what it takes to accomplish something and whether I had it. It wasn't as if there was something in particular I wanted to do. It was the scope that attracted me, the big span, the real thing.

*

"So what do you want?" the man I am seeing asked me when I tried to talk about all this. I'd brought it up because he had just said to me, "Go to Saks and buy yourself something delicious." He meant: Go the lingerie department and get something made of silk. Silk lingerie is the present that men are buying these days, and despite the fact that I knew it was a taste he'd acquired from pleasing other women, it nevertheless pleased me to be seen in such a way. I don't approve of this disposition on my part, which I consider a weakness from my days of magazine reading, but I have to admit that his saying it affected me, still does. I am ashamed to have even the slightest inclination to what I think of as erotic passivity, the thrill of being the object of desire, but there it is. I've seen it in other women, too, not that its prevalence justifies it.

Be that as it may, I was standing on the escalator in Saks, somewhat embarrassed at this mission, when the thought came to me. That is, as I caught a glimpse of myself in the burnished mirror that accompanied my

159

ascent from the first to the second floor, as I was debating what I would buy that would make me look beautiful to him, I began to compose what I thought he would say when he saw me, but what I heard instead was: In illegal prisons all over the world, Jews are being tortured for the crime of being Jews.

To my own surprise I had not forgotten the speech of that Saturday night in the fall. It had not been possible, if you read the paper, because it became a concern for many more people than young journalists looking for whatever I was looking for. But even before that, I'd remembered it at odd times, and more often than I'd expected. In the subway on the way to work, sometimes at lunch, and even as I was about to fall asleep, every once in a while. At the time I'd said nothing to anyone. But when it happened in Saks I began to get worried. After all, I was very proud that I'd allowed myself to be involved with a man to whom pleasure came so easily, as it certainly is not easy for me.

The man I am seeing is a sculptor. He thinks with his hands. He spends all day working his fingers through various substances, and spends the rest of the time eating, drinking and making love. He doesn't mix work and pleasure, but he does give them equal time, which means, of course, that the time he spends with me is devoted to various ways of gratifying the flesh. He would never put it that way. The only way I can explain what I'm doing with him is to remind myself that before I met him I had been determined to live as a nun. Naturally this was a reaction to the end of a long sad love. I'd found one room at the top of a building, furnished with a bed and a desk, and come home after work to look out the window and listen to myself try to figure out what to do with my life. Although at first I went through all the phases that a person living alone in a big city faces — loneliness, panic, squandering time in trivial anxieties — after a while I got good at solitude, I mastered it, so much that I had to remember not to tell my friends that I spent most evenings looking out the window, or they might worry.

Of course, when I had finally conquered the one thing that had frightened me most, when my stoicism had started turning into an active satisfaction — although I still didn't know what I wanted to be — I was persuaded to go to a party, and that is where I met him.

This was a real New York party, and I had dressed as if it were the first time I had gone to a party in months, which indeed it was. I had uncharacteristically taken a bath with a lot of perfume thrown in, and had worn gold sparkles around my eyes and elaborately arranged my hair. I wore an old beautiful dress, cut velvet in a rich dense pattern that was one of a kind. I looked breathtaking. There are times when you know you do, and this was one. Yet it was all for me. I did it to be exactly the opposite of what I was in my daily life. Still, it drew him to me, my dress, my bearing in that dress. Afterwards I felt a kind of obligation: He had been taken by the fanciful creature I was that night, and I could not fail him. Besides, his way of being interested me. The food he shaped with those hands, the bottles of wine he chose lovingly. And, best or worst, the way he moved his hands over me. I know it is said that physical love depends on emotion. Many people have told me that. All I can say is that I had loved others much more, but the sculptor's hands won me.

Grace makes me weak. His long thin fingers, their deliberateness, seeking out the places that would move me most and remembering them: it was a gift. Even when he was distracted he couldn't help doing it well. I think being clumsy, being blunt, would have been intolerable to him, a betrayal of his artistry. You would think that the idea of his feelings being dissociated from his skill would horrify me. All I can say is that I must have wanted to be the way he saw me very badly. He made me feel immortal.

I wanted nothing to interfere with that, because my work offered me daily examples of the precariousness of men's fortunes, not to mention their lives. I was willing to feel the anguish of history from nine to five, or to seven, more often. And I couldn't help being woken up by the story I've spoken of: That is my nature. But I set aside my times with the man I am seeing as a sanctuary from thinking. It was a struggle to suspend myself into his largely physical existence, but I was firm. It was my only hope of a normal life.

He wasn't normal at all. He was an artist. His work was immediately possessing; you knew he had it. But what I meant by normal was eating, drinking and sleeping, three things I am bad at that most people can do. He did them beautifully, and that's why I couldn't resist him.

And that's why I got worried in Saks. My mind should have been thinking only of lingerie, colours like peach, lilac and mint, edges of lace, lots of ribbon. Naked bodies in a room near the sky, not a groaning nakedness in a cell. Every time I imagined us, the picture of him came instead, an older man screaming or shocked into silence. Bleeding gums. Stripped raw skin. I couldn't stop. Twitching limbs. Please don't let me ruin this, I prayed to myself as I walked onto the floor. Rows and rows of silk underwear were arranged before me. The steel tubes on which they were hung reminded me of gun barrels. I'm losing my mind, I said to myself. Don't be a priest, I said fiercely.

I needn't have feared. My fingers were enchanted by the fabric I began to touch. The silk ran through my hands, and as I held the embroidered rim and imagined him taking off whatever I was wearing over this, heard his delight in the feel of it, the bodies in foreign parts dissolved and there was only me with him. I bought it in a daze, more money than I'd ever spent and no regrets. Walking home I pictured him saying, You are beautiful, and saw myself stretch in silent, confirming pleasure. I couldn't bear even the two or three hours until I saw him.

As always when you're looking forward to something in a more than measured way, you are tested. He phoned to say that a client was demanding, and I heard the necessity in his voice. Although I am grown up, there are times when in disappointment I have to count one more day toward something long awaited, and truly, when I first hear of the delay, I don't know how I'll live. The pain catches in my chest and narrows my breathing. That's what happened when he told me no. I had to sit quietly. Come late, he said suddenly, take a cab very late and slip in beside me. The joy in my assent was frightening, the hold of his body and of his desire over me.

I was in for an edgy evening. There were many hours until it was late, and something had to be done about them. I wanted to kill time, not in the conventional sense of wasting it until the true hour arrived, but murder it, for being itself and not in my favour. Of course, I was pacing around my apartment as I thought these things, wandering around the room turning the lights on and off, furious that I was furious. Never did he spend an evening like this, I was sure. And not because he didn't want me. It was my womanness that was responsible for this particular torment, the passion of waiting. I couldn't pretend I had hobbies. I did not smoke a pipe. I had nothing to do with my hands except eat, and no food in the house. My mind was racing, racing, I could not contain it, stop thinking.

What I did in the end was wash my hair, one of the few activities that eases me without destroying anything. There is something about the motion of water through clean hair that is wonderfully hopeful. It is enough trouble that you wouldn't do it if you were planning to kill yourself, for example. It is work, but also a contribution toward the coming night, a self-contained good.

Now I sat wrapped in his large terry robe, taken from him in early days, and turned on the TV. Immediately the restlessness came over me. I flipped from station to station, not knowing what I was looking for, and saw in rapid succession the captain of a boat, a newscaster, a bear. I imagined Daniel's commentary on these scenes, and the next thing I knew I was telling him everything, writing it down in a letter to him. "Dear Daniel," I said, "I'm sitting in my room waiting to wear silk lingerie while in illegal prisons Jews are being tortured." I told him the rest of it, the seduction of hands, a journalist's career, not knowing how to make up my mind about important things, except for the man who'd spoken out and

162

who now lived in Israel. "It seems to me the package from Saks betrays him," I wrote. "Please advise."

The letter was what finally made it late. I was allowed to start to dress and did very carefully, from scent in my hair to the silk on my skin. I covered myself in the opposing order that he'd uncover me, and heard his voice in my mind saying: "Beautiful, beauty." I would enter in silence, I decided, and let him see me in the mysterious half-light of his room on the street. I would say nothing until he spoke to me.

The slam of the car door could have announced me, but the house was quiet when I came in. I walked across the hall and stood in his doorway, waiting for him. But he was asleep. He would not speak.

"I want to accomplish great things," I cried.

"Come to bed." He turned over lazily and drew me in.

What followed was the only thing to be done. I couldn't give up my body, not when it served me so well, not when what I was engaged in, sending me peacefully to sleep, was all for which men in prisons were hoping their bodies would be redeemed.

*

I hadn't heard from Daniel in a long time and was beginning to worry. There was a crisis escalating in the Middle East, the papers were full of it, and I didn't know if his silence was because the mail was more disrupted than usual or because he was in the reserves, or even because he didn't want to talk to me. I sent him a note, but before he could have received it his answer came.

"I don't know what they're saying about us," he wrote, "but whatever it is, don't believe ninety-two percent of what you read. We are here to stay, and that is why we're here, not to make the rest of the world happy. The man on the news came here with that assurance.

"As for your dilemma, all I can tell you is what I saw one woman say on a documentary I watched last week. I turned off the sound to force myself to read the Hebrew subtitles, so I can't promise an accurate transcription, but the essence was this: She was talking about a man who'd saved her life from the Nazis in Hungary. He was a diplomat, not a Jew, and as far as I could tell he did what he did out of a compassionate heart, for mercy. She said: You have to understand, we were treated like animals. And along came this man, this angel, debonair and immaculate, everything about the way he dressed and looked saying to us: You, too, are worthy, each of you, of life. In the middle of degradation he'd suddenly appear, radiant, princely.

"You have to live in the body you're in and do what you can, with no predictions. There is no guarantee of immortality. All you can do is set yourself on course. Above all, waste no time worrying about greatness. What is it? How others talk about you, how they tell your story. We all deserve the right to tell our story. Yes, that's why I've chosen to live here.

"I am the last person to advise you about love. But if each of us has a story, what we want more than anything is that someone else believe it. Believe our version of ourselves, that is, believe that what we're saying we see is true, what we're impassioned about is not falseness.

"And that's the tragedy of the diplomat. At the end of the war he disappeared. It seems the Russians took him, hid him in prisons, where he may have been ill or gone mad. Denied his chance to tell himself to us, he's being created now in other images. His own voice, his beautiful body: silent. Talking is the most important thing."

Mr Silberman Meets the Pope

Stephen Walker

The night before my grandfather died I had this dream where I witness the ecstasy of my own circumcision.

Well, he's there of course, my grandfather, my zaydie I called him, and a lot of other people, and he's telling the joke about Mr Plotnik and the baby. You know the one? Mr Plotnik, he's the circumcisor, and he comes up to Monty Fleischman and Monty Fleischman is carrying this tiny baby in his arms and Plotnik looks at the baby for a long long time, he appraises the baby and he says, Monty Monty Monty that's one beautiful baby boy you got there and Monty Fleischman says to him first it's not a boy its a girl, second let go of my finger.

In the dream everybody bursts out laughing except Mr Solomon (because he's the circumcisor) and me (because I'm the one he's going to circumcise). Mr Solomon busies himself at his table. He has a battered black bag, from which he takes out a knife, a spatula, two pronged needles, a pair of scissors, a test tube, a thick roll of bandage, and a beaker which he fills with Palwins Number Seven Kosher wine. He takes a quick swig of the wine, turns to the assembled gathering and says, "I think gentlemen we are ready to begin."

I watch my mother bring me into the room, swaddled in white cloth, eight days old. I am handed to my grandfather who sits on the Throne of Elijah. I am very small. The room fills with the sound of Hebrew prayer, the men swaying backwards and forwards. Mr Solomon picks up the knife. My eyes are wide open. Mr Solomon approaches me. I notice that his hands are not entirely steady. Also that his eyes are crossed. He bends over me and I can smell the wine on his breath. The knife glints in the candlelight. Then the room goes suddenly very quiet.

And Mr Solomon is just about to cut off the end of my shmekkel when the most extraordinary thing happens. My grandfather suddenly turns into the Pope.

Then he winks at me.

I remember the exact moment my grandfather started to go senile. I remember, because it was his eighty-seventh birthday and everyone was there, the whole family. We all went to his favourite restaurant and everybody told jokes and it was a very lively affair. There he sat, Sammy Isaac Silberman, my grandfather, at the head of the table, my grandmother beside him, his children and grandchildren and great-grandchildren around him, a *mensch* in the community, a somebody, a patriarch. He wore a pink paper hat. Someone brought in this huge cake and we all sang Happy Birthday and For He's A Jolly Good Fellow and cried *Mazeltov* (except my Aunt Gilda who got embarrassed and kept looking at the other people in the restaurant) and then we all asked my grandfather to make a speech and he slowly rose to his feet and everybody in the room quietened down — and that's when I noticed it. I suppose we all did. My grandfather just stood there, swaying slightly, saying nothing. Someone cried speech speech but he didn't appear to notice. He just stood there and his eyes, I remember, his eyes looked blank and uncomprehending, staring into the distance. He was still wearing his paper hat. I think he must have stood like that for five minutes, at least it felt that way. And then, I remember, my grandmother gently took his arm and drew him down to his chair. He didn't resist. He just sat down again, still with that blank look in his eyes, like there was nothing behind them, like he was lost in his own little world. And everybody was silent and my grandmother, her arm still touching his, asked him what was wrong and still he said nothing and I remember thinking at that moment how old he looked, how very very old. Not like a patriarch at all. Not now.

That was six months before I left for Germany. I had a whole summer just before starting school. I decided I wanted to learn German, or at least my parents did. You'll find it extremely useful, said my mother, when you come to choose your career. It's the closest thing to Yiddish, said my father. I went, not really expecting my grandfather to die so soon. In six months he had deteriorated very rapidly, but to me he was indestructible. Some days he still managed to remember my pocket money and he would fish in his pocket for fifty pee and he would give it to me with a little, secret smile and close his hands on mine as he gave me the money and I would look at him and think he was indestructible.

"Little *shnorrer*," he would say. "You'll bleed me dry." And he would wink at me.

Other days, there would be no pocket money and no jokes about bleeding him dry. Other days, he would dribble down his chin and urinate in his trousers and my grandmother would clean up after him like he was a dog or something since she refused to get a nurse.

"What do I need a nurse for?" she would ask. "You think I can't look after my own husband?"

The week before I left for Germany, he was sitting in the lounge in his pyjamas shouting at my grandmother. He never used to shout at her, not before. My grandmother was in a terrible state and kept fussing about him. "Get up," she kept saying, "Sammy please you must get up, you heard the doctor, please you must get up." But my grandfather kept pushing her away.

"I'm not getting up," he said. "Go away."

The doctor had ordered that he take some exercise otherwise his muscles would start to rot away along with his brain. Twice a day, the doctor had said, take him for a little walk around the apartment. Just a few times. But my grandfather was refusing to walk and he kept shaking his head and shouting no no no no, I'm not getting up I'm not getting up over and over again like a child, this man who once owned a flourishing business, this man who was once a *mensch* in the community. "Go away," he shouted, and his mouth dribbled saliva.

"Samuel, please, the doctor...'

"Go away I tell you."

I can still see my grandmother tugging gently at his sleeve, pleading with him, pleading with him to come back to her and look after her as he had done for over fifty years, praying this was all some game and he would suddenly snap out of it and be himself again and take her in his arms and say it's all right now, it's all right. If only he would take a little walk.

A week later I was in Germany.

*

They left a message at the hotel, "In extremis," it said. "Come back at once if possible lots of love." The *concierge* looked grave as he gave me the message. I suppose he must have read it already. I told him I had to leave immediately and he nodded and said of course Sir, I understand, immediately, yes, and hurried to his back room for the bill. I went upstairs and started packing. In extremis. He was dying. Perhaps he was already dead. The message was several hours old. I turned out the light and went downstairs.

There was no plane, all the seats were full, so I decided to take the train. A taxi took me to the station. The streets were empty, everybody had locked themselves in from the rain. I could have phoned home but something stopped me from doing so. I wanted not to know. I wanted not to be sure. I wanted a second chance to say goodbye. My grandfather had been a practical, methodical man but in this business he had been too quick for me. He had left me standing.

"*Lindenstrasse. Der Hauptbahnhof,*" the taxi-driver said.

The next train to Ostend was four hours away. A lot could happen in four hours. I brought a ticket and paced up and down the platform. Like the streets it too was empty, empty and wet. I tried sitting in the second class waiting room but it stank of stale nicotine and unwashed bodies and damp. A woman was stretched out on one of the benches, asleep. I picked

167

up a couple of ancient magazines from a table and started looking though them and I remember how one was full of pictures of some bomb attack, black and white pictures of bodies splintered and torn and bleeding, spread across the pages. My grandfather wouldn't die like that, I thought. Without friends, without family. My grandfather would die with all his limbs attached, I thought, his body intact. And then I remembered how thin he had become, how in a matter of months, mere months, his head had started to shrink and shrink until all that was left were his eyes, his blank uncomprehending staring eyes, and nothing else.

A lot can happen in four hours, I thought.

*

I can see my grandfather's hand shaking as he lifts the spoon to his mouth. This is one of the things he still does by himself, without help. After fifty years of eating my grandmother's famous *lokshen* soup it's become a sort of habit not even senility can break. Except his hand trembles more, and some of the soup ends up running down his shirt and he doesn't seem to notice. My grandmother fusses and scolds and tries to smile but she never dares ask if he needs help. She never dares do that. In this sense, he is still her husband, the man of the family, the head of the house, the patriarch.

*

The boat was late, like the train. The weather, they said. The wind was up, they said. It was going to be a rough crossing.

*

My grandfather is what they call a delicatessen Jew. Instead of going to the synagogue he goes to the delicatessen. In the delicatessen he meets the same people he would have met if he had gone to the synagogue. He waits in line by the smoked salmon counter (this is always a very long line) and he talks *gesheft*. My grandfather is not a very pious man. His idea of faith is a *lox* and cream cheese bagel. He eats unkosher meat. He smokes Cuban cigars. He drives a German car. He drives on Saturdays. Once my uncle told me he even had mistresses.

Another thing my grandfather does is he gambles. My grandmother also does this. It is part of what keeps them together. Each Saturday afternoon they sit down in front of the television set to watch the racing. My grandfather lights the first of his cigars and my grandmother reads out the tips.

Then they argue.

"Solomon's Choice a good runner for the two-thirty," says my grandmother.

"A *nebbish* of a horse," coughs my grandfather, through his cigar.

"Not according to my tipster," says my grandmother.

"A *shmendrick* that one," says my grandfather.

"A *yentz.*"

"A *draykop.*"

"A *shmeikel.*"

"A *shmegegge.*"

"A *kocheleffel.*"

My grandmother once told me my grandfather could swear like a Jewish trooper. She was very proud of him that way.

*

We got to Dover early evening. The train was waiting at the station. I found an empty compartment and sat down. People clattered past the corridor, their voices muffled. But nobody came in. The floor of the compartment was full of cigarette ends and ash. Outside, the light was beginning to fade. A dreary, dingy sort of light. I shut my eyes as tight as they would go and tried to get some sleep.

*

Bits of memory come back to me. Flying past the mind like the houses and the washing-lines and the wet streets outside the window. His best brandy. The stuff he only brought out for special occasions, locked away in glass cupboards above the dining room table. The smell of his cigars. Huge Cuban cigars, exotic names in humidifiers and boxes and cases you weren't allowed to touch. Grown-up country, grown-up smells. My grandfather had a way of talking without ever taking his cigar out of his mouth. I remember practising in front of the mirror with a toilet roll but I could never get the hang of it. Think of all those cigars now, lying unsmoked in all those boxes, and my grandfather in his deathbed. There must be hundreds of them. Worth a small fortune. I wonder what will happen to them. I wonder if they're mentioned in his will. I wonder if they'll be thrown away. It would break his heart.

There seems something terribly wrong, something blasphemous about rifling his cupboards like that. Breaking taboos, like spitting on the grave. And he isn't even dead yet. At least I don't think he is.

169

I got to London about nine and took a taxi straight to the flat. I didn't phone, not yet. The taxi got caught in traffic and took an age getting there. The driver asked where I'd been and I said Germany and he said he didn't much care for Germans and I said I didn't either and we left it at that. I looked steadfastly out of the window and he didn't say anything after that.

It was still raining. People with umbrellas dashing about in the rain, puddles in the streets, the rhythmic squeak of windscreen wipers. I will miss him when he's gone. I will miss the fifty pee pocket money, I will miss the smell of his cigars, I will miss the solid reliable comfort of it all. I don't have to see him all the time to know he's there and that's all that matters, really.

*

In the taxi my grandfather lights up a new cigar and asks me what I want. He calls me the Birthday Boy. And what does the Birthday Boy want for his Birthday, he says. I say I want a Whistling Elephant, please, which you have to wind up and then it whistles. (That's why it's called a Whistling Elephant). My grandfather pats his pockets and says you'll ruin me yet and I'm not making any promises. But I know I'll get my Whistling Elephant. When it comes to things like that my grandfather is as solid as a rock.

*

I paid the taxi-driver and he helped me with the luggage. There wasn't much. Just a backpack and a couple of small bags. The chill bit my face and it was supposed to be the middle of summer. I looked up at the block of flats. They lived on the third floor. I could see the balcony and the window in the lounge. The bedroom I couldn't see. The bedroom was at the back.

For a few moments I didn't move. I stood there, in front of the building, my things jumbled around me on the pavement. A man brushed my shoulder as he walked past. I thought, I must go up. I felt very weary, suddenly. I had come all this way. I had been travelling day and night, hours and hours, in boats, in trains, in taxis. Getting closer and closer. And now I was here. And I didn't know what to do. I didn't want to pick up my bags. I didn't want to nod to the porter in his lodge and smile and say good evening. I didn't want to do any of that, not now.

But I did it all the same.

170

The porter slides from his seat as my grandfather and me go past.

"Lucky Lady," he says. "An absolute treat at twenty to one if I may say so Mr Silberman. This the birthday boy?"

"Daylight robbery," says my grandfather. His cigar is still clamped between his teeth. "Put fifty each way on Roger's Dick for the three-thirty. No wait," he says. "Better make that a hundred. He's eight years old today."

"Eight, eh?" says the porter, looking at me out of the corner of his eye.

I'm nine actually. But that doesn't matter because I'm far more interested in what they're saying. This is what I'm going to do when I'm rich and grown-up like my grandfather. Put fifty each way on Roger's Dick. Or maybe even a hundred.

We get into the lift.

"Boxhill at school says his dad gives him a hundred quid a week pocket money."

"*Fershtinkener kind*," says my grandfather. "He must be a terrible child."

"He spends the whole lot on sweets."

"He should spend a little on his dentist."

"His dad has this sweet factory. I've been invited. His dad drives a Rolls."

"A Rolls *noch*?" says my grandfather. He waits for the lift doors to open. "Nobody ever made money in sweets," he says.

The porter slid from his seat as I stepped into the lobby.

"They're all upstairs," he said and he looked at me out of the corner of his eye. "I am sorry. Such a good man Mr Silberman. If I may say so."

He shook his head.

"I know," I said. "Thankyou." I pressed the button for the lift. The porter wouldn't go away. How much did you have to tip him, just to go away.

"If there's anything I can do," he started.

"No really. Thankyou. Again."

Still no lift for God's sake.

"Well just give me a shout. If you change your mind."

The lift arrived with its bell. The door opened.

"I will. Thank you." The man hovered by the door. "Thankyou," I heard myself say again like a stuck record. Thankyou thankyou thankyou. What else do you say?

171

I knew immediately from their faces. I knew it from the way they looked at me when I came in. They were all there, the whole lot of them. My parents, my brothers, my sister, my aunt, my uncles, the whole lot. And Dr Goldblatt. And my grandmother, sitting in her favourite chair by the television set where they used to watch the races, together. On the table, a bottle of brandy, half empty. My grandfather's brandy. They had all been drinking.

"Seeing him off," said my uncle, the first to speak. "One for the road." He picked up his glass and gestured towards the bottle. "Want one?"

"When did you get in?" said my mother.

"You got my telegram?" said my father.

"I got it," I said. I looked at them all. My grandmother said nothing. She hardly seemed to notice me. The matriarch.

"Hello," I said.

"Have a drink then," said my uncle. "It's his best brandy. The stuff he always locks away. Godspeed and all that you know. What the Irish do."

"Where is he?"

"In his room," said my father. "You'd better go and have a look."

"Say goodbye," said my uncle, "and all that."

I went over to my grandmother and kissed her on the cheek. I was surprised to see that she was not crying. Her eyes were quite dry. She blinked at me.

"I love you," I said, in her ear.

"You just missed him," she whispered. "But he wouldn't have known. He wouldn't have known a thing."

*

My grandparents slept in separate beds. When I was very little, I used to stay the night in their flat as a special treat. My grandmother would let me go to bed much later than at home and then she would find sheets and blankets and tuck me up in bed and tell me a story and kiss me goodnight. And I would always ask her to keep the door open so I could see the walls of my room and I could hear them move softly around the flat until they too went to bed. And the light outside my door was turned out and suddenly everything was quiet and dark except for the noise of cars outside and sometimes a slow, rasping cough from my grandparents' bedroom. My grandfather's cough.

*

He was lying in his bed. I stood quite still at the door, not daring to go in. His face was turned away from me. The sheets were pulled right up to his

172

neck. I thought how clean and crisp and new they looked next to his head, next to the tangled grey hairs that fell over his ear and on to the pillow. They said he had a great head of hair, once. Thick black hair. They said he looked like Douglas Fairbanks Junior. He did not look like that now. Now he looked like what he was. Old and dead.

I went up to him. There was a glass of water beside his bed. I noticed it wasn't full. He must have drank a little before he died. I suddenly felt terribly thirsty. I hadn't had a drink since I got off the boat, ages ago. Fourteen hours on the train, five hours on the boat. I had paid my respects, I thought. I'd done my bit. I picked up my grandfather's glass and swallowed the rest down.

I remembered this bed. He told me stories from here. He gave me his racing tips. He tipped his cigar all over these sheets. He spent whole mornings in here. I wondered how much longer he would spend in here now.

From where I stood I couldn't quite see his face, only the back of his head. I had a strong desire to see his face, just once more, for the last time. I went round the other side of the bed. His body looked so small. His feet were at least two foot off the end. He looked like a dead dwarf. His face had shrunk even since I last saw him, had stretched and tightened round the brittle bones like a sort of mask, not his face at all. I saw the stubble on his cheek, grey ragged bits of wire hair. He needed a good shave and I wondered if he would get one. I felt a bit silly standing there. I thought I ought to do something, say something, maybe pray a little. How do you say goodbye to a corpse? What do you do? I didn't know what to do except that something made me reach out and touch his skin with my hand, touch his lips and nose and cheeks. He felt quite warm.

I stood like that a few more moments. I stood and looked at that face and tried to think of the right things to think about. I thought if I didn't stay there a reasonable length of time the others would think I didn't love him enough. When all I really wanted now was to wash, change, get some sleep. I looked across at my grandmother's bed. It looked almost inviting. The same crisp sheets, the same plumped up pillows. I could have done with a little nap, with what he used to call a little *shluf*. Just an hour or so in the other bed, that's all. He wouldn't have minded. He was always very practical about things like death. He called it a fact of life. It's a fact of life, he used to say. Like having a meal. We all eat, we all die. So what?

So what indeed.

But I couldn't tear myself away from his side. Something held me there, something stronger than me. The idea of seeing him for the very last time. The idea of never seeing that face again, of never touching him again, of never being in the same room as him again. I couldn't bring myself to go.

173

I had to remember once and for all what he looked like, the nose the eyebrows the mouth the deep lines in his forehead. I had to remember it all. There could be no second chances, no going back.

So I bent down to kiss him as I had kissed my grandmother. And as I did so the most extraordinary thing happened.

My grandfather winked at me.

*

Everybody looked up.

"He *what*?" said my Uncle Sidney.

"He did *what*?" said my Auntie Gilda.

"You say he *winked* at you?" said my Uncle Manny.

For a moment nobody said anything. Then they all shouted at once.

"What is the boy crazy?" said my Auntie Gilda.

"Crazy nothing," said my Uncle Manny. "He is *oysgematert* after his long journey."

"*Oysgematert* nothing," said my Auntie Gilda. "I tell you the boy is mad." ·

"Stupid."

"Dumb."

"Drunk."

"*Winked,*" he says.

"A sense of humour he calls this?"

Then my grandmother spoke up. "What happened?" she said. It was the first time she had spoken.

I told her. "I tell you he's still alive," I said. "People don't wink once they're dead."

"Who says they don't?" growled my Auntie Gilda.

*

Everybody went to the deathbed. I followed them in. My grandfather was in the same position as before. His eyes were closed but his mouth was now half-open. You could see his tongue between his false teeth and, if you listened very carefully, you could just make out the sharp intake of his breath, rapid but regular, and the rhythmic movement of his body under the sheets. He was alive.

"Jesus Holy Christ," said Doctor Goldblatt.

My grandmother stood there, shaking her head.

"It's a miracle," she said. "It's a miracle from Heaven."

"I've read about this," said my Uncle Manny, "in the *Reader's Digest.*

174

It happens from time to time."

My Auntie Gilda turned accusingly to the doctor. "But for the boy here," she said, "we should have buried my father alive."

"He was quite dead when I last checked."

"Not dead enough, clearly," said my Aunt Gilda in the voice she used to servants just before she fired them.

"I tell you," said Doctor Goldblatt, "he was perfectly dead when I last looked. Anyway," he added, "you should be thrilled. Your own father, he's come back from the dead."

"Assuming," said my Aunt Gilda, "he was ever dead in the first place."

At this point my Uncle Sidney spoke up. "My God," he said. "He's even drunk the water!"

*

For four hours my grandfather stayed that way. His eyes never opened again, but his breathing remained rhythmic, and some of the colour even returned to his face. We waited with him, taking it in turns to sit by his bedside in case anything happened. My grandmother did not go back into his room. She had already seen him die once, she said, for what did she want to see him die again? "It's not natural," she said, and made us all a cup of tea and took the bottle of brandy away from my uncle and locked it back in the cupboard where it was always kept.

The doctor, closely watched by Auntie Gilda, felt my grandfather's pulse and checked his blood pressure and listened to his chest through his stethoscope and said he didn't have much longer to live anyway. But Auntie Gilda only sneered and said we'll see about that, like it was her decision one way or another.

So the night dragged on into the early hours of the morning, and we sat there, drinking endless cups of tea and wondering how it was that my grandfather — a practical man by all events and not what you would call the spiritual type — should have managed to rise from the dead.

My Uncle Sidney said maybe it was because God like gamblers, but my Uncle Manny disagreed and said not if they kept on losing all the time and he never knew anyone who lost as often as my grandfather. My Auntie Gilda said in her opinion all gambling was disgusting and that anyway my grandfather had not risen from the dead since he had not been dead in the first place.

At almost one o'clock in the morning, my mother called us back into the room. My grandfather, she said was on the way out. We heard a rasping sound from his lips, we saw a slight, barely perceptible stiffening of his body under the sheets, and then he died for the second time. Doctor Goldblatt made double sure this time, checking his heart, feeling his pulse, writing little notes in his notebook, before he finally straightened up, turned to face us and said (maybe a little defensively), "this time, he really is dead."

Auntie Gilda stepped forward. "What makes you so sure then?" she said.

"Because I am sure," said Doctor Goldblatt.

"Maybe," said Uncle Manny, "we should wait a while and see if he wakes up again."

"He won't wake up again," said the doctor, "because he is not alive. He is quite dead."

"Don't you think," said my Uncle Sidney, "we ought to toast him on his way, again? I mean. you never know."

*

My grandmother took it all very well, though it must be said she had already had, as it were, a dress rehearsal. She did not cry, just as she had not cried when I first saw her that day. She seemed to be the only one strangely untouched by what had happened. I suppose in her eyes my grandfather had already left her months before, when his mind had started to wander and his bladder had started to leak and his dignity had started to die. She had been in mourning longer than any of us. She had just kept it to herself.

A miracle, she called it.

But of course, all that was before we found out about the Pope.

*

You can imagine the shock.

It was my Uncle Sidney who broke the news. Locked up for hours in that flat, waiting for my grandfather to die first once then a second time (and who knows, maybe a third time) we were completely cut off from the outside world. We had other things to think about. So you can imagine with what surprise we discovered that His Holiness Pope Paul VI, surrounded by all his physicians, his counsellors, his cardinals, had died that very same day in Rome.

Now you may ask what my grandfather, a Jew (albeit one who could never say no to a cooked breakfast) has to do with the Pope but I believe a great deal. According to my Uncle Sidney, my grandfather died the first time just a few seconds before the Pope. Mere moments separated the Vicar of Christ, the Prince of the Apostles, the Supreme Pastor of the Universal Church from Sammy Isaac Silberman, my grandfather.

'Now that's what I call *chutzpah*," said my Uncle Sidney.

*

Perhaps my grandfather and thousands like him were already well on their way to Heaven that night when all of a sudden the Pope dies. So what happens? So everything happens. Such confusion, such excitement, such a *shlemozzel*. This I need like a hole in the head, says the Archangel Gabriel, standing before the entrance to Heaven. *Stop!* he yells at my grandfather (who already has at least one foot in the door). *Stop! Turn round! Go back! Enough already! The Pope is coming!* Meanwhile this huge traffic jam builds up. It's crazy up there. Nobody knows what's going on. Everybody had to turn back and wait for the Holy Pontiff and all his angels, cherubs, hangers-on, etc, to be processed. This takes time, Popes being Popes, and not ordinary mortals like my grandfather. In fact it takes about four hours whilst my grandfather and all the others temporarily return to their bodies and wait for the Pope to pass through. Four hours, then they are free to go. And my grandfather once more leaves his body. Only this time for ever.

I tell you one thing. He would have loved that story.

The Devil in the Cupboard

Michelene Wandor

The first time I saw the devil in the cupboard was at four o'clock in the morning. I had just finished painting the flat — white walls, white doors, white ceilings. White dust covers hooded anonymously shaped piles of furniture; cardboard boxes full of books created square and oblique khaki mountains; the beds in the spare room were piled high with shapeless mounds of clothes. It was like being in a timeless world.

Everything was fresh. Pure. New. Wonderful. That night I walked barefoot up the warmly varnished wooden stairs, made the bed with clean sheets, flung my clothes over a chair and got into bed naked. Cooled by the white cotton, I fell asleep, in a home that was cleansed of the clutter and turmoil of the past.

I don't know what wakened me. I sat up in bed, hot, the sheet crumpled. The luminous dial on my clock said four a.m. The moon was casting bright shadows through the curtainless windows. I straightened the sheet and was about to lie down again, when I noticed that one of the cupboard doors was open. I got up to close it, and as I put my hand on the door, the devil said, "Hang on a minute."

I knew it was the devil because I could see he had two little protuberances, like a baby goat's horns, on his forehead. I knew it was the devil because he had cloven hoofs neatly crossed in front of him. I knew it was the devil because his tail was neatly wrapped round his left arm. And I knew it was the devil because I was starkers, and not in the least self-conscious about it.

"What the hell do you want?" I asked.

"Hell is the operative word," he said.

"Have you woken me up in the middle of the night for a theological debate?" I asked.

"Sit down," he said, "I want to talk to you."

I sat on the end of the bed. "This had better be good," I warned.

"You're unhappy," he said.

I was wide awake now. "You've got a nerve," I said, "I'm a woman of the nineties. I've got a rewarding job. I own my flat. I have a balcony on which I can have coffee and croissants for breakfast on Sunday. I've got wooden floors, and as many books and CDs as I want. I go to the theatre with my friends. I save money and go on exciting holidays. I've trekked the Himalayas, tramped through the jungles of Ecuador and scaled the

179

pyramids. I am not unhappy."

"Oh?" said the devil. "And what about love? Passion. Romance, the marriage of two minds?"

"I have lots of good friends," I countered. "Anyway, what does the devil know about love."

"More than anyone," he said. "And I know a loveless creature when I see one."

"Takes one to know one," I riposted — and then realised what I had said. "OK," I sighed. "My life lacks true love. But that doesn't mean I'm unhappy."

"Wait," he said. He was out of the cupboard, and sitting beside me on the bed. "I can show you the way to true love and happiness," he said, his sharp green eyes holding mine.

"Pigs might fly," I said.

"I need your help," he said.

"Me, help the devil?" I laughed in disbelief.

"I am at the end of my time in limbo," he said. "I have endured the tortures of hell, and now I have to do a good deed, and then I can be admitted to paradise."

"And I'm it?" I asked. "I'm your good deed?"

I blinked. I saw now that he was cradling a bowl of fruit and vegetables, and the scent of lemon and basil and garlic filled the room. "I will set you three tasks," he said, "and then we shall both be free. We are in limbo. We are both searching for true, heavenly happiness. Together we can find it."

His voice drifted hypnotically over me. "Your first task is to become the best cook the world has ever known, the chef to end all chefs, the gourmet to end all gourmets..."

And I did. I travelled to the mountains of Tibet and learned the secrets of spiced lentils washed in icy mountain streams. I travelled through the searing deserts of Africa, learning the cooling draughts that soothe the night-time palate. I plumbed the succulent depths of the potato *latke*, the infinite variety of the Turkish delight, baby carrots and courgettes from French valley farms. I baked and steamed and chopped and marinated, and soon I was a celebrity, famous all over the world.

Then I met him. A dark, brooding man, with melting brown eyes. A painter. When he painted the fronds of the dill plant, you could smell its caressing flavour. You wanted to put your hand out to catch the over-ripe cherry before it tumbled. We fell passionately in love.

I left my flat and we moved in together. He was a man inspired and possessed. I cooked and he painted. I soon learned to love sitting silently in a corner of his studio as he worked, making him dark, fragrant coffee in a white swirling jug, and then creeping away to the bed in the spare room, lest my breathing disturb the dreams he needed for his work.

After a year, I woke up one morning, saw my recipe books with their pages unturned, my copper pans dulled, my herb garden overgrown. I realised I no longer loved him. While he was still asleep, I dropped a kiss on his nose and left.

*

I moved back into my flat. My friends had watered my plants and kept the furniture free of dust. I painted everything white. Fresh. Pure. Wonderful.

On my first night there, I stretched luxuriously between freshly ironed cotton sheets, and fell into a calm, dreamless sleep.

I sat up suddenly. It was four o'clock in the morning. There was the devil, sitting at the bottom of the bed, the same sharp green eyes, the same cloven hoofs.

"Well," I said triumphantly, "that didn't work, did it?"

"Three tasks," he reminded me. "Are you ready for number two?"

I could see now that a length of shimmering blue-green silk was draped around his neck. In one hand he held a large pair of tailor's shears, and in the other a chunk of tailor's chalk.

"You," he said, "will become the greatest designer in the world."

"You've got to be joking. I can't even thread a needle."

"You will establish the taste of nations; you will invent colours and shapes that will astound everyone..."

And I did. I dipped my batiks and silks in colours drawn from the earth and trees and plants from all over the world. I tacked and back-stitched and ruched and smocked and gathered and lined. I learned to love the silkworm and the rayon-yielding tree bark. By simply smelling and feeling a piece of wool, I could tell you from which country, region, farm, and even field, its animal donor had come. I invented synthetic fabrics that transformed the lives of those in need. No-one lifted a needle before my spring and autumn designs had hit the fashion pages.

It was at a fashion show that I met him. A finely boned face, blue eyes, long, wavy, deeply auburn hair. My sculptor. He had seen my work, and my shapes and patterns had inspired him.

We fell passionately in love. He took my real colours and shapes and transformed them into wild and mysterious sculptured forms, which captivated the art world. I loved watching him work, and he loved having me near him while he worked. I loved brewing him dark, fragrant coffee in a swirling white jug, and I made him brightly coloured smocks to wear while he worked. At night I crept away to the bed in the spare room, lest

181

my breathing interrupt the dreams he needed for his work.

After a year, I woke up one morning, and saw my sketch pads unopened; I saw piles of fabric gathering dust, and I knew I no longer loved him. I dropped a kiss on his nose and left.

*

I moved back into my flat. My friends had watered the plants and kept the furniture free from dust. I painted the walls white and revelled in their fresh purity. Wonderful.

That night, I fell asleep immediately between the crisp white cotton sheets. At four in the morning I sat up suddenly. There was a sound in my room, a sweet, soaring, poignant sound.

There was the devil, sitting at the foot of my bed, his sharp green eyes looking at me as he drew a bow across a string instrument of a kind I had never seen.

"I know what you're going to say," he began —

"Good," I said. "Because I've had enough."

"One more task," he said, the bow drawing the most exquisite sound I had ever heard. It filled my head and ran through my veins to the tips of my toes and the ends of my fingers. I had no power to protest any more. I knew what my task was. I knew what I had to do.

And I did. I learned to play every instrument ever made. I learned to draw any sound I wanted from the most subtle clavichord to the largest, most resonant church organ. I trumpeted and fluted and drummed. I played the old and the new: the cello and the viol, the recorder and the saxophone, the racket and the euphonium. I was as content and adept on the folk instruments of South America as I was with the Indian raga tradition and the repertoire of Beethoven and Mahler.

I performed and recorded, from plain-chant to freeform jazz. At one of my concerts a man waited patiently until all the fans had dispersed. Then he came towards me, diffidently holding a sheaf of papers. He was stocky, vibrant with energy.

"I wrote this for you," he said. "I hope you will have the time to look at it."

It was as if he had read my inner being and written music designed to touch my soul and to make me want to play it and to touch the soul of others.

At the premiere he was modest, only taking his well-deserved bow when the audience refused to stop applauding.

We fell passionately in love. He wrote and I performed. I grew to love hearing the way a piece moved from sketch to completed form. He loved playing his work to me and listening to my reactions. I loved making him dark, fragrant coffee in a white swirling jug, and then creeping away to the bed in the spare room, lest my breathing disturb the dreams that brought him new melodies.

One morning I woke up and saw the broken strings on my instruments. I heard my piano play out of tune. My reeds were dry and brittle, my music dusty. I knew I no longer loved him. I dropped a kiss on his nose and left.

*

Back in my flat, the plants were watered, and my friends had kept my furniture free from dust. But this time, before I painted the walls white, there was something I had to do.

When everyone else in the street was asleep, I collected all my cookery books, pots and pans and dishes, and piled them in the middle of the road. Then I took all my design books, all the brocades and lawns and linens and added them to the pile. Then, with the strength of ten, I pushed the pianos and the harps, carried the lutes and guitars and lyres, the oboes and sackbuts, and added them.

It was a dry night, and the flames quickly took hold. A warm wind blew the petals off the blood-red roses and purple clematis, each of which caught fragrant fire as it landed in a rain of light and colour.

Behind me a voice said: "Well done."

I didn't need to look round.

"True love?" I yelled against the roar of the fire. "I've wasted the best years of my life looking for the impossible. I'm sorry if you can't make it into heaven because of me. You picked the wrong person."

"You can cook, you can sew, you can play," he said.

"That's right. I can cook, I can sew, I can play. Big deal. The perfect little housewife."

"Isn't that enough?"

"Of course it isn't enough," I shouted. "I want to paint. I want to sculpt. I want to compose."

"Well," he said, "what's stopping you?"

"What's stopping me?" I was beside myself. "What's stopping me?" I stood still and thought for a moment.

"Nothing," I said calmly. "Nothing at all when it comes down to it. If they could do it, then I can. If I inspired them, then I can inspire myself. I can paint. I can sculpt. I can compose."

I smiled at him. It was four o'clock in the morning.

I do hope that you can come to the wedding. The cupboard looks small when you first open it, but believe me, that's an illusion. Inside, it's heaven.

The Vote

Shelley Weiner

There was once a poor young maid who found work in a great house in Johannesburg. The maid's name was Martha and her employer's name was Juliette, and each of them thought how very lucky she was to have come upon the other. Juliette, a renowned hostess who was married to one of the city's leading financiers, had been searching far and wide for a malleable, presentable servant whom she could train for the eventual position of cook-general in her Lower Houghton home. And Martha had been seeking stability. She'd been looking for a live-in position with good prospects so that a regular sum of money could be sent to the black township where her children were growing up. Despite her apparent youth and innocence, Martha had already produced two offspring — thanks to a feckless lad called Jim, who'd kept wooing and impregnating her. But, she assured Juliette, she was finished with all that now.

"That's over, madam," she declared. "I tell you, madam, I've had it with men."

"And who looks after the children for you?" Juliette had had bitter experience of maids with dependents. They tended to let one down.

"My sister," said Martha. "She's very reliable."

"Ah," said Juliette. She knew all about sisters. And so-called cousins and aunts. They usually turned out to be professional childminders who lacked long-term commitment and eventually dumped their charges on their natural mama. Or worse. Anyway, one couldn't cater for all eventualities, and Martha seemed keen and unspoilt and reasonably intelligent. She decided to take her on.

"Thank you, madam," said Martha, with effusive gratitude. "You won't be sorry, madam — you'll see."

"I hope not," Juliette said — not in quite the right sort of tone for an artistic soul with liberal inclinations. So she added a few pretty phrases about Martha's future happiness and the excellence of the staff quarters in the Keller home and the mutual benefits that would result from their working relationship.

"If you're fair to me, Martha, I'll be fair to you. I see you have an excellent reference from that Mrs ..."

"Mrs Swart, madam. I was there three years, but the family had to move to Krugersdorp and it was difficult for me, with the children here in Soweto ..."

"I understand. Now let me show you round the house and explain the sort of thing I'll expect you to do. As you can see, we have many valuable things around here and, if there's one thing I can't stand, it's a clumsy girl ..."

Martha started work the following Monday. The day before, she had arrived with a single small suitcase and taken occupation of her room. Juliette had introduced her to the facilities. Everything, she'd pointed out, was of the very best.

"Here's your toilet and your basin," she'd said. "And very soon you'll be getting your very own bath. Mr Keller and I have always believed that servants should be treated properly — we're not like some people."

"Yes, madam. I can see that." She could indeed. At the Swarts, she'd had to drag buckets of water from the kitchen to her room at night and there had been no prospect of a basin — let alone a proper working bath. It seemed that she'd been lucky with this job. Very lucky.

"I'll leave you to settle in now, Martha," Juliette had said. "At six o'clock I want you to come to the kitchen to meet Mr Keller — he should be back from golf by then. Our daughter, Joanne, will also be here I expect. She's at university, studying dentistry — God knows why a girl like her would want to do something like that. We tried to put her off, but she's stubborn. No-one's ever been able to tell Joanne what to do ..."

Martha had arranged her possessions and tried on the uniform which was provided with the job. A nice one, too. Pink overalls with a frilly white cap and apron. Mrs Swart had never stretched to anything like that. And as for Mr Swart — he'd hardly acknowledged that Martha existed except when the food was overcooked or his shirt not properly ironed. Mr Keller, though, struck her as a gentleman. A proper gentleman.

"How do you do, Martha?" he'd said. "We hope you'll be happy with us."

"Yes, master."

She was absolutely sure she would, for the job offered more than any girl could reasonably expect.

Meanwhile Juliette, in her turn, was equally certain that she would derive long-term satisfaction from her new employee. "I think we've got a winner here, Stanley," she confided to her husband at the end of Martha's first week. "I have a feeling that she's exactly right for us."

It was a perfect match. Juliette was convinced — and she never had reason to change her mind — that Martha was heaven-sent. It amused her to think that God must have set aside a moment from his interminable sorting of man and wife to allocate this maid to her madam.

As the years passed, Martha became an integral part of the Keller home, renowned for her loyalty, her sobriety, her celibacy and — most of

186

all — her excellent Duck l'Orange. Her cooking, generally, had blossomed under Juliette's guidance and she had soon become capable of producing lavish dinners for up to twenty without additional help. She was never clumsy and invariably cheerful and, all in all, an asset whom Juliette prized even more than her three-carat diamond engagement ring. She always made sure that Martha's salary was well above the market rate.

And Martha, whose appreciation of her good fortune in finding a position with the Kellers never dimmed, repaid her madam with steadfast fidelity.

"You can count on me, madam," she avowed, when Juliette expressed apprehension about a forthcoming dinner party or a houseful of guests or when Mr Keller (who worked exceedingly hard to support their Lower Houghton life-style) was taken to hospital with a heart attack. He recovered, but Juliette's confidence in his reliability had been shaken. The fixed point in her life had become Martha. Martha, who turned up each day in the kitchen, rain or shine.

Joanne, meanwhile, had graduated as a dentist and married another dentist called Geoffrey and — in her strong-headed way — had announced to her parents that she and her husband had decided to emigrate to England. The future looked more promising there.

"I can't tell you how upset I am," Juliette confided to Martha. She had started confiding in her maid more and more as the years went by. "Not that we've seen very much of her recently — once a week if we've been lucky. Still — England's so far away. You know how one worries about them ..."

"I know, madam. Children can be such a worry."

Martha's two were growing up under the tutelage of a series of sisters and cousins and aunts. Their mother saw them regularly and was proud that — thanks to the Kellers — she could afford to have them well educated. But Jason, her son, had started running with a wild crowd, a political crowd, and was in danger of getting into deep trouble with the police. And Angel, her 14-year-old daughter, was pregnant.

"Children," sighed Martha. "You're lucky, madam, that you only have the one." She didn't share with Juliette her anxieties about Jason and Angel for that was not the way things worked. And Juliette, who also knew the rules, rarely asked.

Instead, she kept Martha closely informed about Joanne's preparations for life abroad and wept profusely on her shoulder when the day of her daughter's departure finally came.

"Don't cry, madam," Martha said. "I'm here. I'm not going anywhere."

"Thank goodness for that," said Juliette, meaning it with all her heart. And she said it again — even more fervently, if possible — on the awful day of Mr Keller's second coronary. This time he died.

So Juliette and Martha remained alone in the great Lower Houghton house. Juliette was the sole occupant of the vast master bedroom with its 'his and hers' dressing-rooms and spacious en-suite bathroom, while Martha still resided in the same little room she'd been allocated 16 years before. The bath that had been installed soon after her employment had commenced was cracked and discoloured.

But Martha didn't complain. On the contrary, she still believed implicitly in her good fortune and, with her madam, bemoaned the upsurge of violence in the country and the fact that Lower Houghton was no longer a safe place in which to live. By now, many of Juliette's friends had left South Africa and, despite all the measures she had taken to secure her home, Juliette confessed that she was often frightened at night.

"You mustn't worry, madam," said Martha with her usual show of conviction. She didn't let on that she'd heard Jason and his friends threatening to plunder the suburbs, to kill the whites, to reclaim their rights. They were wrong. She'd tried to tell them they were wrong. But it seemed they were talking a different language. How strange it was that she could understand her madam's fear better than her children's anger. How much more effective she felt consoling her madam than trying to calm all that bitter young wrath.

So she spent more and more time in Lower Houghton, even on her once-weekly day off. A panic-button was installed to link Juliette's suite with that of her servant and, as a show of appreciation for Martha's devotion, the maid's room was enlarged and a new improved bath (with shower unit) was installed. Martha was delighted.

Her delight was somewhat dampened, however, when — a few months later — Juliette announced that, despite all the security measures and the staunchness of her servant, she had decided she couldn't continue living in South Africa any longer. Her nerves were at breaking point.

"I'm a reasonable person, Martha," she declared. "You know how reasonable I am. And it's not as though I don't believe that things could be shared more equally — that the blacks don't have any rights."

"Of course, madam," said Martha, who had long stopped associating herself with the blacks. She'd stopped thinking of herself as anything but Juliette's maid. That was all.

"It's just the way things are being handled," Juliette continued. "The violence. The chaos. Now that Mandela's been let out of prison, I don't know where it will all end ..."

"Who knows, madam? Who knows ..."

That was when Juliette made her proposition.

"Joanne and Geoffrey have found me a flat in London," she said. "It's a very comfortable place, I believe, in a smart part of London called St John's Wood."

"I see," said Martha.

"And I was thinking that if you wanted to come with me — there's a place for you there as well."

"For me?"

"Well, we've been together a long time, you and me, and I was hoping..."

"Me in London, madam?"

"Why not, Martha? I'd take care of you — you know that."

"I know that, madam. It's just ..."

"You'd be much better off with me in London than with all the trouble about to break out over here. Think about it. I'd never force you, of course, but I believe it would be best. For both of us."

Martha thought about it. She pondered for days. So distracted was she that she broke an antique vase and forgot to add seasoning to the meatballs and finally, one morning, arrived in the kitchen more than half-an-hour late for work.

"You're not getting careless, are you?" asked Juliette, who had begun voicing her concern about Martha's latter-day absent-mindedness across various bridge tables in Lower Houghton. "It's not like you, Martha. Is something the matter?"

"It's ..."

"What? Tell me."

"This London business, madam. I can't decide."

"Well, time is getting short. You're leaving it very late. The packers are due in three weeks."

"I know, madam. I know." She paused, frowning, and rumpled her apron uneasily. "Maybe if madam can give me the weekend off, I can go and speak to the children ...?"

This was was not a convenient request, for it required the postponement of a dinner party. The urgency of the situation, however, called for adaptability, so Juliette — who saw herself as infinitely flexible — agreed.

Martha went to Soweto, feeling alien and rather frightened on the crowded train. She wasn't accustomed to it any more — the crush, the smells, the noise. Her life had become so tranquil, so orderly, while her people, it seemed, had grown wild. The children had turned into crazy, drunken creatures. There was madness in their eyes. "Change is coming," they exalted to Martha. "Black South Africa. Can you imagine it? South Africa for all."

She tried to talk to them, to discuss her predicament with them — but instead of listening, they jeered at her. "Madam," they taunted, laughing hysterically. "Madam. Just wait. One of these days she'll be calling you madam."

"Sshhh," said Martha warningly, but they continued to tease. And finally she left them, she made her way home. Home to her room and her bath, which she filled with steaming water and the jasmine-scented grains Juliette had given her for Christmas. "Ahh," she luxuriated, lying back. "That's better."

The next day she told Juliette that she had decided to accompany her to London.

"Good," said Juliette briskly, successfully hiding her immense relief lest Martha should imagine she was irreplaceable. That never worked, with servants. "We'll have to get ourselves organized. Tomorrow I'll start making lists."

It was a brilliant campaign, orchestrated by Juliette with Martha, tireless Martha, carrying out the duties of a medium-sized regiment. Within weeks, the contents of the flat had been sorted, listed, pruned, packed and despatched for shipping in two vast containers. Juliette's personal possessions had been desposited into seven suitcases, five of which were being sent ahead as unaccompanied luggage.

"There," said Juliette with satisfaction when the final item had been packed. Martha was released to see to her own belongings which, fortunately, were not copious. The bulk fitted into a spare suitcase inherited from the late Mr Keller and the excess was taped into a large cardboard box.

All that remained was for the madam and her maid to be transported to the airport and for Juliette to be installed in her first class seat on South African Airways and for Martha to squeeze into the economy accommodation at the rear.

It was unbelievable, she thought, holding her breath while the air hostess fastened her seat belt. Astonishing. She couldn't believe her luck. A girl from Soweto, to be travelling so far, in such style? If only her friends could see her — her aunts, her sisters, her children.

But no-one saw her. No-one noticed her much at all. Undeterred, she kept marvelling to herself as the aircraft climbed to its cruising altitude and dinner was served — served! To her! — and the lights dimmed and she dozed and was woken for breakfast — again! Served again! Oh, how clever she'd been to have found such a job, to have kept such a job, to be flying here high above the clouds into a new world. Clever and lucky.

The new world, though, turned out to be remarkably similar to the old. With its towering apartment blocks, St John's Wood seemed to Martha much like Lower Houghton, and the flat in London almost replicated Juliette's Johannesburg abode. Much smaller, of course — but Juliette appeared delighted with it.

"It's gorgeous — don't you think so, Martha?" she gushed over her shoulder, as Joanne and Geoffrey led the way inside.

"Yes, very lovely, madam," Martha panted, following with the suitcases.

"Madam?" echoed Joanne, disbelievingly. "Surely, mother! You can't have her calling you that here."

"No, no. Of course not." Juliette patted her daughter placatingly, remembering the whithering force of Joanne's scorn. "Martha, I forgot to tell you — you'd better call me Mrs Keller from now on. It's not — er — done in England to use the word madam. Things are different here."

"Yes ma... Mrs Keller."

But things didn't turn out very different at all. Not really. Amost immediately, Martha slipped into the familiar routine. The laundry on Mondays, the kitchen on Tuesdays, the silver on Wednesdays, and so on. The only real change was that Juliette took to referring to her as "the domestic" rather than "my maid" — but that was only when other people were present. Alone, they remained on the same easy terms. "Don't worry, madam," said Martha, when Juliette at times grew tearful over the hurts inflicted on her by Joanne. "You mustn't take these things to heart. Children will be children."

Children. Martha couldn't prevent her own heart constricting when her mind dwelt on her own. Despite her huge efforts to keep her attention focused on her job and kind madam and great good fortune, she was lonely sometimes. She missed the sound of her language and the fellowship of other servants and the African light and the sun. But still — who was she to complain?

"So — aren't you glad you decided to come to London?" Juliette asked her after a few months. She had purchased new curtains for Martha's room and presented her with a portable black and white television set which Joanne and Geoffrey had discarded. Martha had thanked her effusively.

"Of course, madam. Of course I am."

"I tell you — South Africa's a good place to be out of at the moment. Everyone says so. With that election coming up, who knows what will happen. It's an explosive situation."

Juliette had read that in the papers. She'd always considered herself an apolitical person. Much more the creative type, she'd always said. But now, in London, everyone seemed to think she had to have an opinion on South Africa. More than an opinion — a passionate desire for equality, for justice, for peace. Which of course she had — in a theoretical way. At any rate, she wished the country well. It would be churlish not to, after all the material advantages it had lavished on her. And although she was happy

191

to be in London, at odd moments she was beset by a tight knot of longing, an indefineable sense of loss.

"An explosive situation?" repeated Martha, alarmed. "Does madam really think it's going to be bad there? Mandela was on the television last night and he seemed calm, madam. He was talking about peace, forgiveness. Maybe it will be all right?"

"Oh, Mandela," Juliette said dismissively, leaving the room. How she wished she could stop thinking, talking, hearing about bloody South Africa. She had left it. Her life was here, in London. Surely a person was entitled to start afresh. Nelson Mandela, Nelson Mandela. Honestly — everyone singing his praises. What did they know? How could anyone who hadn't lived there begin to understand the complexities? Every day, in almost every news bulletin, there he was with his saintly face. And Juliette watched him and sometimes, despite herself, found she was believing, hoping, wishing, longing to be there, to be part of it. Then she caught herself, remembering how very fortunate she was to have got away.

And now they were saying she ought to vote.

"You are voting, aren't you Juliette?" everyone asked her.

"Naturally," she said, wishing they'd mind their own business.

"It must be such a privilege to be able to take part in something so historic."

"Oh, it is, it is."

"And your housekeeper — what's-her-name...?"

"Martha."

"Yes, Martha. She must be excited. Is she going to vote?"

"I'm not sure. We haven't really discussed it."

"You really should."

"I suppose so," said Juliette.

So they did.

"Martha," she began that evening as the supper plates were being cleared. "Martha, I was wondering — about the elections, you know."

"Madam?"

"The elections in South Africa next week. For the new government. Apparently, South Africans living abroad can vote too. People like me and..." She paused momentarily. "And you."

Martha didn't appear to notice the hesitation. She continued to clear the plates.

"Martha?"

"Madam?"

"Martha, are you going to vote? Do you want to vote?"

"Is madam going to vote?"

"Of course," said Juliette quickly. "Joanne and Geoffrey have offered

192

me a lift. I'm sure you could come along too."

Martha carried on clearing in ponderous silence.

"Or else," Juliette continued, suddenly desperate to elicit a proper response from this woman who had — damn it, she had just about shared the best years of her life with her. Surely she, out of everyone, understood the conflict, the belonging, the not-belonging? "Or else — if you'd prefer it — we could go by taxi, me and you. We could go and vote together."

Martha stood still. She turned to Juliette and met her gaze. "Let's do that, madam. The two of us can go and vote together."

They sat alongside one another in the taxi. Only a few miles separated St John's Wood from Trafalgar Square, but the journey seemed longer and even more momentous than the flight from Johannesburg. At last they reached the South African embassy and joined the queue. An excited, jostling queue.

"All right, madam?" asked Martha, noticing for the first time that her employer was growing old. She seemed frail and uncertain in the boisterous crowd. Martha took her arm. Juliette didn't resist.

"I'm fine, Martha," she said, as they walked in step, side by side. "And you? How about you?"

Dead Ringer

Jonathan Wilson

Henry, lying on a table in the ultrasound room, felt the young nurse spread warm jelly over his testicles. He tried to fight back an erection and, somewhat disappointingly, succeeded with ease. "See anything so far?" The nurse click, clacked on the machine and slid a probe over him. The screen flashed black and white; there were constellations of electronic blips, universes, black holes. "The doctor will talk to you afterwards." The nurse was on automatic pilot. What possible interest could middle-aged balls hold for her?

"Turn on your side please. No, the other side."

Henry turned, and the pain throbbed through him. He was there because of the pain. And the pain was there because... well, because pain comes and takes you by surprise. Sometimes, as in his case it persists.

He had spoken with Dr. Vikrami. She was his wife's doctor first, but because he was too lazy to search for someone else Henry had signed on too. On most matters Dr. Vikrami was straightforward, to the point, almost brusque, but she seemed to regard Henry's private parts as just that. Once a year she lifted the band of his underpants, took a quick look, then snapped the elastic back without comment, as if what she had seen had somehow offended her. Last March, as Henry was getting dressed, she had muttered

"And how is your sex life? Everything alright?"

Henry had begun to reply but as soon as he did so Dr. Vikrami left the room.

Back home, he complained to Arlene.

"But what do you want her to do?" his wife responded in an exasperated voice.

"I want her to examine me thoroughly."

"You should go to a male doctor."

"That's ridiculous. All doctors should provide the same treatment."

" They're doctors, it's like being a neutral country." When Henry called Dr. Vikrami and described the pain in his testicles she did not ask him to come in.

"See," Henry put his hand over the receiver and hissed at Arlene who was working in the kitchen.

"I think we had better set you up with the radiologist right away."

"Do you think it's serious?"

195

"Let me make a phone call and I'll get right back to you." She was as good as her word.

"Tomorrow. 8.15. At the hospital. Can you make that?" Henry couldn't sleep. He channel surfed for an hour and thumped his pillows. Arlene woke up.

"I'm going to die." Henry said.

"So's everyone else", Arlene murmured and turned her back to him.

The pain, like so much that had effected Henry's life in a big way, was connected to sex. For some time Arlene had been complaining of sore breasts; she didn't want to be touched. Henry and her had fought terribly, sadly, after her father had died six months previously. She had accused him of being insensitive, indifferent to her suffering, unable to take care of the children properly. He continued to be sexually demanding, he hadn't allowed her time to herself, time to mourn. Henry thought the accusations unjustified. He had liked his father-in-law and he missed him too. The sore breasts had arrived within two weeks of the funeral. But last week, after watching a repeat episode of "The Jewel in the Crown" on PBS Arlene had suddenly relented and let him push her nightdress up. At the sight of those gorgeous orbs Henry ejaculated, and with the hot spurt came searing pain. He lay face down on his pillow.

"Too much for you?" Arlene asked, tucking herself back into a cocoon and rolling onto her side.

He didn't want to mention the pain, it seemed like a defeat.

The radiologist came into the room. She was even more attractive than the nurse. A lion's mane of tawny hair, freckles on her snub nose. He lay there in his hospital johnny, trying to tug the bottom down like the hem of a skirt.

"Mr. Newman?" Henry nodded.

"How are you feeling?"

He thought "Tell me the worst."

"Well, I'm happy to say we can't find much wrong with you. Your epididymis is inflamed, but not remarkably so."

"What's the epididymis?"

"It's the mass at the back of your testes. You've got some convoluted tubes back here," she prodded under his skirt with her fingers, "and they've got inflamed. It's not uncommon in men of your age."

"Is it curable?"

"Possibly, or it may be that you have developed a chronic condition. In which case, I'm afraid, it's just something that you're going to have to live with. Are you under stress?"

"All the time." The radiologist laughed, a sweet, melodic laugh. Henry wanted to say "Marry me."

196

"You should probably consult a urologist. Just to get some advice. I'll give you a name before you leave."

The route home took him past the Star of David Convalescent Home on VFW Parkway. Without realizing that he had made a decision to do so he pulled into the car park. An old man with an aluminum walker inched away from the car next to him. Henry tried to stop himself from springing out so as not to emphasize the terrible difference between middle and old age.

His mother was sitting up in bed eating a green apple. Her roommate, Mrs. Sonnenthal, bolt upright in a chair, held a magazine in her lap, but didn't look as if she had been reading it.

From her window his mother could see the fake gingerbread roof of a Pancake House. Two weeks ago someone had been shot dead in the parking lot. The police suspected a drug deal gone bad.

"What, no boyfriends today?" Henry asked teasingly.

"Your son has a virile imagination." Mrs Sonnenthal replied, not smiling.

"How are you doing Mom?" Henry tried to keep up the light-hearted tone.

"I'm on my way out."

"Mom, you're not even dressed."

"Not outside, lummox. Out of this earth. Death."

"Your mother's very tired," Mrs Sonnenthal added "She's had a visitor."

"Who?"

"Mr. Flu."

"Why didn't you tell me?"

His mother shrugged her fragile shoulders.

"One week we could be here," Mrs. Sonnenthal continued, "The next you'll find an empty room."

Henry felt his heart empty out like a burst dam.

"But the doctor. I had a word with him on the way in. He said you were doing fine."

"Since when have they known anything?"

Henry wanted to say "They know the difference between epididymitis and testicular cancer."

His mother pulled her bed jacket tighter around her and shivered. The skin at her neck hung loose and red.

"Never mind all his," she said "Have you been *there*?"

There was the heart of the matter. She repeated the question on his every visit. Three months ago, shortly after her eightieth birthday, his mother had suddenly become concerned about Henry's brother's grave.

197

Henry had lived forty-seven years without it ever being mentioned, but now here it was, in the foreground of things.

His brother had died as a baby two years before Henry was born. He lived seven months then he caught an infection and died. It was shortly after Pearl Harbor. His father had been mobilized and his mother left alone. When Henry was growing up the baby was rarely mentioned.

No one visited his grave. No memorial candle was lit. Henry couldn't remember learning the name until he was about ten: Aubrey. His mother and Mrs. Sonnenthal were looking expectantly at him, waiting for a reply.

"No Ma, I haven't been yet. I've been busy. I've got things to do." The two women sighed, simultaneously it seemed, old, exhausted sighs that appeared to test their lung capacity and rattle something inside them.

"I'll go. I promise."

"You'll go." Mrs. Sonnenthal was scathing.

He wanted to say "This has nothing to do with *you*" but he was afraid to offend her. She was his mother's only friend, only confidante. What if she abandoned her, or requested a room change?

His mother picked up a comb from her bedside table and pulled it through her thin grey locks.

"Pass me that mirror," she ordered him. Henry did so and she seemed to relent.

"And how are you? You alright? You look a bit fat."

"I'm O.K. I'm swimming." The throbbing in his epididymis caused Henry to shift in his seat.

"The children?"

"Fine."

"Arlene?"

She didn't wait to hear his reply.

"Why aren't you at work?"

"I'm on my way. I thought I'd stop..."

"You're coming from a strange direction at this time of the morning. Where have you been?"

"Nowhere. I just thought I'd drop in."

A young girl in blue overalls came smartly through the door pushing a trolley laden with brooms and pans.

"Time to get up," she announced in a thick Irish brogue, "I've got to clean this room out."

"Come back in five minutes," Mrs. Sonnenthal ordered her, "This one's visiting his mother."

When the girl left the room Mrs. Sonnenthal whispered

"She's illegal. They all are. She's got no Social Security. What if she gets sick, that's what I want to know?"

Henry left down a corridor choked with slow moving individuals in bathrobes, some with sticks, some on metal walkers, all bent or stooped; making the effort.

He decided to take the morning off. He called Angela at the office. Things were slow anyway. No one had any money, not for the kind of investments he specialized in: low-cost housing programs for corporations who wanted to get a tax break and look good at the same time.

He went early to the swimming pool at his health club. Swimming brought temporary relief from the pain, something to do with gravity.

In the large room next to the pool women in brightly coloured spandex stepped up and down on tiny stairways. He watched through the big picture windows until all the women suddenly turned at once. He held up his hands in a futile gesture of surrender and walked on through a double set of padded swing doors.

Swimming was boring. Worse, the club insisted that you wear a cap, which he hated. Henry's was black, with a sharp red logo on the side connoting muscularity and athleticism, but even so. This morning, in order to entertain himself, he tried to recall what it had been like to be the age of his lap number. One through four were entirely lost to him, but on five he remembered the first day of school and by ten his memory banks had begun to release some funds. On lap eighteen, late for a boy, he knew, came sex. Henry was breathing hard now, and he took in a mouthful of water halfway down the lane. When Carol Anne Muske appeared before him on the beige couch in the basement of her parents house he was embarrassed to feel the erection that had eluded him at the radiologists begin an underwater rise. In the next lane a man with a shaved head (no cap required) and a Sumo stomach heaved himself out of the water to be replaced by a man with a withered arm who dragged himself up the pool in slow side strokes.

When Henry was done he went and sat in the whirlpool. Two women, submerged up to their necks in bubbling water, were discussing surgeries (it was the endless topic.) Henry closed his eyes and felt white water beat against his back.

"Excuse me," one of the women shouted across at him "Can you help us out? What do you call the operation that men have in the groin area that begins with a P?"

"Prostate," Henry yelled back confidently.

"Is it in the penis or in the balls?"

Henry realized that he didn't know. He was pretty sure it wasn't in the penis, but he didn't think it was in the balls either. But then where could it be? And why hadn't the woman said "testicles?" Penis and balls didn't go.

He pretended that he hadn't heard and sank deeper into the tub.

When he had showered and dressed he called Arlene from a booth outside the cafeteria.

"What did the doctor say?"

"There's nothing wrong."

"Well that's good."

"Not exactly nothing. Epididymitis."

"Oh that's just an inflammation."

Henry had seen a sign once stapled to a telephone pole near his house. It said "For Sale, Full Set of Encyclopedia Britannica, Perfect Condition, Unused, Wife Knows Fucking Everything."

"Are you at the office?"

"Yes."

"What time are you coming home?"

"I don't know. Later. I've got a lot on."

Henry put the phone down. He didn't know quite why he had lied. He had nothing to hide.

He got in his car and drove aimlessly, or so he thought, but as the neighbourhoods changed and the houses became noticeably less affluent he knew that he was headed towards the cemetery where his brother was buried.

He listened to the DJ on the radio announce WJXP Boston, no rap and nooooo hard rock. Every time he heard these words Henry felt crushed. He wanted desperately to be with the rap and rock listeners, to eschew the endless loop of James Taylor and Fleetwood Mac. It was a problem for people in his generation. Even those with teenage children couldn't get it into their heads that they weren't young anymore, so the radio stations had taken it upon themselves to remind them.

Henry stood in the cemetery office on one side of a high desk. A short woman detached herself from conversation with a man in a black silk *yarmulke* and came to talk to him. Henry explained the situation. She reached under the desk and extracted a battered ledger with the legend 1942 embossed in gold on the front.

"Newman, you say."

"Or it could be Neuman. My father changed his name, but I'm not sure exactly when. It was before I was born."

"And this is your brother your looking for?"

"Yes."

"Sad for you."

Was it? Henry wasn't sure. Sad for his parents, certainly. But what was Aubrey to him? A chimera, a figment of the imagination, and not a very powerful one at that.

200

"Was it January 1942?"

"January or February. Sometime in winter. My father was away. They gave him leave to come back."

The woman pored over the handwritten pages.

"Here we are. Aubrey Neuman. 2/16/1942. FF73. That's in the old cemetery. You'll have to walk across the street. Mr. Gesell will direct you."

Henry walked past rows of graves, some freshly dug, some with fresh cut flowers in small glass vases, others with small pebbles placed as tokens of memory. In the lower half where his brother lay, the tombstones were smaller and the chisel work less elegant. The community had been poorer then.

In a far corner where the paved paths gave way to gravel walkways Henry found the marker FF. It had begun to rain, a warm drizzle that misted and sparkled the stones. Heading down the line 51-100 Henry tripped and stumbled to the ground. When he stood and brushed himself off he noticed that his hand was bleeding from a small cut. He found a tissue in his pocket and pressed it to the wound.

FF73 was overgrown with weeds and the tiny tombstone, chipped and streaked with birdshit, had tilted to one side. Taking care not to step on the grave Henry tugged with one hand at the high sprouting tendrils that clutched at the stone and obscured it's inscription. At the top were some words in Hebrew that Henry couldn't understand and below them his brother's name and the dates of his short life. His parents had left a simple message of bereavement:

Deeply mourned by... followed by their names.

Henry stood for a few minutes letting the rain dampen his head. He tried to concentrate on the grave, to feel something about his brother's death, but all that took his attention was the throbbing in his left testicle. The sound of footsteps diverted him and he looked up to see Gesell, the man from the office approaching zigzag through a line of graves. He had swapped his *yarmulke* for a green felt hat.

"I followed you down," he shouted from a couple of rows away, "I thought you might need a prayer."

"A prayer?"

"I can say a prayer for you. For the departed."

Henry didn't respond.

"A donation is required. At your discretion, but ten dollars is the usual amount."

"I don't think so," Henry replied and began to walk back down the path. The rain picked up in earnest and came down in heavy, fat drops. Gesell pulled down the brim of his hat.

"I'll say something anyway."

Henry continued to walk away. He decided to go home for lunch. When he walked in the door Arlene was on the phone. She acknowledged him with a glance and carried on talking. In recent years he had noticed she spent more and more time on the phone to her friends. Women, he felt, grew closer together as they got older whereas men drifted further apart. Arlene was part of a tight group, an empathetic circle in which each member helped the other through crises: childrens' sicknesses and broken limbs, problems at work, divorce, the loss of their parents. Henry barely even spoke to the neighbors anymore. His best friends, or the people he liked to imagine were his best friends, lived miles away, in California, or upstate New York.

He went to the fridge, removed a chunk of cheddar and began to make himself a sandwich. Arlene, watching him, pointed toward his heart and mouthed the word "cheese."

Eventually, she put the phone down.

"What are you doing here?"

"I went to check out my brother's grave."

"Obedient boy. How did it go?"

He knew he had to be very careful — hence, the nonchalance of that "check out" — any indication that he had been moved and Arlene would have pounced, accusing him of trying to play the sympathy card, accruing emotional capital that didn't belong to him. But in truth the grave had not touched him, so why not say so? Because, after the business about her father he did not want her to think he was hard-hearted.

"It needs some work. I'll go out there with a scrubbing brush and rake. Clean it all up. Then I'll take Mom and Mrs. Sonnenthal."

"I have to get back to work."

Arlene taught speech pathology in a local school. When she had gone Henry dialed the urologist's number. The secretary told him that she had a cancellation and he could come in right away. Henry thought that he'd had enough of doctors for one day, but then he changed his mind. Why not get it all over with?

The urologist's office was on the top floor of a new medical building only a mile or two from Henry's suburban home. The chairs in the waiting room were tubular chrome and leather; there were two glass tables covered with up-scale magazines that had single initial titles.

"I'm here for Dr. Balter."

"Dr. Malcolm Balter or Dr. Stuart Balter?"

"I'm not sure." Henry handed over the piece of paper that the radiologist had given him.

"Dr *Stuart* Balter, he'll be right with you. You can go through."

When the doctor came into the examining room, tall, angular, with gold-rimmed glasses, Henry thought that he recognized him.

"Does your son play Little League?" he asked.

"You may be thinking of my nephew. I have a daughter."

"But you watch him, right, I've seen you at the games."

"That's my brother Malcolm. We're identical twins."

"You're kidding."

Dr. Balter smiled. He had had this conversation before.

"Dead Ringers!" Henry announced excitedly.

"Excuse me?"

"The movie. Surely people must have mentioned it to you. With Jeremy Irons. Only they're not urologists they're ..."

"Gynecologists."

"Yes."

There was a pause while Dr. Balter reviewed the part form that Henry had filled out.

"And you've had this problem how long?"

"About three months."

"Well shall we take a look?"

Dr. Balter took a look, then he rested Henry's left testicle gently in the palm of his hand like a bird's egg.

"I'm going to press in various places and you tell me if it hurts."

Balter pushed with his finger.

"No. No. No. No."

"Not at all?"

"No, nothing." Henry felt like a fraud. After the fourth "no" he was hoping for pain. A shooting serious pain, something to justify his visit to a specialist.

"OK turn on your side please. Now we come to the part that nobody likes." At this moment Henry always thought the same thing: but what if you did like it? Did that mean you were gay? The truth was that he had never not liked it; he had only worried that he would be unable to control his bladder.

Henry pulled up his pants and tucked in his shirt.

"Your prostate is fine."

Henry took a deep breath. He knew how Balter had got there, but where was the prostate located? Henry was too embarrassed to ask.

"Now let me show you something."

Dr. Balter sat down in a chair next to Henry. He held up an anatomical drawing and used his finger as a pointer.

"Here's the area of your problem."

Henry looked at the swirling contours of blood and muscle. For all it meant to him he might just as well have been studying a relief map of the

Mekong Delta.

Balter more or less repeated what the cute radiologist had already told him then asked abruptly

"Any questions?"

"How do you get on with your brother?"

Balter was taken aback, and Henry too, by his own question. Nevertheless, he proceeded.

"I mean are you close? As twins? You must feel responsible for each other." And suddenly Henry knew what he was asking and he wanted to shout "His grave. Would you maintain his grave if he died?" But instead he murmured "I'm sorry" and fled the room.

The following evening after work he returned to the cemetery. He knelt by the tilting tombstone in late summer light and scrubbed at the stone. There was dirt in the crevices of his brother's name which he used a toothbrush to get at. As soon as he began to exert himself his testicle throbbed and after a while he had to pause to let the pain subside.

An hour passed, the sky streaked a kind of industrial orange that he associated with the toxic glow that rose over power plants on hot and humid days. Henry, who had forgotten to bring gloves, tore at the bushes that surrounded and overgrew the grave. He pulled some up by their roots and cast them aside; earth slid into his shoes and beneath the cuffs of his rolled-up shirt-sleeves. Henry smoothed the ground and scoured the stone. By the time he was through his face was running sweat and smeared with mud. He felt surprisingly pleased with himself and thought that, yes, now he might cry. It wasn't tears that came next but words.

"OK now?" he asked the stone.

He washed in the bathroom nearest the entrance of the Star of David Home then took the elevator up to his mother's floor. It was late and she wouldn't be expecting him. The light in the corridor was the sickly fluorescent yellow that substituted for dusk in hospitals and old people's homes.

The door to the room was closed. He knocked then gently pushed it open. Mrs. Sonnenthal was sitting in her chair: she held her purse in her lap and her legs were pressed tightly together. The room was illuminated only by the tiny blue emergency lights above the bed. She turned her eyes toward Henry.

"Your mother's gone," she said quietly.

"When will she be back?"

"Back? Back is for Christians."

Henry stared at his mother's empty bed. The white sheets were folded down and the pillow had been removed.

A shiver ran down his spine. One of the orange call lights above the bed began to blink.

"But I did it," he murmured to Mrs. Sonnenthal, "I went there."

Mrs. Sonnenthal remained immobile, an ugly grimace of contempt frozen on her face.

Henry, dazed, turned back into the corridor. The oblong light seemed to pass right through him, like an X-ray. He leaned against a wall and breathed deeply. Then he saw his mother shuffling in slippered feet out of a bathroom. She approached him slowly not recognizing or acknowledging his presence until she was right in front of him.

"I couldn't stand it any more," she said, "I asked for a move." She toppled a little to one side; Henry gripped her under the elbow.

"I cleaned up Aubrey's grave," he said.

"That's good," his mother replied, "Don't speak to that woman."

Kafka in Brontëland

Tamar Yellin

My parents belonged to the lost generation, and when I was growing up their drawers were full of old letters, stopped watches, bits of broken history: a Hebrew prayer book, an unblessed *mezuzah*, nine views of Budapest between the wars. I drew pictures on the prayer book, mislaid the *mezuzah*, swapped the postcards for Peruvian stamps; and when my parents were dead and I was fully grown I looked at the hoard and saw it was nothing but junk. Then I hired a skip and threw the lot — watches, pictures, letters and prayers — onto the heap of forgotten things, and came up here to start a new clean life; but I rattled the cans of the past behind me willy-nilly.

*

There is a man in the village, they call him Mr. Kafka. I do not know if that is his real name. He does not often speak to people. He is very old. Every day he walks down the village in the company of an elderly and asthmatic wire-haired terrier.

He does not speak to people. But he smiles occasionally: a faint and distant, somewhat dreamy smile. In this respect, but in no other, he resembles a little the Kafka of the photographs.

Eric the builder says that he is Dutch. Kafka is a Dutch name. No, no, I tell him, it is Czech, it is the Czech for jackdaw. It is like the writer Kafka, who was born in Prague. Who? The writer. Kafka the writer. The one who wrote *The Trial*.

Well, you never know, says Eric. And he tells me a story of how people die and come back to life. How young Philip Shackleton, who used to work at the quarry over Dimples Hill, fell into the crusher one day and disappeared. "Never found his body. Just traces of blood in the stones. Next year he turns up in Paxos."

The main question, however, is whether there are beams behind my cottage ceiling. Eric taps the plasterboard with his implement.

"Yes, I should think you've got a nice set of beams under there. Pine. Shall I go whoops with the crowbar?"

I say we had better wait a little.

When he has gone I dart across to the Fleece for a box of matches. Mr. Kafka is sitting in the corner over a pint of dark beer. He wears a dirty mackintosh and a buff-coloured hat like James Joyce, and he stares into his beer as though time has ended for him. I consider making conversation, but I haven't the courage.

*

When I was a girl I wanted to be Emily Brontë, but this summer I am reading Kafka with all the new enthusiasm of an adolescent. I walk the moors with a book, utterly entranced. I have fallen in love with him. Sometimes I imagine that I am him.

These literary obsessions are hardly innocent. My urge to be Emily, for instance, has altered my entire life. That is why I am here, alone in Brontëland. I grew up determined to live in haughty isolation. Only recently did I realize I had been misled: that she never spent a single day of her life alone in Haworth parsonage.

And now I have chosen to fall in love with Kafka. Kafka, child of the city. Kafka the outcast, Kafka the Jew. He wasn't inspired by spaces, he didn't belong in the hills. He didn't care for weather. He would have hated it here.

*

Emily Brontë called these mountains heaven. Today they are referred to as the white highlands. Down in the valley, in the poor town, live the Asians, Pakistanis, Muslims from Karachi and Lahore.

Eric tells me about the first time he ever laid eyes on a Black man. "I just stared." It was in the next village. "Nothing so exceptional now." "Yes," nods Hilda. "You don't see that many here still; but they're creeping up the valley road."

Hilda is a Baptist, Eric a Wesleyan; or it might be the other way round. They are always sparring. When she hears that I play the piano, she lends me a copy of *The Methodist Hymn Book*. "You're not the only Jew round here, you know. Mr. Simons who runs the off licence, I think he's half-Jewish."

I ask about Mr. Kafka. Kafka, I say uncertainly, is a Jewish name.

"I thought he was Polish. Isn't he Polish, Eric?"

"Dutch," says Eric, with conviction. He lights his pipe. "Some sort of a writer fellow, so I've heard."

Then he tells a story about the Irish navvies who helped to build the reservoir. One of them, who was in love with the same lass as his neighbour, took the brake off one of the carts one day and ran him over, and they carried him up to the village, dead. "They said it was an accident,"

208

he concludes, "but you ask Ian Ogden and he'll always tell you, murder was committed in this village."

The Greenwoods and the Shackletons all have Irish blood. Eric's great-grandfather was a Sussex landlord. Hilda's used to make boots for Branwell Brontë.

*

Twice a week I ride down from the white highlands to the black town. In fact it is more of a grey colour. It has a shopping centre, a cenotaph and a community college. I am learning Urdu.

> *Ap ka nam kiya hai?*
> *Mera nam Judith hai.*

On Tuesdays I teach English to a young woman from Lahore. She is recently married: at the moment she seems to spend most of her time rearranging the furniture in the lounge. Every time I visit we sit somewhere else.

As a matter of fact her English is rather more advanced than my Urdu. She has a degree in Psychology. I decide we will read *Alice in Wonderland* together.

Mrs. Rahim has lovely tendrils of hair at the nape of her neck, and I spend much of the lesson watching her play with them. I also stare at a framed picture of the Ka'ba done in hologram. The mad dream of Wonderland, taken at such protracted length, makes no sense whatever: we might as well be reading Japanese.

Mr. Rahim pops his head around the door: a cheerful face, a white *kurta*. He is carrying a live chicken by the legs. Shortly afterwards I hear him killing it in the kitchen.

As I leave the house at five the children are making their way to mosque to learn Koran: boys in white prayer caps, solemn little girls in long habits. I remember that a Jew should not live more than half a mile from a synagogue, to prevent the desecration of the sabbath; nor can he pray the services alone. Ten men are required for a congregation; though they do say that a Jewish woman is a congregation in herself.

It is getting dark, and all the shops, the Sangha Spice Mart, Javed Brothers, the Alruddin Sweet Palace, are lit up like Christmas. I am filled with nostalgia for something I never had.

*

209

Today I read the following lines in my *Introduction to Kafka:*

> *More than any other writer, Kafka describes the predicament*
> *of the secular alienated Jew. Yet his work, so personal on one*
> *level, remains anonymously universal. He has no Jewish axe*
> *to grind. Nowhere in any of his fictions does Kafka mention*
> *the words Jewish, or Jew.*

This seems to me remarkable. Can it be so? I resolve to make a thorough survey. There must be the odd Jew somewhere that my commentator has missed.

I cannot escape the impression that this is a pat on the back for Kafka. Yet they seem rather a sad conjuring trick, these disappearing Jews. A bit like that author who composed an entire novel without using the letter e.

The Brontë sisters did not recoil from mentioning Jews. I know all their references by heart. *Villettette* has an 'old Jew broker' who 'glances up suspiciously from under his frost-white eyelashes' while he seals letters in a bottle; but at least he does a satisfactory job. Charlotte describes her employers, 'proud as peacocks and wealthy as Jews,' but I have never liked Charlotte much. There is a 'self-righteous Pharisee' in *Wuthering Heights*, and in some ways I am grateful Emily did not live to finish that second novel.

The Brontës, of course, are often praised for the universality of their work. Especially *Wuthering Heights,* which is extremely popular in Japan. All of which goes to disprove our professor's thesis: to be universal you don't have to leave out the Jews.

*

I may change my mind about ripping down the ceiling in my cottage. It is a perfectly good ceiling, after all. A little low, perhaps — it gives the room a constricted feeling — but it covers a multitude of problems. Exposed plumbing, trailing cables, not to mention the dust, the spiders. And there may not even be any beams behind it.

"Can you assure me categorically that the beams are there?"

"Put it this way, I'm ninety-nine percent certain." Then Eric tells me how once, when he was pulling down a ceiling at Egton Bridge, he found a time capsule hidden in the joists. "One of those old tin money boxes with a lock. But it wasn't mine, so I gave it to the owner and he broke it open." What did they find? "A bit of a newspaper, five old pennies and a picture of a naked lady."

I say we will hold off on the ceiling for the time being. I ask him to tell me more about Mr. Kafka. Has he lived in the village long?

"I can't rightly say. Have you seen his place? That cottage on back lane with the green door: looks like a milking shed. The one with thistles growing out of the doorstep." In winter the thinnest trail of smoke came from the chimney. Sometimes the children played round there, but their parents didn't like it. Sometimes the old man tried to give them sweets.

No doubt the council were trying to get him rehoused. But, though he was a foreigner, he had Yorkshire tenacity: he wasn't moving for anyone.

I stop asking questions about Mr. Kafka. I am suddenly embarrassed, as though by taking a special interest I have linked myself to him. It is a kinship I would prefer not to acknowledge.

*

Not long before she got married, Mrs. Rahim's father died. She nursed him herself for three months before the wedding. When he died she felt a great peace in her heart, as though she could sense him entering the gates of paradise.

Even so, he was always very close. Sometimes she was certain she could hear him talking in the next room. When she opened the door there was nobody there, but the room was filled with a feeling of warmth and love.

We are talking about death, and we are not making much progress with *Alice in Wonderland*. Death is less perplexing: we share many certainties regarding it.

"I think they are still here: I think they are listening," says Mrs. Rahim. "My father suffered very much. But he is happy now."

Mrs. Rahim reaches for her big torn handbag and brings out a man's wallet, worn, old-fashioned, foreign-looking. It is stuffed with papers covered in tiny handwriting. She clasps the wallet between her palms and holds it to her nose: sniffs deeply as though it is some redolent flower.

"I always keep it with me. It is like him."

I have a cold. She makes me milky tea boiled with cardamom, ginger and sugar. She slips a dozen bangles up my arm. Later, in an aura of almost sacred comradeship, we look at the Koran, which she carries to the table wrapped in a silver cloth.

She cannot touch it, she explains, because she is menstruating. Nevertheless I turn the pages for her reverently as she reads. She reads beautifully. I dare not tell her I am menstruating too.

*

"Kafka. K-a-f-k-a. Kafka."
"What sort of a name is that, then? Is it Russian?"

211

"No, it's Czech."

"Have you tried under foreign titles? I don't think we have any books in Czech."

"He wrote in German, actually. But he's been translated."

"Oh, look, it's here, Jean: someone must have put it back in the wrong place."

A robust copy of *The Trial*, wrapped in institutional plastic: they leave me to it. Avidly I check the date stamps and the opening page.

Why do I do this? It's a symptom of the literary obsessive: merely the desire to see the cherished works in as many editions as possible. As though one could open them up and discover new words, new revelations. I myself possess four different copies of *Wuthering Heights*. With Kafka, it is something else. I need to see which translation it is. This I can tell immediately, from the first sentence. "Someone must have traduced Joseph K., for without having done anything wrong he was arrested one fine morning." I don't like 'traduced.' It's an immediate stumbling block. A lot of people don't know what it means. "Someone must have been telling lies about Joseph K., for without having done anything wrong he was arrested one fine morning." That's better. Comprehensible. This copy is a traduced.

I didn't expect the people of Brontëland would have much call for a book like *The Trial*. There would be a few lonely borrowings, half-hearted attempts, defeated best intentions. But I get a surprise. The label is a forest of date-stamps, repeated and regular, going back years: there are even a couple of old labels pasted beneath with their columns filled. I pick up *The Castle*. That will be different, I think: everybody reads *The Trial*. *The Castle* is, if anything, just as popular. There is a kind of frenzy in the frequent date-stamps which suggests, even, a profound need for Kafka in Brontëland.

It could all have been the same borrower, of course.

I leave the library with a strange reverence. It is as though the town and its cenotaph carry a peculiar secret, which I have stumbled on in the pages of a book. I see them for a moment with different eyes.

*

Having soaped my arm to remove Mrs. Rahim's obstinate bangles, Hilda has lent me another book, *John Wesley in Yorkshire*. I thank her politely. I have not yet learnt any of the pieces in *The Methodist Hymn Book*.

My front door is open. Eric strides in, a big rangy man, and without a word he buries his pickaxe in my smooth white ceiling. It smashes up like papier mâché. He grins a long sideways grin.

"By heck, I hope I'm right about this."

He heaves at the plasterboard with all his strength and it comes crackling down, along with a shower of dirt and beetles which covers us both.

My beams are there. My revelation. The double crossbeam, backbone of the house: the ribwork of joists between. One has a blackened bite taken out of it where the oil lantern used to be. All are hung with a drapery of webs. Not so beautiful just now, perhaps: but when I have scrubbed them and scraped them, sanded and stained them, varnished them three times with tender loving care, they will be magnificent.

Eric stoops and picks out something from the heap of dirt: a piece of metal wrapped in a strip of cloth. "Old stays," he mutters. He raises his eyes to the ceiling. "Lady of the house must have been dressing herself up there," he says, "and dropped 'em through the floorboards. An heirloom for you."

He hands it ceremoniously to me. I use it as a bookmark.

*

When he has left I go for a walk on the moors. The sun is setting: lights are coming on in the valley. Someone is walking towards me down the moorland track.

It is Mr. Kafka. He is following his slow dog down the hill to the village. He has nearly finished his walk, and his head is bent, contemplatively.

I wonder whether to acknowledge him. I am afraid to disturb his silence. He does not often speak to people. Sometimes he nods a greeting to those he knows.

As we pass each other my voice chokes in my throat, I can say nothing; but I manage a smile. Our eyes meet; he smiles back at me.

It seems a smile of recognition, and for the briefest moment he resembles once more the Kafka of the photographs.

The Slow Mirror

Richard Zimler

Pedro was from Buenos Aires.

Yet it was only after his death that I stopped to consider what that might mean. I was in Argentina for the first time, attending an ornithology conference, and I was walking down the Avenida Santa Fe when it suddenly occurred to me: so this is what he saw and heard while growing up. Did he think of this place often after making love with me?

There was an accompanying vision of oncoming black taxis and wide, endless boulevards, a sense of strolling through perfumed breezes toward obelisks and military monuments. But the important thing was not the actual character of Buenos Aires. It was only vital that the city was real, that it was always present whether or not I was aware of it, and that Pedro had come from there.

I was on my way to the address of his childhood (torn down to make way for a utilitarian concrete monster) when all this condensed inside me as if from the cloud of a forgotten dream. I stopped as if confronted by a riddle. And when I looked around again, I found myself in front of an over-crowded antique store. I entered to think my confusion out, nodded to the owner and walked to the back to get out of the light. There, past a shelf of books and numerous hat racks, I discovered the mirror. It was sitting on top of a dusty 17th-century Portuguese dresser in the twisted-and-turned style made popular following Vasco da Gama's first trip to India, and it caught my attention because it was shaped like a lyre. I am a professor of ornithology by trade — with a specialty in North American seedeaters *(Passeriformes Fringillidae)* — but an amateur lutanist at heart. And I am fascinated by antique instruments. Naturally, then, I approached this lyre-mirror and brushed my hand along its frame. And when I stared into its reflection, I discovered a Chinese camphor-wood trunk whose front was carved with a serpent brandishing a lantern in its mouth. The trunk sat directly opposite the mirror, atop a curious English desk with handles made from lapis lazuli. It was the magical alliteration of lapis lazuli, lantern, lyre and lute that finally impelled me to obey my original instincts and make an offer for the mirror, and I was able to bargain the dealer, an ancient Uruguayan from Paysandú smelling of pistachio nuts and brandy, down to a reasonable price.

That evening, back in my tiny room at the Hotel Estrella, I noticed, for the first time, the mirror's singular powers of retention. Following a shower, I had taken out my brush with the intention of combing my hair into a semblance of reason. I lifted the mirror out of its wrappings and discovered that the camphor-wood trunk and the surroundings of the antique store — and not I — composed the entirety of its reflection. From all angles, no matter whether I moved to the side, knelt or stood on the hotel's monstrous desk chair, the silver surface of the mirror still gave to me the various surroundings of the Uruguayan's store.

After a momentary fright during which I made an aborted call to the desk clerk, I watched the reflection for quite some time, coming to two possible conclusions: the first (and more obvious), that this was not a normal mirror; the second (and, naturally enough, more disturbing), that I might very well be going mad.

I dreamed of the mirror that night, imagined that it reflected the image of a Rose-Breasted Grosbeak — the bird on which I did my dissertation at Cornell University and after which my daughter, Rosalie, was named— flying through green clouds evaporating from giant oak trees. This bird was a messenger, had been sent by Pedro to pick Rosalie up and carry her to heaven.

In the morning, I fully expected to see a reflection of the bird or even my face, but found once again the antique store. In consequence, I cut short an appearance at a symposium on tone displacement among wood warblers and went back to the Uruguayan dealer. I informed him of my two possible conclusions.

"Let me assure you, *Señora*, you are not going insane," he said with a smile of solidarity. "There is indeed a time lag. The mirror seems to retain images. They seep in and take a long while coming out. I call it the 'slow mirror'" (In Spanish, he referred to it as the *"espejo atrasado."*)

"How long does it take for the mirror to give its images back?" I asked.

The dealer shrugged. "I took over the store four years ago from another Uruguayan, a man from Punta del Este, and the mirror has yet to reflect anything but the Chinese trunk," he said. "Of course, it has also given back the images of some people who have lifted it up and passersby who have headed toward other antiques." He laughed and twirled his mustache. "But the selfish thing has not yet given my image back. So it must be slow by at least four years."

"And do you know where it came from?"

"Brazil, I believe. Of Portuguese craftsmanship, perhaps. Although maybe it's Japanese. Might have come over with the immigrants. I was told by a Korean agronomist that the wood forming the lyre frame is Japanese Maple."

The antique dealer generously offered to buy the mirror back if I were disappointed with its slow reflections. But I assured him that I still wanted it, thanked him for his help and returned to the hotel.

The mirror, although perched on a simple writing desk by my bed, still insisted, of course, on reflecting the Chinese trunk and the antique store. And by standing far to the right, I could now see the first Uruguayan dealer from Punta del Este, a small, withered man with eyeglasses held together by tape. He sat behind a table centered by a baroque candelabrum with the sinuous arms of a Hindu goddess. A strong sunlight that seemed to be distilled through billowy clouds shone in through a window on which a gilded Byzantine crucifix was hung. I watched, mesmerized, and after some time a tall woman in black entered the store, toured and left without making a purchase. The dealer ate lunch from a white bag as if the contents were to be kept secret. He read a large book bound in leather. Later, hard-edged shadows from unseen furniture crept across the floor as if seeking the night. A man in a brown fur coat entered, admired an azure-glazed Persian vase and wrapped it in white handkerchiefs from his pocket before letting the Uruguayan package it. Just prior the store's closure, two large women holding bursting packages came in to ask directions.

And it was then, alone with the antiques, that I felt a sudden tremor of joy. It was as if, while watching the store, I'd left my body behind for a time. And now I had returned to discover the wonder of fingers, hands, lips, of a woman who could touch the world, feel her place at the center of life, breathe, kiss, talk. I picked up my phone to share this discovery with Rosalie. Yet upon hearing her quivering voice, I decided it best to simply inquire about her health.

"But where are you?" she asked.

"Buenos Aires."

"Still there... then why are you calling?"

"To see about you. I'm sorry if I woke you."

Rosalie was silent. I imagined her tears reflecting a sepia world leached of colour, pictured a lone child facing a German fairy-tale forest. Without an answer, she let the phone down. Our line disappeared. I sat with my head in my hands. Regretting so much. Watching the antique store submerged in night. Finding the mirror now quite normal — an impossible artifact to be sure, and certainly a gift, but just one of many impossible objects all around me. I imagined it had been pulled through a magician's hat from the same invisible land that had given rise to Rosalie's leukemia and my own helplessness.

Time crept very slowly to me that night. I slept in and out of cold, endless dreams bordered by water. And when I woke in the morning, it was with the great energy of escape. I was gripping the silver Star of David which Pedro had hung around my neck when we were engaged. Dressing

217

madly, I ran out of my room to catch a lecture on male incubation.

Two days later, when the meeting's concluding cocktail party had finished, I packed up the mirror, boarded my night-time plane and headed back to San Francisco.

There, inside our Richmond District home on 12th Avenue, I placed the slow mirror atop my rosewood dresser. When Rosalie had awoken from a nap, I showed it to her. "From your father's city," I said. She returned my smile absently, stared into the reflection for a few moments following my explanation and said: "It's too slow." She patted my arm, refused to elucidate on her comment and returned to bed.

Only later did I understand what she meant: *I haven't enough time left to wait for the mirror to return my reflection.*

Despite the dark canal of dread this realization cut through me (or perhaps because of it), I began to follow the life of the antique store avidly, compulsively I must say, becoming an expert on the habits of the Uruguayan from Punta del Este and the lascivious tastes of his Saturday store manager, a weedy looking man with a penchant for atavistic blonds in elastic clothing. I also came to enjoy the idiosyncrasies of several regular visitors, particularly those of an elfin Native American woman living in La Boca who came in once a day to sniff the camphor-wood trunk because of her sinus problems (I read her lips once while she discussed her misery with the Uruguayan).

Often, I would watch the tale of the mirror upon waking and just before going to bed, and for some time it took the place of reading, lute-playing and films for me. And yet, as one can well imagine, after a year of the store and customers — and the Chinese trunk in particular — I grew decidedly bored with the life of a Buenos Aires antique store and moved the mirror to the floor by my linen closet where I could check on it from time to time but rarely be encumbered by its constant story.

Rosalie was growing weaker at the time. And she was in more pain. Chemotherapy was helping very little, if at all. Often, she spoke to me in the voice of the tiny, winged being I imagined trapped inside her limp body. I realized at such moments that it would not be long before this entity would fly free from her and disappear from both our lives like a Thomas Campion sprite. Although I am frightened even now to admit it, I surely hoped for this to come to pass quickly.

Soon after I had put the mirror away, Rosalie asked me in a trembling voice if I would hang the mirror on the wall directly opposite her bed. "Something impossible I saw in it," she said. She refused to say more, showed me by way of explanation a book from her childhood that she must have hidden away. It was Italian, with illustrations of birds by Bruno Munari in reds and blues and yellows that seemed distilled from actual feathers. It was the only book Pedro had brought with him from Argentina when his family had fled the persecution of an anti-intellectual, anti-Semitic dictatorship. All the others had been left behind and had perhaps gone up in smoke. When Rosalie was a child, Pedro used to sit with her for hours and show her the pretty pictures. "What did you see?" I asked again.

Rosalie put her finger to her lips in a gesture of silence, smiled as if to comfort me and squeezed my hand.

Two days later, she was dead.

I found her holding the lyre-mirror to her chest, face down, as if she were seeking to incorporate the silver reflection in her body. Underneath was her children's book. How she found the strength to take the mirror down from the wall I had no idea.

The past recedes from me after that, as if my personal history were pulled out to sea for a period of years. I know I must have worked and ate and talked with people — done all the things one is expected to do in order to survive. But my thoughts from that time are bounded by the impenetrable black ocean of an ancient epic. When my history finally does emerge up through this dark landscape again, it is with Rosalie's face as its masthead; a week ago, almost four years to the day after her death, I saw her reflected in the slow mirror. From her surroundings, I could tell that she was standing in the doorway of my linen closet. She was staring straight ahead with what I can only call the face of a woman adoring a child. After some time, she kneeled down and kissed the surface of the looking glass.

I watched all this in her room. From inside a warm ether that seemed to be composed of tears. From under her blankets. For I had re-hung the mirror on her wall after her death and begun to sleep in her bed.

The next day, I watched myself in the reflection carrying the mirror to her room and hanging it on the wall, exactly as I had done nearly four years earlier.

After that, I lived Rosalie's final hours without pausing for sleep. I believe it was peace I saw in her face more than anything else. Was it simply the antique store that was helping her so? I hadn't a clue until I saw her rise from the bed with the childhood book she was keeping on her night table and glide with the ease of spectre across the floor. She stopped to the right of the mirror and stared for quite some time, then climbed onto the dresser and took it down. She brought it into bed with her and gripped it as one might hold a sick child.

A few moments later, there was only the darkness of her unwavering chest. On the evening I witnessed all this in the mirror, I flew down to Buenos Aires. Upon my arrival, I took a taxi directly to the antique store.

219

The ancient Uruguayan dealer from Paysandú was still there. *"El espejo atrasado, no?"* he asked when I entered.

"Si, may I look around?"

"Please."

The Portuguese dresser in the twisted-and-turned style was still at the back of the store. Another mirror was resting on it now, a normal one which reflected my hand when I held it up as an experiment. I stood where Rosalie had and stared. From my angle, I could see a bookshelf. It seemed clear that whatever she had seen, she had spotted there.

I passed over the books as quickly as I could till I was stopped by the name Munari. It was another of his children's books. On the cover, a scarlet finch perched on a sunflower. I pressed it to my chest and closed my eyes, was suddenly dizzy with a mixture of amazement and fear. My booming heartbeat was swaying me from side to side. My feet felt rooted at the very center of the world. I gripped the Portuguese dresser in case I sensed myself going faint.

When I gathered to courage to caress the book open, I found an inscription in Ladino to Pedro from his mother dated: Purim, the 14th of Adar, 5707 (1947). I sounded out the message in a whisper: *"Para mi pequeño pájaro con amor. El imposible es la prueba."* (For my little bird with love. The impossible is the proof.)

The strange sensation that these words were meant for me seemed to suspend my breathing. From deep inside an armour of body, I felt as if I had happened upon an understanding of the world grounded in belief. Was it this belief that had given Rosalie the serenity she possessed before death? Pedro must surely have passed on his mother's words to her years ago. Did they assure her that she'd be joining him in God?

When the movements of another customer tugged me back into consciousness of the store, I paid for the book. The dealer said, "Isn't that the mystery of life. We had this lovely thing displayed prominently for many years and no one bought it. Now that it's hidden away, you come in an find it. You figure it out."

"Maybe this has something to do with it," I said, showing him the book's inscription. To his wide-eyed look of bewilderment, I said: "It's Ladino. A Jewish Spanish written with Hebrew letters dating from before the Inquisition." I read him the message from Pedro's mother.

"What do you think it means?" he asked.

I unfurled my arm to indicate the store, the street, the antiques. I pointed at him, then at myself. "Has the unlikeliness of the world itself... or something absolutely impossible that's occurred never made you feel that there's more to this than meets the eye?"

"Ah, I understand," he said. He puffed out his lips and held up his hands in a gesture of passive scepticism. As he started to speak, I raised my index finger to my lips and offered him Rosalie's soft smile of silence.

On my return to San Francisco, I took the mirror down and sold it to a Chilean antique dealer in the Mission District with brilliant blue eyes. And flew to Cornell. I walked in the woods during several days, holding the children's books, not knowing what I was after, until an arrow of pastel pink streaked by in front of me. It was a Rose-Breasted Grosbeak, a female, and she had alighted on the branch of a gnarled oak tree directly above me. She was staring at the ground. When I looked down, I discovered a puddle of water atop a bed of moss. It was reflecting the face of a tearful old woman, a sudden winged shimmer of pink passing through green clouds into a sunlit sky. And I thought: *Dreams, too, are impossible.* And: *Whether I know it or not, this woods, this place, is here all the time.*

Afterword

Richard Zimler's haunting and enigmatic story extends the central metaphor of revelation and reflection afforded by the mirror; it suggests that seeing ourselves sometimes steals upon us in a more artful (or is it artless) fashion, the slow mirror only yielding its secret message, its moment of recognition, at a time of its own choosing and by degreees.

The secreting of images, their suspension in time, their delayed transmission into an alien context, — how rich a metaphor for the post-Holocaust Jewish experience. We look into the glass, expecting to see the present, and we see the past. For the Jewish writer, this is particularly resonant, since images of the past are often released at times and places altogether unexpected.

Stepping back from the mirror, we wonder what images lie suspended in the silver glass to be released at some future time: a purloined fork, perhaps, or an iron bar, a gold tooth, a broken typewriter key; a tattooed wrist, a set of pink-tinted glass seder dishes, a silk shift or a pair of red, leather shoes with thin shining gold threads.

The multifariousness of these images bear witness to the multifariousness of this anthology.The editors are reminded of a set of images at the entrance to the Museum of the Diaspora in Tel Aviv. These images flash down on the visitor from a host of screens alongside which is posed the question:What is a Jew in today's world? The answer lies in the multiple images on the screens, all of them of faces vastly different in age and disposition, in colour and ethnicity, yet all of them Jews. It is a collection of faces that defies stereotypes. This anthology, we hope, fulfils the same role.

Biographies

Carol Bergman is a child of Holocaust survivors and was born and raised in New York City. After living as an expatriate in London for more than a decade she returned to America. Her essays, features, profiles and reviews have appeared *The New York Times, Cosmopolitan, Family Circle, German Life, Cineaste, Jewish Currents* and elsewhere. Carol is the author of biographies of Mae West and Sidney Poitier and numerous short stories. A memoir, *Searching for Fritzi* is pending publication. She teaches at the Gotham Writers' Workshop in New York City.

Tony Dinner is both a painter and a poet. His first one-man exhibition was at Gallery 26 in Highgate, London and he has work hanging permanently in La Brasserie, Highgate and at Yakar Educational Foundation. His first collection of poetry, *Forbidden Texts*, was published in 1992 by Whitethorn and he is preparing his second collection, *Ecstatic Confessions,* also to be published by Whitethorn. He is the director of the London Academy of Playwriting and co-director of a newly formed theatre company, Imago Mundi. He was born in South Africa and has lived in Northern Ireland and Israel, and for many years now in London.

Rachel Castell Farhi was born in London in 1965 to a Jewish mother and a gentile father. After postgraduate qualification in teaching, she worked in Israel and continued to write. Her work has appeared in several publications, including *Jewish Quarterly* and the poetry anthology *The Dybbuk of Delight*. She is married and has a daughter.

Moris Farhi, a Sephardi, was born in Ankara in 1935 and moved to Britain in 1954. He has worked as a scriptwriter for television for plays and series, including *Menace* and *Out of the Unknown*. His poetry has appeared in numerous journals and he has written one play, *From the Ashes of Thieves* — a modern Greek drama in verse. His three novels are *Pleasure of Your Death* (1972), *Last of Days* (1983) and *Journey Through Wilderness* (1989). A fourth, the subject of which is the Gypsy Holocaust, is near completion. Moris Farhi is married with one step-daughter.

Elaine Feinstein is a poet and a novelist and was made a Fellow of the Royal Society of Literature in 1980. She received a Cholmondeley Award for her poetry in 1990, and in the same year, an Honorary D. Lit. from the University of Leicester. Her *Selected Poems* was published by Carcanet in

224

1995 and her latest collection, *Daylights,* is due this autumn.

Ellen Galford is a member of many different and possibly incompatible tribes — an Ashkenazic, half-Litvak half-Galitzianer, Lesbian, secular and/or heretical *treif*-eating Jew who still lights *Shabbos* and *jahrtzeit* candles and has an ancestral *mezuzah* on the doorpost. She was born into a now-dispersed but once very lively Jewish community in Newark, New Jersey but migrated to Scotland a quarter-century ago. Her loyalties are 100% Scottish, even if her accent is not. Ellen Galford has written four novels so far: *The Dyke and the Dybbuk* (Virago) won a 1994 Lambda literary award in the USA. The others are *Moll Cutpurse: Her True History, Queendom Come* (both Virago), and *The Fires of Bride* (The Women's Press).

Since his early thirties, **Jack Gratus** has earned his living as a writer and lecturer. His novels include *A Man In His Position* (Hutchinson) and *The Jo'burgers* (Corgi); his non-fiction, *The Victims, The Great White Lie,* (both published by Hutchinson) and *The False Messiahs* (Gollancz). He has also written features and drama for BBC Radio. He scripted and presented two series on management training for BBC TV, and has written a number of books on interpersonal skills including *Successful Interviewing* (Penguin). He is a co-director of a video production company whose first training video, *The Numbers Game,* was launched this year. Recently he returned to his first love, the short story, and is hoping to maintain the love affair long enough to give birth to a collection.

Dan Jacobson was born in Johannesburg, South Africa. He worked as a teacher and journalist before the publication of his first novel, *The Trap,* in 1955. For the next twenty years he lived by his pen, apart from periods spent at various American universities. In 1976 he became a member of the English Department, University College, London. He has published many novels, among them *The Rape of Tamar* and *The Confessions of Josef Baisz,* two collections of short stories, and two critical works. His most recent book, *The Electronic Elephant: A Southern African Journey,* recently came out in Penguin. Literary prizes given to him include the John Llewellyn Rhys Award, the W. Somerset Maugham Award, and the J.R. Ackerley Prize for Autobiography.

Zvi Jagendorf was born in Vienna in 1936 and came to England in 1939. He read English at Oxford and moved to Israel in 1958, now teaching English and Theatre at the Hebrew University. His fiction and essays have been published in many journals including *The London Review of*

Books, Kenyon Review, Tikkun, Raritan, Midstream and *Ariel*. At present he is completing a sequence of stories about refugees and ghosts. He is married and has three children.

Gabriel Josipovici was born in Nice in 1940 of Russo-Italian and Romano-Levantine parents. He lived in Egypt from 1945 to 1956, when he came to Britain. Since 1963 he has been on the faculty of the University of Sussex, where he is now part-time Professor of English in the School of European Studies. For the year 1996–7, he is Lord Weidenfeld Visiting Professor of Comparative Literature at the University of Oxford. He has published over a dozen novels and collections of short stories and half a dozen critical works, and his plays have been performed in London and Edinburgh and by the BBC and RAI (Germany). A new critical book, *Touch,* is published by Yale University Press this year and a new novel, *Now,* by Carcanet in 1997.

Robert Lasson was born in Philidelphia in 1922. Most of his professional life was spent as a copywriter. After hours he wrote humour which appeared in several American magazines as well as *Punch. The Tale of a Shamos* was written 20 years ago and resided in a drawer until it was published in *The Jewish Exponent* (Philadelphia) in 1982. Robert Lasson describes himself as a Jewish atheist with an abiding love for the Yiddish language. He lives in New York with his new wife, Meta.

Shaun Levin is a South African writer who has lived in Israel since 1978. He holds a degree in English Literature from Tel Aviv University, where he has done graduate work on African American literature and taught English and American literature. He writes book reviews for the literary supplement of *Ha'aretz* and has published short stories in Hebrew and English. His work has appeared in *The Evergreen Chronicles, Queer View Mirror* and *Stand. Shoes* (under the title *Imagine*) first appeared in *The Evergreen Chronicles.*

Deena Linett, a 1996 Hawthornden Fellow, grew up on the Gulf coast of Florida and teaches writing and literature at Montclair State University in the USA. She is the author of two prize-winning novels, *On Common Ground* and *The Translator's Wife.* Twice a Yaddo Fellow, her poems and essays have appeared in many magazines and her travel writing will feature in a forthcoming title from New Rivers Press.

Marci López-Levy is a native of Buenos Aires, was a teenager in Barcelona via Patagonia and has been unsettled in Britain for a long time.

She feels at home in any city cafe which allows prolonged reading over an expresso. She has worked locally in communities and internationally for human rights and social justice. She is currently narrowing her chances of gainful employment by writing, travelling and studying anthropology.

Sonja Lyndon was born in London of German and Jewish refugee parents. She studied languages and linguistics, which she taught for many years before becoming a free-lance editor and writer. She recently co-edited *The Dybbuk of Delight* (Five Leaves Publications), the first British anthology of Jewish women's poetry. Her most recently performed play, set in the Terezin Ghetto, toured nationally in 1995. Her new play *Gradiva or The Love Cure,* a comedy featuring Freud and Jung and the women in their lives, will be produced in the spring of 1997 by Imago Mundi theatre company, which she co-founded this year in association with The London Academy of Playwriting. Sonja Lyndon sits on the editorial board of *Jewish Quarterly* and is currently compiling her first collection of short stories.

Carole Malkin is a fiction writer, critic and the author of a critically acclaimed biography, *The Journeys of David Toback* (Schocken), based on her grandfather's Yiddish memoir about his life in Czarist Russia. She was raised in Brooklyn and attended college in Ohio. Married and the mother of three, she currently resides in Berkeley, California. She studied with the poet William Dickey at San Francisco State. Malkin says, "I'm not religious, and yet, I know I'm Jewish from the top of my head to the soles of my feet. Whatever I write bears the imprint of my Jewishness."

Sylvia Paskin is a lecturer and writer on film and television. She has co-edited *Angels of Fire* — an anthology of radical poetry (Chatto and Windus), *Dancing the Tightrope* — an anthology of women's love poetry (Women's Press) and *The Dybbuk of Delight* — an anthology of Jewish women's poetry. She is currently working on another fiction anthology and a longer work of her own.

Rozanne Rabinowitz was born in the Bronx in 1957, emigrating to New Jersey when she was 9. For years she has lived in South London with two flatmates, two dogs and four cats. After various forms of wage slavery she is now a full-time — and occasional part-time — dole scrounger. She works on *Bad Attitude*, a feminist publication devoted to "the overthrow of civilisation as we know it". Currently Rozanne is writing a vampire novel set in Brixton called *Blood on the Dole*.

Frederic Raphael was born in 1931 in Chicago, he came to England in 1938. He has written more than twenty novels, four volumes of short stories, biographies of Byron and Somerset Maugham and three volumes of essays. He won an Oscar for his film *Darling* and was Television Writer of the Year for *The Glittering Prizes*. Frederic Raphael also writes for radio, translates from Latin, Greek and Spanish and writes for *The Sunday Times* and a number of other publications. *Going Back* is one of a sequence which will be published in the spring of next year.

Nessa Rapoport was born in Toronto, Canada. She graduated from the University of Toronto and the University of London. She is the author of a novel, *Preparing for Sabbath,* and of *A Woman's Book of Grieving*. Her short stories and essays have appeared widely. With Ted Solotaroff, she edited *The Schocken Book of Contemporary Jewish Fiction*. She co-wrote the screenplay of *Saying Kaddish*, a network drama aired nationally in the United States. Nessa Rapoport speaks frequently on Jewish culture and imagination. *Great Men* was originally published in *The Forward* (New York). Reprinted by permission of the author, all rights reserved.

Stephen Walker read History at Oxford and Philosophy at Harvard, joining BBC TV as a graduate trainee. He directed films in a variety of series including *Heart of the Matter, Everyman* and *Inside Story*. His films ranged from South Africa to Vietnam and Beirut. He has also directed films on a number of Jewish subjects, including the Mengele Twins, the French Nazi Paul Touvier and the Middle East. In August 1995 his drama *Prisoners of Time* was broadcast on the anniversary of VJ Day on BBC 1. Work in progress includes a collection of Jewish short stories. Stephen Walker is currently making a film on Jewish weddings for *Modern Times* on BBC2.

Michelene Wandor is a poet, playwright, critic and musician. Her selected poems, *Gardens of Eden* were published in 1990. Her prolific work for radio includes dramatisations of *Jane Eyre, The Mill on the Floss, Persuasion* and *The Jungle Book,* which was a runner-up for a Writer's Guild Award. More recently, her play, *Orlando and Friends*, for which she arranged the music, was broadcast on Radio 3. Some of her poetry was included in the Five Leaves anthology *The Dybbuk of Delight,* the title coming from one of her poems. *The Devil in the Cupboard* was originally commissioned by Radio 4.

Shelley Weiner was born in South Africa and worked as a journalist for many years before turning to fiction in 1990. Since then she has had three novels published (*A Sister's Tale*, *The Last Honeymoon* and *The Joker*) and another awaiting publication. She is presently engaged writing a fifth. Her short stories have appeared in *Winter's Tales* and other anthologies. Shelley Weiner is a co-director of *Writers' Block* and tutors at creative writing courses in the UK and abroad. She is on the editorial board of *Jewish Quarterly* and lives in London with her husband and two children.

Jonathan Wilson was born in London in 1950 and educated at the universities of Essex, Oxford and the Hebrew University of Jerusalem. He is the author of *The Hiding Room*, a novel and *Schoom*, a collection of short stories. His fiction and essays appear frequently in the *New Yorker* magazine. He is Associate Professor of English at Tufts University and lives in Newton, Mass. with his wife, the painter Sharon Kaitz, and two sons, Adam and Gabriel.

Tamar Yellin grew up in Leeds and studied Hebrew and Arabic at Oxford. After teaching in Bradford she lived in Toronto for two years. She now works as a Jewish Faith Visitor in Yorkshire schools, walks on the moors every day and translates Hebrew for pleasure. Her stories have appeared in *Writing Women, London Magazine, Metropolitan, Panurge* and the anthology *Best Short Stories*. Current work includes a collection of short stories and a novel.

Richard Zimler was born in New York in 1956 and has lived in Porto, Portugal, since 1990. *Unholy Ghosts*, his second novel and the first to come out in English, was published in September 1996 by GMP Publishers. Richard's first novel, *The Last Kabbalist of Lisbon*, was published earlier this year in Portuguese. To his surprise it received an enthusiastic reception and reached the top of the Portuguese best seller list. In 1994, he was awarded a Fellowship in Fiction by the U.S. National Endowment for the Arts. *The Slow Mirror* first appeared in *London Magazine* and reflects the author's interest in mysticism and Sephardic culture.

ALSO AVAILABLE FROM FIVE LEAVES

THE DYBBUK OF DELIGHT: AN ANTHOLOGY OF JEWISH WOMEN'S POETRY
Edited by Sonja Lyndon and Sylvia Paskin
236 pages, £9.99/$15, flapped paperback, 0 907123 57 0
Published in association with the European Jewish Publications Society.

A major celebration of Jewish women's creativity. This is the first such poetry anthology and covers the interests of contemporary Jewish women, religious and secular. Themes include assimilation, emigration, the festivals, family life and family pressures, the Holocaust, Jewish artists... and food.

In Jewish folklore a dybbuk is a restless, wandering soul, compelled to take possession of a living person and speak through them.

The Dybbuk of Delight is a remarkable collection of poems: passionate, witty, often heartbreaking.
The Ham and High

Among the 62 contributors are Wanda Barford, Janet Berenson-Perkins, Nadine Brummer, Liz Cashdan, Tricia Corob, Ruth Fainlight, Rachel Castell Farhi, Elaine Feinstein, Nini Herman, Sue Hubbard, Lotte Kramer, Jane Liddell-King, Gerda Mayer, Alix Pirani, Myra Schneider, Valerie Sinason, Michelene Wandor and Tamar Yoseloff.

THE SKIN OF YOUR BACK
by Michael Rosen
64 pages, £5.50/$9.00, 0 907123 66 X

Best known as a children's writer, Rosen's second volume of poetry (for adults) is pithy, tragic and bizarre. He reflects on church-front nativity scenes where the wiseguys are foreigners and Mary and Joseph are English and suburban. He writes of going on Ban the Bomb marches at the age of 13 and his parents stuffing his bag full of chicken and fresh fruit. His free form structure is deceptively simple and the magic is a result of his precise choice of concrete words and accurate observation.
New Moon

YOU ARE, AREN'T YOU?
by Michael Rosen
72 pages, £4.99/$8.00, paperback, 0 907123 09 0

Michael Rosen's first collection of poetry for adults, featuring material on Jewish and socialist themes is as sharp as a pickled cucumber.

POEMS FOR THE BEEKEEPER
Edited by Robert Gent
144 pages, £6.99/$11.00, paperback, 0 907123 82 1

An introduction to the range of modern poetry in Britain today. 38 contributors, almost all of whom are "household names" on the modern poetry circuit, including Danny Abse, James Berry, Carol Ann Duffy, Elaine Feinstein, Jackie Kay, Henry Normal, Tom Paulin and Jon Silkin.

WATER
by Sue Thomas
162 pages, £7.99/$12.00, paperback, 0 907123 51 1

"In the end, she was forced to take her chances on the open ocean and there, off the coast of Scotland, she drowned him because she thought he deserved it. He probably did..."
Water is a novel of a daughter's revenge.

The Los Angeles Times described Water as *"...a dreamy novel that is pulled along by a thread of emotion."*

LAUGHING ALL THE WAY
by Liz Cashdan
72 pages, £5.99/$9.00, paperback, 0 907123 46 5

Liz Cashdan's poems convey a strong sense of personal identity and this collection includes the acclaimed Tyre/Cairo letters, a dramatic reconstruction of the life of an 11th century Jewish family.

THIS IS NO BOOK
by Gregory Woods
112 pages, £6.95/$10.00, paperback, 0 907123 26 0

A collection of review essays by one of Britain's leading experts on gay men's literature.

DESTROYING THE BABY IN THEMSELVES: WHY DID THE TWO BOYS KILL JAMES BULGER?
by David Jackson
46 pages, £3.50/$6.00, paperback, 0 907123 31 7

That blurred, foggy frame of the security video has become engraved on the public conscience. We can never know the whole truth of what followed, but a critical re-focussing on the Bulger case is essential if we are to challenge the paralysing horror of what happened.

All books published by Five Leaves are available through bookshops or, post free, from PO Box 81, Nottingham, NG5 4ER, UK. Trade distribution: Central.

Please send a card if you wish to go on Five Leaves' mailing list.